MURDER ON THE MENU

THE 1ST NIKKI HUNTER MYSTERY

Nancy Skopin

Copyright March 2015 by Nancy Skopin.

All rights reserved.

No part of this book may be reproduced, scanned, or distributed in any printed or electronic form without permission. Please do not participate in or encourage piracy of copyrighted materials in violation of the author's rights. Thank you for respecting the hard work of this author.

This is a work of fiction. Names, characters, places, and incidents either are the product of the author's imagination or are used fictitiously, and any resemblance to locales, events, business establishments, or actual persons—living or dead—is entirely coincidental.

Dedication

This book is for my husband Max and our dogs Buddy, Malcolm, and Turq. You are my inspiration.

Acknowledgements

I'd like to thank Juliann Stark for her superb editing skills and endless patience, Detective Mark Pollio for his insight into the world of law enforcement, and my agent Adam Chromy for his brilliance and tenacity.

CHAPTER 1

MY NAME IS NICOLI HUNTER. I know it sounds like a cliché, a private investigator named Hunter, but it's not what you think. My father chose the name when he arrived at Ellis Island. It's just a coincidence that I ended up making my living as a kind of hunter.

Most of my work involves bar and restaurant surveillance, although I do the odd insurance investigation and on rare occasions agree to follow unfaithful spouses. Tonight my friend Elizabeth and I were dining and barhopping at the expense of four of my regular clients. We'd started our evening at a Microbrewery in the Union Square area of San Francisco, and had worked our way around the city.

At the moment we were standing in the lobby of a somewhat famous eatery on Montgomery Street. We were both slightly underdressed for this establishment, and the hostess (read queen bitch) was studiously ignoring us. This is part of the plan for many of my clients. They want to know how their employees behave when management isn't onsite.

After waiting almost five minutes to be noticed, I approached the desk and asked the QB in my sweetest tone of voice if we could be seated. She looked me up and down, and replied with the expected, "Do you have a reservation?"

"Of course," I responded. "Nicoli Sinclair, for eight o'clock."

She made a show of reading the reservations ledger, then picked up two menus and showed us to a table directly outside the kitchen. Perfect, for my purposes at least. Every detail of each employee's behavior would go into my report for the owner, not to mention the quality of the cuisine, the temperament of the crowd, copious notes regarding the condition and cleanliness of the establishment. You get the idea; attention to detail is critical.

Elizabeth looked around the room, trying not to stare at the rich and famous patrons while I observed the staff. Waiters were milling about taking orders and checking on customers who had already been served. It was still early in the survey, but at this point it appeared that the only fly in the soup was the hostess.

We were approached by a young man in black tie, minus the jacket, who, after introducing himself as Brad, asked if we'd like anything from the bar. Brad must be a new hire. I didn't recognize him from previous surveys.

"I'd like a glass of something red. What would you recommend?"

Brad produced a wine list and asked a few pointed questions to help him narrow it down for me. "Do you prefer light, fruity, meaty...?"

I smiled at his etiquette and said, "The meatier the better."

Brad made his recommendation and I acquiesced. He turned to Elizabeth who ordered a tall Mudslide. Brad hid a grin and said, "Very good, ladies," before departing for the bar.

I momentarily turned my attention to my best friend, Elizabeth Gaultier. We'd met two years ago when I moved aboard my yacht and opened my PI office in the marina complex where we both currently live. She's a pixie with a stratospheric IQ, just over five feet tall with strawberry blonde hair, a curvy figure, and a very slight accent left over from her childhood in New Orleans. Elizabeth is a walking paradox. She's brilliant (though she insists she's nothing special), outspoken to a fault yet incredibly kind and generous, and has a bawdy streak a mile wide. All attributes, in my opinion. She's currently single, as am I, which is why she has time to occasionally accompany me on these little 'shopping' expeditions.

Brad returned and served our drinks, expectantly watching our faces as we each tried a sip. The wine he'd selected for me was exceptional. A combination of black currant and bell pepper notes, it was so dense I almost had to chew.

"Is it satisfactory, madam?"

"Outstanding. Thank you, Brad."

He turned his inquisitive gaze toward Elizabeth who smiled around her straw and said simply, "Yummy."

Brad nodded politely, but his eyes were twinkling. Most men twinkle at Elizabeth.

"Would you like to hear this evening's specials?" he asked.

We listened attentively to the specials, (at least I did, since Elizabeth was people watching again), and ordered. As Brad departed I felt my cell phone vibrate in my purse.

"Shit. Who calls a PI after eight o'clock on a Wednesday?" I muttered as I pulled the Nokia from my bag. I didn't recognize the number, but since it might be important I trotted into the hallway outside the restrooms rather than committing a major faux pas by answering at the table.

"Hunter Investigations," I intoned.

"Ms. Hunter?"

"Yes, this is she."

"My name is Kate Howard."

I recognized her name instantly. Kate's daughter, Laura, had been killed two weeks earlier. I'd been following the story on the evening news. Laura's body had been found behind a dumpster on Bay Road, less than two miles from my office. According to the news reports, no persons of interest had yet been identified by the police.

Finally something more challenging than catching till-tapping bartenders. I grabbed the pen and notebook I keep in my purse as Kate spoke.

"I'd like to hire you to investigate Laura's murder," she said. Her voice was a soft monotone, which is often the case when people are in shock. "The police won't tell me anything, except that they don't have any suspects yet, and that is not acceptable."

"I can imagine how you must feel," I said, although of course I couldn't. "Why don't you come to the office tomorrow so we can talk about it in person."

Kate and I scheduled an appointment for the following morning and I gave her directions to my office in the marina complex. I slipped my phone and notebook back into my purse and returned to the table just as our Caesar salads were being served.

"What's up sweetie?" Elizabeth asked.

"You won't believe this," I whispered. "Holy shit, *I* don't believe this. Someone wants me to investigate a homicide. Have you heard about Laura Howard's murder on the news?"

Elizabeth stopped with her salad fork halfway to her mouth and nodded.

"That was Kate Howard, Laura's mom, on the phone. She's coming into the office tomorrow."

I entered the appointment in my PDA, then set my excitement about the new case aside so I could focus on the meal and the service.

The Caesar salad was the perfect combination of fresh greens, croutons, and anchovies, served with a piquant dressing which had been prepared at the table. My coulotte steak was so tender I could cut it with a fork, and the bordeaux reduction sauce contained diced morel mushrooms. I closed my eyes as the medley of flavors hit my tongue and almost had an orgasm. Elizabeth was very happy with her stuffed lamb chops, and we were both delighted with Brad. He was attentive without hovering, and absolutely charming.

When he delivered the check, in a black leather folder on a silver tray, I was ready to insert my credit card when I noticed something was amiss. The folder contained a time stamped register receipt, but it showed that it had been printed at 7:42 p.m. It was now almost 10:00 p.m. My steak and the two Caesar salads were listed, but rather than showing Elizabeth's stuffed lamb chops, the second entrée listed was frog's legs. The wine shown on the receipt wasn't what I had ordered, and the tall mudslide wasn't on the receipt at all. Brad had apparently held onto someone else's receipt and was reusing it, so that our meal would not be recorded on the register. I tucked my credit card back in my wallet and slid a stack of cash into the folder instead.

When Brad returned with my change I pocketed the bogus receipt and left a tip in the folder. I was disappointed by my discovery. Brad was a really good waiter and he'd lose his job over this. Not that he didn't deserve to lose his job, but I wasn't looking forward to being there when it happened and sitting in on termination interviews is part of my standard protocol. Fortunately, most people are so embarrassed about being caught and so relieved that they aren't being arrested, they never mention my identity and profession to their former coworkers.

We completed the bar survey in record time, and decided to call it a night.

Elizabeth was in a Mudslide stupor on the way home, so I shifted my focus back to Kate Howard. The police were probably already doing everything possible to investigate Laura's murder, and I might be wasting my time if I took the case. I dislike wasting time. I am not among those fortunate individuals who can relax and allow life to happen while they placidly observe, although learning how to placidly observe is on my long list of things to do. Nevertheless, it sounded *so* much more interesting than anything else I was working on at the moment. The most excitement I'd had in several months involved videotaping a chef who was stealing frozen calamari from his employer. The Howard case would give me an opportunity to expand my area of expertise. Besides, this woman had lost her child. I couldn't just turn her away.

What if, I thought, *the detectives working the case were incompetent? Or what if they just didn't care?* It could happen. How much death and destruction can one individual absorb before becoming desensitized? I would listen to what Kate had to say with an open mind, and perhaps even speak with the RCPD homicide detectives handling the investigation, before making a decision.

CHAPTER 2

THURSDAY MORNING ARRIVED WITHOUT fanfare. Sunny skies, with a light breeze, and only seventy-five degrees at 8:00 a.m. The air conditioning in the office complex was on the fritz again so I opened a couple of windows to create a cross draft.

The marina where I live and work is in Redwood City, California. I live aboard a forty-six foot Cheoy Lee motor sailor called *Turning Point*. Two years ago I qualified for my private investigator's license, got divorced, and moved onto the sailboat. It was definitely a turning point in my life.

The complex consists of five office buildings, one exceptionally good restaurant, and six gates, or docks, within which are housed approximately five hundred yachts. About two hundred and fifty of the yachts are owned by individuals and families who live aboard, as I do.

Across the street from the marina is the Bair Island Nature Preserve. It's a safe place for egrets and herons to roost, in spite of the fact that people come from all over the county to walk their dogs there.

Redwood City is a small town by California standards. The weather is generally mild, although in the summer the temperature occasionally climbs to over a hundred degrees, and the coast gets a lot of wind.

I'd heard on the news that Kate Howard and her husband lived in Atherton, an affluent community just south of Redwood City.

Since our appointment wasn't until 10:00, I had time for a workout. I finished typing the reports from last night, then locked up the office and drove around the corner to the gym.

I work out regularly and I try to live on the Zone Diet, but sometimes I cheat. Coffee is not on the Zone Diet, it turns out, and neither is Guinness, but I make an effort. I don't do these things because I'm obsessed with my appearance. I do them because my self-esteem is affected by my behavior. Being a trained observer, I've noted with some dismay that I exhibit guilt symptoms when I drink to excess, don't work out often enough, or eat unhealthy food. The guilt undermines my self-confidence, which leads to additional self-destructive behavior. It's a vicious circle.

After an exhaustive workout I drove back to the marina and showered aboard the boat, scrunched up my curls, applied mascara, lip gloss and my usual work clothes, and hiked back up to the office complex.

Kate Howard was punctual, dry-eyed, and one snappy dresser. She was probably in her late forties, but she didn't look a day over thirty-five. Her hair was shoulder length, honey blonde with highlights, and expensively cut to frame her heart-shaped face. She was about five-eight, her eyes were blue, and her skin was like porcelain. She was dressed in a teal silk shell and form-fitting David Kahn jeans. Her shoes were Stuart Weitzman leopard print flats and they matched her belt and her microscopic shoulder bag. In spite of the compassion I wanted to feel for this woman, I thought there might be something wrong with anyone who looked this put-together while enduring such a monumental loss.

I was dressed in Eddie Bauer cargo shorts, a short sleeve white cotton shirt, and New Balance Cross Trainers. I had tidied up the office, but I rarely alter my dress code even for socialites from Atherton. I do my best thinking when I'm comfortable.

I stood up as Kate drifted toward my desk, and shook her hand. It was limp, cool, and felt as though it had recently been exfoliated. I always make a point of shaking hands with someone I'm meeting for the first time. I've found that my intuition kicks in when I make physical contact, as long as I have no preconceived opinion, and providing the individual in question doesn't remind me in some way of my mother, my father, or my cousin Aaron – the three people most likely to push my buttons. Any similarity to one of them disables my objectivity.

I offered Kate coffee and she declined when she found out I didn't have decaf. I don't believe in decaf. Either it's coffee or it's not, and decaf isn't coffee.

Kate carefully examined my visitor's chairs before selecting the one on the right and sitting down. She heroically resisted the urge to dust it off. For the record, the chair wasn't dirty, it was just old.

My little ground floor office isn't elegant, but it's not shabby either. Two of my four walls are almost floor-to-ceiling windows that slide open, and the double front doors have glass panes in them. The view from my desk encompasses a substantial portion of the marina, including my boat and those of my neighbors, as well as the lush grounds of the office complex. I can see the sky, the earth, and the water. The view satisfies a fundamental need I have to stay in touch with nature.

My carpet is only three years old and a rich shade of forest green. I have a safe concealed behind a framed photo of the Great Wall of China, three file cabinets, a fax machine, one black-and-white and one color printer, two straight-backed visitor's chairs, and my own ergonomic swivel chair behind the desk. The desk itself is solid oak and it took four of Bekins's burly movers to get it in from the truck.

On top of my desk is a Dell desktop computer, a three-line telephone, an in-tray, an out-tray, an ashtray, and a few stacks of file folders. The files I keep atop my desk are not of the confidential variety. Those I lock in my Pendaflex drawer.

I keep a Ruger revolver in a Velcro holster strapped to the bottom of my lap drawer. I haven't needed it yet, but I grew up watching Mom's Thin Man videos so I feel more secure knowing it's there.

I have a kitchenette equipped with a toaster oven, a coffee maker, and a small refrigerator, as well as a sink and garbage disposal. I keep a portable cabinet with a TV and VCR/DVD player in the kitchen, so I can view surveillance tapes and discs. I store the TV in the kitchenette so my clients won't think I spend my days watching *soaps*. I have a private bathroom, unlike most of the offices in the complex. This was a major selling point, along with the fact that the office is only a hundred and fifty yards from my boat.

Kate's face was expressionless as she sat before me. Maybe that was how she avoided getting character wrinkles – no expression, no wrinkles. I waited silently. After looking around my office, she took a deep breath and volunteered a summary of her deceased daughter's life.

"Laura was a luminous child," she began. "When she smiled it was like the sun coming out. She was intelligent and affectionate, and she did well in school. She was the center of our universe, Ms. Hunter. But when she turned twelve something changed. Suddenly she was drifting away from us. She stopped studying, and her grades fell...she became defiant.

"Laura didn't finish college," she continued, in an apologetic tone. "She went to Stanford and got her BA, but then she just dropped out."

In what cosmos, I wondered, *does getting only a Bachelor's degree mean you're dropping out?*

"She still lived at home, but we didn't see much of her. Derrick has his company to run, and I do a lot of charity work."

I took notes while Kate spoke, but I was already having some doubts about taking the case.

"Laura was our only child," she said wistfully. "I loved my daughter, Ms. Hunter, but I haven't been able to reach her for years."

Kate stopped talking and looked at me expectantly.

"How did you hear about me?" I asked.

"I looked in the yellow pages. I wanted someone local and I wanted a woman. I thought a woman would be more sensitive."

She had me there.

"And what do you hope I'll accomplish?"

"I want to know why..." She finally broke down. Her perfect face seemed to collapse in on itself, her eyes and lips squeezed shut as if to contain her emotions. She opened her purse, desperately searching for a Kleenex. I pushed the box I keep on my desk toward her and she gratefully accepted two tissues, which she applied underneath her eyes to keep her mascara from running, and to her nose, which she delicately blew.

I had been wrong about Kate. She was using every ounce of strength she possessed to stay in control. After a minute, she continued. "I want to know why my daughter was killed. And I want to know that someone is dedicated to finding the person who did this to her. I want him to pay for taking her life."

"Do you have any ideas about that?"

"No, but I didn't really know her anymore. I don't know any of her friends." Her eyes grew distant.

"Have you already had the funeral?"

"Three days ago."

Damn. I had always envisioned handling a murder case where I'd catch my first glimpse of the killer at the victim's funeral. I read a lot of mystery novels.

"I've had our attorney request that you be shown the police file on the investigation," Kate said. "When you're ready to look at it you can call Detective Bill Anderson at the Redwood City Police Department."

A look at the case notes would be a tremendous help. It's next to impossible to get your hands on an open homicide file. I know this from watching television. Kate's attorney must have some serious clout.

I made a note of Anderson's name and asked Kate for her home address and phone number, her husband's work number, a picture of Laura, and the names and phone numbers of any family members with whom Laura might recently have been in touch. As an afterthought, I asked if she knew Laura's social security number. This would allow me to do additional research through Criminal Investigative Services, a.k.a. CIS, the service I use for background checks.

She gave me a wallet-size picture of Laura, and wrote down her address and phone number. She took out her BlackBerry Smartphone and read me the home number of Derrick's sister Sylvia, who lived in Los Angeles. She also had to look up her husband's number at InSight Software.

"New number?" I asked.

"No. I just don't call him very often."

I raised an eyebrow.

While I waited, Kate made a call, asking the person who answered for Laura's social security number. She jotted down the number and handed it to me, slipping the phone back into her bag.

"I'm willing to do a preliminary investigation," I said, "after which I'll let you know if I'm going to take the case." Kate nodded.

I told her my hourly rate, adding ten percent for hazard pay. This would be my first murder investigation and I had no idea what kind of risk might be involved. Before I could ask for a retainer, Kate took out her wallet and wrote me a check for two thousand dollars. More than adequate. I entered her name and the amount of the retainer on a standard contract, dated, and printed it. We both signed, and I gave her a copy of the agreement.

"I'd like to look at Laura's room this afternoon, if that's all right with you."

"That should be fine," she said. "I plan to be home all day."

After Kate left I looked at the photo she'd given me. It was Laura's high school graduation picture. She had been a lovely young woman with long blonde hair, her mother's perfect complexion, and unnaturally bright blue eyes.

I called the Redwood City Police Department and asked for Detective Anderson. After I held for almost three minutes he came on the line.

"Anderson."

"Hello, Detective. My name is Nicoli Hunter. I'm a PI working for..."

"I know who you are," he interrupted me. "You can come by and look at the binder anytime in the next hour. I may not be available after that."

"I can be there in fifteen minutes."

"Fine." He hung up without another word.

Of course he wasn't happy about showing me *the binder.* I couldn't blame him, but he didn't have to be snarky about it.

Before leaving the office I brushed my teeth and put on fresh lip gloss. I photocopied the check from Kate so I'd have a record of the information it contained, then dropped my Cyber-shot mini-camera into my purse. I didn't know if Anderson would leave me alone with the binder, but if he did, I didn't want to waste time taking notes when I could just point and shoot.

Outside, the blue sky was reflected in the still water of the marina making it look almost clean. There was a slight breeze and the temperature was seventy-nine degrees according to the thermometer I keep on the wall outside my office.

I decided to walk. The Redwood City Police Department is located on Maple Street, which is just a footbridge, a second marina, and a boatyard away from my office. As I walked, I smoked an American Spirit organic cigarette. I'm ambivalent about fresh air.

Going over my conversation with Kate in my head, I automatically compared the family portrait she had painted to my own. She had said Laura was the center of their universe. I'm the only child of a Cossack and a former nun. My mother was a sister, a thirty-year-old virgin holy woman, when she met up with a haunted Russian soldier so in need of salvation that she devoted the rest of her life to his spiritual rescue.

The mingling of these two unlikely sweethearts explains to some extent my cynicism about organized religion, my compulsion to save people, and my predisposition to stand and fight when the wiser course of action might be a hasty retreat. I also have an overdeveloped sense of justice coupled with an inherent distrust of authority figures. It works for me. I am not, however, nor have I ever been the center of my parent's universe. In spite of the fact that Laura was dead. I kind of envied her family's devotion to her.

Chapter 3

THE RCPD IS HOUSED in a building worthy of a layout in *Architectural Digest.* The entrance is surrounded by a semicircle of steps leading gracefully up to a covered landing with an abstract metal sculpture reminiscent of the Madonna and Child. I think of it as good advertising. *We may be the law, but we care about nurturing the community.*

I entered the lobby and looked around. No employees were visible, in fact, the place seemed to be deserted. There were several doors leading into the heart of the building, each of them labeled and undoubtedly locked, but the foyer was so well appointed that I almost felt welcome. I approached the reception counter and waited a moment before a woman in the back noticed me and came forward. Her nametag read *L. Ketteridge.*

L was a petite blonde in her early fifties and she was smiling. "What can I do for you?" she asked in a cheerful voice.

I had the impression that L either enjoyed her work or was the kind of person who would enjoy almost anything that came her way. I handed her my business card and told her Detective Anderson was expecting me. She tilted her head to one side and wiggled an eyebrow, said she'd be just a minute, and disappeared for maybe two. When she returned she told me Detective Anderson would be right out, and then she winked. I was a little nonplused by the wink. Did she think this was a date?

Detective Anderson was not right out, but when he entered the lobby four minutes later he looked like his wavy black hair had just been combed and his breath smelled of wintergreen. I had no idea what L had said to him, but I decided to be flattered.

I'm thirty-five years old, about five-seven, and a hundred and thirty-three pounds. My hair is long, curly, and chestnut brown with a few strands of white that look like highlights, but aren't. My eyes are sea blue with black rims around the irises; a combination I've only seen on one other person, my father. It's what discouraged me from challenging his paternity when I was a teenager and we were battling over things like curfew, dating, and make-up.

Detective descriptions of each subject encountered during an investigation are automatically recorded in a good PI's memory. This is something Sam Pettigrew, the crusty old PI who trained me, drilled into me during my internship. *What kind of shoes was the subject wearing, Nicoli? If you don't notice the shoes, how can you accurately estimate height?*

I checked out Detective Anderson. He was almost six feet tall, in his late thirties, lean but muscular, and clean-shaven. He had intelligent brown eyes that bordered on hazel with wicked long eyelashes, and his black hair was just beginning to gray. His complexion was dark, like someone who spent a lot of time outdoors or maybe had some American Indian heritage. His lips were full. There was no ring on his left hand, but his shirt looked clean and wrinkle free. His shoes were Ecco Track IIs. I knew this because I owned a pair.

Now here was a handshake, firm, but not a bone-crusher, dry, and warm. After we introduced ourselves he led me into one of the interview rooms where suspects are detained. There was probably a surveillance camera concealed somewhere, but it wasn't obvious at first glance.

When the door was closed and we were both seated, he asked to see my I.D. and my license. I showed him my private investigator's license, wishing I'd been having a better hair day when the picture was taken, and also handed him my driver's license and one of my business cards. He took a long look at my licenses, then handed them back to me and pocketed the card.

"I'll be right back," he said, and left the room.

I took the opportunity to scan the ceiling for cameras. I didn't see any, and there was no two way mirror like you see on TV crime dramas, but I remained convinced that there was a camera and there would be a viewing room somewhere nearby.

Less than a minute later Anderson was back, carrying a large black ring binder.

"You understand everything in the book needs to remain confidential," he said. It was a statement, not a question.

"Of course," I said.

He offered me the binder, holding it in both hands, and I noticed the thumbnail on his right hand was longer than the one on his left. That was a little weird. He continued staring at me after giving me the binder, as though he expected me to read the whole thing while he watched.

"We've managed to keep most of the details from the press," he said.

I looked him in the eye. "I understand," I said.

Did he think I was stupid or just a total sleaze?

I have to admit that up until now I had not made an effort to cultivate a relationship with the RCPD. I had only a few regular clients in Redwood City and since none of them had chosen to prosecute the employees I'd caught stealing from them, I'd had no need to do so. Most of the police departments I deal with are very cooperative and even refer clients to me. I had heard mixed evaluations of the Redwood City men and women in blue, but, as always, I would form my own opinion.

I opened the binder, glanced quickly at the autopsy report, and winced at the pictures of the crime scene. Laura was almost completely naked and her chest had been savaged. That, combined with the plastic bag over her head, caused my breath to catch in my throat. I closed the book and looked at Anderson.

"Can you give me ten minutes alone? I can't concentrate with you watching me."

He gave me an intense look, nodded once, and left the room. I whipped the camera out of my purse and snapped pictures of each page in the binder, front to back. There were fifteen in all. It took me about twenty seconds. I slipped the camera back into my bag and took a deep breath. I hoped I had finished before Anderson made it to the observation room. I doubted he would have asked any of his co-workers to watch me for him, so I was probably safe.

Now that I had photos of all the data, I could take my time reading through it. I looked over the crime scene report and the interviews with local merchants and business people who populated the neighborhood where Laura had been killed. I glanced quickly at the photos of the scene, noting how few there were in the binder, and that they had all been taken from a distance. Anderson was holding back, not showing me everything.

I started reading the autopsy report. Kate hadn't told me the details of the murder and they hadn't been publicized. According to the report, Laura had been suffocated, after which she had been stabbed in the chest three times. I looked more closely at the photos of her body and started feeling lightheaded. I pushed away from the table, dropping my head between my knees.

After a minute of deep breathing I heard the door open and saw a pair of Eccos approaching.

"Are you okay?"

So he *had* been watching.

I sat halfway up and leaned on my knees.

"How embarrassing is this? I guess the pictures kind of got to me. Do you have time to go out for coffee?"

That's when I got the smile. Detective Bill Anderson has a great smile. It extends from one side of his face to the other and includes some very white teeth and those little laugh lines around the eyes that look so good on men.

"Let's take my car," he said. "You're not gonna pass out are you?"

"God, I hope not."

We walked through a maze of cubicles to Anderson's desk, where he locked up the binder. Then he escorted me through an atrium in the center of the building and out a back door to the secure parking lot. He unlocked the passenger door of a fire engine red classic Ford Mustang. I wanted to smoke, but I couldn't bring myself to defile such a well-maintained vehicle.

"Is this your personal car?" I asked.

"Yes," he said. "I can't use it when I'm undercover. Too conspicuous."

We drove out through a security gate and made a right on Maple. Anderson drove to a restaurant called Otto's on El Camino Real. I knew this place well, and I knew the coffee would be terrible. Otto is one of my regular clients.

We seated ourselves in a booth in a corner of the restaurant where we could have some privacy, ordered coffee, and waited until it had been served.

When we had our coffee and the waitress was out of earshot, I asked Anderson if he'd seen anything similar to Laura's murder before.

"No."

A man of few words.

"Have you developed a profile?" I asked.

"Based on this case, I'd say the killer has a lot of anger toward women. Probably Caucasian. The knife wounds suggest the killer may have known the victim."

"What do you mean based on this case?" I asked.

"Well, I assume you watch the news."

I nodded. There had been another murder in Redwood City the week after Laura's. A librarian had been killed in an alley behind the I-Ching bar.

"Are you talking about the librarian?" I asked. "Is there a connection?"

He took a sip of coffee and looked into the cup as though he thought there might be a cockroach swimming in it, then set it down on the table.

"Both victims were female and they were both killed in Redwood City. No relationship between them that we can find. Not yet anyway." He started to raise his cup again, thought better of it, and pushed it aside. "I shouldn't be telling you this. You'll have to keep it to yourself."

"No problem."

He looked at me, probably trying to decide if I was trustworthy.

"I took some pages out of the binder before I showed it to you," he said. "There was something unusual about the weapon."

He paused and I held my breath.

"There were two puncture wounds on either side of each stab wound to Laura's chest." He was watching my face intently. "Can you handle hearing this?"

"I'm fine," I said, blushing. I am *such* a wimp.

"We think the knife had a sharp spike on each side of the hilt," he said. "The librarian who was killed had her throat cut, and there was a second, more shallow cut, just below the one that killed her."

I thought about that for a minute, trying to picture it.

"It was the same *knife!*" I said, a little too loudly.

We both looked around to see if anyone was paying attention.

"Sorry," I whispered. "But Laura was suffocated before being stabbed."

I had read that much of the autopsy report before I got woozy. To me, this meant that after she was dead the killer still had enough rage left over to need the additional release of stabbing her.

"Any prints on the plastic bag?" I asked.

"Just a few unidentifiable partials, some smears and smudges. Probably wore gloves."

"Laura's prints weren't on the bag?

"No."

If someone put a plastic bag over my head I'd reach up and touch it, and, given the opportunity, I'd yank it off or tear holes in the plastic so I could breathe.

"Any indication she was restrained?"

"No ligature marks."

"He could have used something soft that wouldn't leave marks."

Anderson looked at me with interest. He nodded, but said nothing.

"Were her clothes removed from the scene?"

"We found a leather halter top in the dumpster. No panties, but she may not have been wearing any. We got a partial print from the zipper pull on the halter top."

"Wait a minute. If the killer wore gloves, how could you get a partial print?"

"We couldn't if he'd been wearing gloves the whole time. Or, if there was more than one assailant, one could have been wearing gloves and one not. The print on the zipper pull may not even be related to the murder. All we know for sure is that it's not Laura's print."

He looked upset.

"How long have you been a homicide detective?"

"I handle crimes against persons," he said. "We call them body crimes. That includes homicides, assaults, sex crimes, and robberies. I've been a detective for seven years. Local homicides are usually a lot more straightforward than this. Gunshots, rival gangs killing each other over colors, domestic violence, that kind of thing." He paused. "She was so young."

Detective Anderson was opening up to me, which was not standard operating procedure. Most cops of my acquaintance are extremely formal and reserved. With any luck he'd care enough to keep me posted on new developments in the investigation. That could save me a lot of time.

"Does the mother think you're more likely to find the killer than we are?" he asked.

"She wants someone dedicated to the investigation reporting directly to her. And yes, she hopes I'll find the killer and ask him why he murdered her daughter."

"You think you can do that?"

I like a man who's not afraid to ask straightforward questions. I searched his face for any sign of sarcasm, and saw none.

"I don't know. I'll talk to the family and any friends I can locate, and then see how I feel about going further."

"Well, be careful."

I asked Anderson for his direct-dial number at the station and he gave me his card after writing his cell number on the back.

"I don't normally give this out," he said. "I keep my cell on twenty-four hours a day. I hope you'll let me know if you discover anything useful."

There it was. He thought I might find something he had missed. I could appreciate that. I took back the business card I'd given him earlier, and wrote my home and cell numbers on the back while he pulled a ten from his wallet and left it on the table. I thanked him for the coffee. It was bad, but he had paid.

Anderson drove me back to the station and before leaving I shook his hand again, just for fun. Then I walked to the marina, got in my own car – a vintage 1972 British racing green BMW model 2002 – and headed for Atherton.

Chapter 4

Tuscaloosa Avenue is in one of Atherton's average neighborhoods where the more humble houses start at three million dollars. I couldn't help wondering how many of the residents were from old money, never having to do anything but manage their stock portfolios, and how many had worked sixteen-hour days building businesses that eventually allowed them to live in these homes.

Everything in life is a trade-off. I gave up the security of working for someone else and took on the stress of managing my own business, covering my own medical insurance, and paying for my own office space. Now I can't leave the job behind when I go home, but I get to make all my own decisions. I keep asking myself if it's worth it. So far the answer is yes.

I like the independence of working alone, although sometimes it makes me feel isolated. Living in a community of boat dwellers helps quell the loneliness. People who live aboard are, for the most part, gregarious. And of course my best friend, Elizabeth, is also my neighbor. She lives aboard a forty-six foot trawler berthed at the base of the companionway that leads from the shore down to the docks.

I pulled into the Howard's circular driveway and parked in front of the enormous white colonial. I felt slightly out of place, but discomfort brings out the bulldog in me, so that was okay.

When Kate answered my knock I was surprised. I'd been expecting a butler in a tux.

"Good afternoon," she said.

"Hi, Kate. Is this a good time for me to look at Laura's room?"

"Of course. Please come in."

She was composed and gracious. Probably a great hostess.

I stepped into the foyer and shivered as the frigid air enveloped me. Maybe having the air conditioning on high was one of Kate's strategies for keeping her skin youthful. I know...*meow*.

As she led me up a broad staircase I admired the architecture, but I would never want to be responsible for anything so spacious. If I ever get tired of living aboard my sailboat I'll probably look for a one-story, two bedroom cottage with a small fenced yard. Something easy to maintain, where I can have a dog or two.

Laura's suite of rooms was at the top of the stairs. Kate opened the door and said, "I'll leave you alone."

"Thank you," I said, and I meant it. It's really hard to snoop with someone looking over your shoulder.

The first thing I noticed was the faint scent of roses. A quick look around told me there were no long-stemmed beauties present. Maybe Laura had used an air freshener or a rose-scented perfume.

The room was pristine. I needed to know if Laura had kept it that way or if the maid had cleaned up after her death.

I stopped Kate on her way down the stairs. "When was the last time this room was cleaned?"

She turned toward me and raised an eyebrow. "I have no idea," she said. "Our staff was instructed never to go into Laura's room. She liked her privacy."

"Have the police been in here?"

"Yes," she said. "But they didn't find anything. At least they didn't say they were taking anything."

I stepped back into the room and closed the door behind me, allowing the experience of being in the murdered woman's space to sink into my consciousness. The room had been painted a soft mint green and the molding and window frames were a pale violet. An unusual combination of colors, but somehow it worked.

I moved my gaze around the room from left to right. Near the door was an elaborate entertainment center with shelves of CDs, DVDs, and VHS cassettes.

The wall beyond the entertainment center was covered with mirrored panels, and the floor was polished hardwood. There was an open door beyond the mirrored wall through which I could see an elegant bathroom. To the right of the bathroom door was a cheval glass turned at an angle toward the mirrored panels.

There were two large windows, and between them stood a mahogany dresser over which hung another mirror. Centered on top of the dresser was a heavily varnished wooden box.

The king-size bed against the wall to my right was covered with a patchwork quilt that looked handmade and homey. Propped up against the pillows was a stuffed Shrek doll. Above the bed was a framed photograph of a tropical island, azure water and waving palm trees. There were end tables on both sides of the bed, each with a mission-style lamp on top of a white lace doily.

A set of double doors to the right of the bed had been left open, allowing me a glimpse of the huge walk-in closet. Shoes were lined up in pairs with the toes pointing toward the wall, and the clothes were all on hangers, nothing on the floor.

If the space you live in reflects your self-image, keeping your bedroom tidy might suggest that you feel good about yourself. Of course, if that was true I was in big trouble. Maybe neatness was a futile attempt to control the chaos of everyday life. That sounded better to me.

On the other side of the closet was a small desk, on top of which I spotted a framed family photo that looked like it had been taken at least ten years earlier. Laura, Kate, and Derrick, all facing the camera with their arms around each other, all of them smiling, but none of their smiles reached their eyes.

I crossed the floor and stepped into the luxurious bathroom. I flipped up two light switches, one of which started an overhead fan. I turned that one off, since I didn't need the distraction. The other switch illuminated a sun lamp bulb mounted in the ceiling and a row of very bright lights over a mirror that spanned the wall behind the sink. The oversized tub was equipped with Jacuzzi jets and the adjacent shower had two heads, plus a hand-held massage unit. It looked to me like the bathroom of a very sensuous young woman.

The contents of the cabinets and drawers told me that Laura had purchased expensive cosmetics and rose-scented, French-milled soap. The medicine chest contained the usual items including a bottle of Excedrin PM, but no other drugs and no type of birth control. I lifted the lid of the toilet tank and looked inside, finding nothing that didn't belong there. As I came out of the bathroom I flipped the cheval glass over and checked the back.

I moved to the dresser and opened the varnished box. The theme song from *Titanic* began playing as I examined the contents. The box contained some expensive jewelry and some garish costume pieces, separated by a divider in the center. I pawed through the assortment with interest, but the music was getting to me. I hate sad movies. I closed the box and opened the top dresser drawer.

I was once again struck by the fragrance of roses, and discovered that Laura had used sachets in her lingerie drawer. On the right was a collection of sporty white cotton briefs, sox, and jogging bras. On the left were black, purple, and red lace demi-bras, thongs, and a strapless navy blue bustier. In the other drawers I found Laura's neatly folded sweaters and tee shirts.

I turned my attention to the bed. Picking up the Shrek doll I turned it over in my hands. There was a Velcro closure on the back. As I tugged at the Velcro I inadvertently squeezed the belly of the doll and a raspy voice croaked, "This is my swamp." Smiling, I pulled open the Velcro at the back and Shrek said, "Thank you very much. I'm here till Thursday." There were two AA batteries and a tiny speaker inside the doll, but no evidence that would lead me to Laura's killer.

I set the doll aside and looked under the pillows, inside the pillowcases, between the sheets, between the mattress and box spring, and under the bed. I stood on the bed and carefully removed the framed photo from the wall, checking the back for anything hidden there. After straightening the bed I peeked under the throw rugs.

On one of the bedside tables was a Nora Roberts paperback. I flipped through the pages wondering if Laura might have been hoping to meet up with a hero and live happily ever after. I have mixed feelings about romance novels. I think the unrealistic expectations they create are responsible for a lot of failed relationships, but I also love the happy endings.

I emptied the nightstand drawers, then looked behind them, finding nothing of interest. I tugged the heavy bed away from the wall so I could see behind the headboard.

I was feeling frustrated and my lower back ached. I wondered if a quick dip in Laura's Jacuzzi would be inappropriate.

I entered the walk-in closet. Laura had everything the well-dressed débutante would wear, plus an assortment of spandex and leather garments that almost made me blush. I wondered if Laura had separated the aspects of her life as successfully as she had separated her wardrobe choices. I was glad Kate had chosen not to join me while I searched her daughter's room.

I checked all the pockets, and then pushed the clothes aside and looked behind them. *If you're going to do something, do it well.* That was my maternal grandmother speaking. She passed away when I was thirty, but I still hear her voice.

I finished my search of the closet finding nothing more fascinating than a pair of navy and white T-Strap Ferragamos.

I rummaged through the desk and found an assortment of mundane office supplies. In the Pendaflex drawer was an accordion file of bank statements. I opened the most recent envelope and scanned the deposits and withdrawals. There were two automatic deposits listed, noting that the source of the deposits was the '*Fanny Pack*'. That was interesting. The *Fanny Pack* was a local strip club. I wondered if I should bring this up with Kate, and decided to wait until I knew more, and perhaps until Kate was suffering less. I set the file by the bedroom door.

I removed each drawer from the desk and checked the bottoms, sides, and backs, hoping something had been taped there like in the movies. No such luck. I got down on my hands and knees and looked under the desk. I hauled it away from the wall, careful not to disconnect the telephone. As I was pushing it back it occurred to me that there was one essential item missing from this room. Laura didn't have a computer. Her father owned a software company. Maybe it was her way of showing contempt for him or for what he chose to do with his life.

Nothing in the room provided any insight into why Laura had been killed. I don't know what I'd expected to find. Maybe a hidden stash of methamphetamines. It wasn't likely she'd had advance knowledge of her impending death. Not like she could leave some kind of a clue behind. That would be too much to hope for.

I sat down on the bed and studied the entertainment center. Most of the videotapes and DVDs were in cardboard or plastic boxes advertising the enclosed movies, but there was one VHS box without a label. I got up, turned on the VCR, and inserted the Fuji cassette. After I got the TV on the right channel and remembered that I had to push *play*, the video began.

On the screen I saw Laura, dressed in a brown jumpsuit and wearing some kind of helmet. There was a parachute strapped to her back, and she was seated in what appeared to be the cargo hold of a small airplane. In spite of the helmet her long hair blew fiercely around her face as she leaned forward looking out the open door. The camera remained focused on Laura and a male companion who was similarly attired. The man was wearing goggles, obscuring his features.

After a few minutes Laura put on her goggles and smiled at the camera, then stepped out of the airplane as casually as I get out of bed in the morning, although somewhat more gracefully. The man jumped out behind her and was closely followed by the person with the camera.

During about thirty seconds of free-fall the camera remained on Laura. She was grinning wildly. Of course it was probably impossible to fall at a hundred and twenty miles per hour without the corners of your mouth reaching for your ears.

I watched the video until Laura and her friend were safely on the ground. The tape ended before the guy took off his goggles, so I never got a look at his face. All I could say for sure was that he was above average height, and appeared to be in pretty good shape.

I rewound the tape, took it out of the VCR, and tucked it into my purse.

I glanced through the rest of Laura's movie collection. It was predominately Disney, but included *Miss Congeniality*, *You've Got Mail*, and, of course, *Titanic*. She read romance novels, slept with a Shrek doll, and watched Disney movies. She also got automatic deposits from a local nudie bar. Human beings are riddled with contradiction, but what I was seeing here suggested that Laura fantasized about a return to innocence, at least while she was at home.

I was tempted to snoop around the other upstairs rooms, but I'd already been there for two hours and I didn't know who else might be home, so I retrieved the file of bank statements and went downstairs.

I found Kate in the living room. She was gazing at a large flat panel TV, mounted above the fireplace. The home movie she was watching had been paused. On the screen I saw a younger Kate Howard, her arms around a chubby toddler who was gazing up into her mother's eyes. Laura's cherubic smile was indeed as Kate had described it; like the sun, shining adoringly on her mother.

I felt my heart catch in my throat. What must it be like to have endured the loss of that child's affection years ago, and now to live with no hope of ever reclaiming the perfect love they had once shared?

I softly cleared my throat to announce my presence. "I'm finished," I said.

Kate slowly turned to face me. Her eyes had a faraway look.

"I'd like your permission to take Laura's bank statements and this skydiving video." I took the cassette out of my purse and held it up.

"Of course," she said.

"I noticed Laura didn't have a computer in her room."

Kate smiled wistfully. "No. She refused Derrick's offers to buy her one. I guess she was old-fashioned in some ways."

Laura might have been old-fashioned in some ways, but I didn't think that was why she'd refused Derrick's offer of a computer.

I told Kate I'd be in touch. She walked me to the door and thanked me for coming. She sounded sincerely grateful, and I searched her face before stepping outside. I had expected to see grief in her eyes, but what I saw there looked more like guilt. She felt responsible for her daughter's death, whether directly or indirectly. I'd have to dig into that eventually, if I took the case.

I started up my little 2002, and drove to the bad part of town.

Chapter 5

I HAD DRIVEN PAST THE *Fanny Pack* often enough to know where it was, but I was surprised to find the parking lot crowded at 12:30 on a weekday. Maybe they served a lunch buffet. I locked the 2002 and approached the front door, stepping around bits of broken glass and gummy patches on the pavement.

The club was housed in a two-story, box-style building that was painted slate blue. There was a brass plaque on the front door that read *Twenty-one Years and Older Only - No Minors Allowed - Open for Business 11:00 AM - 2:00 AM*

When I opened the door I was struck by the smell of cigar and cigarette smoke mixed with the odors of beer and human sweat. Apparently the patrons of this establishment chose to ignore the *No Smoking* signs and management was disinclined to enforce the ordinance. The music was almost painfully loud and I could feel the bass vibrate in my bones.

I surveyed the room and felt the urge to flee. This took me back to high school when the girls' and boys' gym classes happened to pass each other on the way to or from the locker rooms. I spend a fair amount of time in bars as part of my work, but I had never been in a strip club before. It felt different from a regular bar. Probably the pheromones.

The doorman seated on a stool to the left of the entry reminded me of Jim Belushi. He was dressed in khaki slacks, a Hawaiian shirt, and a baseball cap worn backwards. He smiled when I glanced his way. It was a nice smile.

A number of people had turned when I entered and were now staring at me, probably because I was holding the door open and letting the daylight in. Not surprisingly, there were few women present, apart from the one on stage. The dancer was a redhead with milky-white skin. She was slender and she wore nothing but a pink G-string and pink high-heels. She looked about sixteen. I felt my stomach clench, and I was momentarily overwhelmed with concern about the young woman's welfare. There are some things I'm not open-minded about.

The red-haired teenager was dancing on an elevated platform equipped with a pair of fire-station-type poles that extended floor to ceiling. As she danced, she watched herself in the mirrored walls. She seemed self-conscious, maybe even embarrassed, but who wouldn't be under the circumstances?

The female spectators looked like working girls and they sized me up with what I interpreted as professional curiosity. The men were sizing me up too, probably wondering how much I charged. I controlled my discomfort by telling myself that if I was inclined to charge for sex, no one in this crowd could possibly afford me.

I let the door close and moved toward the bar, taking everything in. The soles of my shoes made sucking sounds, sticking to the floor as I walked. I tried not to think about what the sticky substance might be. The walls were lined with pinball machines and video games, and a pool table was positioned in a corner to the left of the door. There was a flat panel television above the bar, tuned to a sports channel, but all eyes were either on the dancer, or on me.

The men who populated this establishment could have been a cross section of Americana. Some wore white shirts and dress slacks and looked like businessmen or possibly car salesmen. There were guys in jeans and tee shirts, and there were a couple of leather-clad bikers. The age range went from early twenties to mid sixties.

I noticed two cocktail waitresses dressed in pastel string bikinis standing in the back of the club; a pretty blonde and a zaftig brunette. I wondered if they were cold. The air conditioning was on high, and it was chilly. They were both smoking cigarettes and each held a large round serving tray.

The bartender on duty looked young. He was close to six feet tall, a little chunky, and wore a goatee. He placed a cocktail napkin on the bar in front of me, briefly made eye contact, and gave me a shadow of a smile. I asked for coffee, raising my voice to compete with the music. I paid for my coffee and then placed a twenty-dollar bill on the bar and took Laura's picture from my purse. As soon as he saw the photo his expression hardened.

"Were you close?" I asked.

"You a cop?"

"No." I leaned across the bar so I wouldn't have to shout. "I'm a PI. Laura's mother hired me. My name is Nikki." I held out my hand.

He hesitated for an instant, and then shook my hand. His was massive, soft, cool, and a little damp. "Frank Waters," he said, his eyes still suspicious.

"How well did you know her, Frank?"

"Pretty well. We used to see each other, you know, outside the club." His voice cracked and his eyes filled with tears. "Excuse me." He turned away, picked up a handful of cocktail napkins from the back-bar, and wiped his face.

While his back was turned I reached into my purse and switched on my tape recorder. California law requires that all parties consent to the recording of a conversation, but I was the only one who would ever listen to it. I set my purse on the bar between us. It would be hard to pick anything up because of the volume of the music, but it was worth a shot.

Frank took a few deep breaths and came back to me. "Sorry," he said. "What do you need to know?"

I like men who cry, so Frank had scored points in my book and I didn't want to upset him any more than I had to.

"I need to know what kind of person Laura was," I said. "How she felt about life. What she did for fun. Who her friends were."

He looked down at the picture, considering, then brushed at his nose with a napkin.

"Laura was a good person," he said, "but she wasn't happy and I don't think she had many friends. We dated for a while. She was pretty and smart, and a great dancer." He looked away and stopped talking.

"But?" I prodded.

"It's hard to talk about." He was tearing up again.

"Is there any place we can speak privately?" I asked.

Frank looked around the club and spotted the cocktail waitresses. He walked over to them, leaned close to the brunette, and said something to her that caused her to glance in my direction. She nodded and went behind the bar.

Frank motioned for me to follow him. He led me down a hallway to a small office that smelled of stale cigar smoke and housed a wall of blank video monitors.

"We can talk in here," he said. "But I can't be away from the bar too long."

"Okay," I said. "I know this is painful for you, but the more time that goes by the more likely it is Laura's killer will get away with it. Anything you can tell me will help, but whatever you don't want to tell me will probably help the most."

With a little prodding and encouragement some subjects will spill everything they know during a spur of the moment interview. If you come back to the same person a week later they'll clam up. Others will tell you nothing during the first encounter, and after their conscience works on them for a while they'll answer all your questions. I had a feeling Frank fell into the first category.

He took in what I had said, blushed, and averted his eyes. I waited. Eventually he spoke.

"She didn't like sex. That was a problem for me. I tried to talk to her about it. Don't tell her mom this stuff, okay?"

"Okay. What did she say?"

"She said it just didn't do anything for her. She liked to be held though, you know, to cuddle. Anyway, we dated for about three months and then decided to just be friends. And we were, good friends. We'd go out to breakfast sometimes after closing, or go to a movie. Things like that."

“What made you think she was unhappy?”

“Little things, mostly. She didn’t smile much, except when she was dancing. She really got off on dancing.”

“You don’t have to answer this if you don’t want to, Frank, but I’ll find out anyway. Was Laura into drugs?”

He looked around the office and fidgeted a little before saying, “She liked crank.”

“Did she do a lot?”

“No. Just once in a while when she was feeling down.”

“Did she ever talk about her family? How things were at home?”

“Only once, when we first got together. She got pretty drunk one night and started crying. I asked her what was wrong and she said she had no family. I asked her what she meant, ’cause I knew she lived with her folks, but she just wanted me to hold her. So I held her, and she fell asleep. I didn’t bring it up again.”

“Can you think of anyone who would want to hurt Laura? Anyone who had a grudge against her or who was angry with her?”

“Oh jeez, I gotta work here you know?” He popped his head out into the hall and looked both ways. “You didn’t hear this from me,” he whispered. I nodded. “There’s this other dancer. Candy. I don’t know her real name. Candy was the big draw here before all the regulars started saving their tips for Laura. That cut seriously into Candy’s take-home. One of the other girls told me Candy threatened to scratch Laura’s eyes out.”

“Was Laura afraid of her?”

“I don’t think so. But Laura liked to take risks.”

My ears perked up. “Excuse me?”

Frank leaned out the office door again, apparently checking on the bar, and then returned his attention to me. "When we first started going out, sometimes she would drive," he said. "She was a crazy person behind the wheel, almost like she had a death wish or something. After a while I started driving everywhere we went together. I just couldn't handle it."

"Was she dating anyone recently?"

He looked surprised at the question. "I don't know."

"Okay," I said. "You've been a big help, Frank. Thank you."

I gave him my card with the usual request that he call if anything else occurred to him and asked where I could find Candy. He said she didn't come in until 8:00 p.m. I asked if the owner was in and Frank said I should check back around 6:00 or 7:00. He said the owner's name was Alfred Miner. He was about five-foot-three and heavy set. The office we'd been using was his.

When I stepped outside into the daylight, I put on my sunglasses and compulsively filled my lungs with smoggy air. What a relief. I switched off my tape recorder and drove to the marina.

CHAPTER 6

BACK IN MY OFFICE I unloaded my purse, placing the tape recorder, the camera, the skydiving video, and Laura's bank statements on my desk. I listened to the tape of my conversation with Frank while I booted up the computer and made a pot of Kona coffee. I lit a cigarette, and typed up some of Frank's comments about Laura; she was unhappy, she felt she didn't have a family, she wasn't into sex, but she was into risk.

I wanted to collect my thoughts before showering and going back to the *Fanny Pack. Ugh.* I started with a log of my time and expenses, then entered my hypotheses about Laura. Her parents had apparently offered her every advantage, but she had chosen to take a huge symbolic dump in the faces of her benefactors by working as a stripper. Why? Did she feel her parents had somehow neglected her? And if she hated her parents, why had she continued living at home? Maybe she loved her parents but resented the lack of attention she received from them, so she stayed at home to be near them, but chose a career she knew would embarrass them if they found out about it. Even negative attention is better than no attention at all.

I had no idea what kind of money exotic dancers made, but I felt certain Laura's parents would have been happy to supplement her income so she could afford a place of her own. It had to be a conscious decision on her part, to live at home with Mom and Dad while stripping five nights a week.

Laura was turned off to sex according to Frank, but a lot of women don't reach their sexual peak until they're over thirty. Besides, Frank seemed like a nice, sensitive guy, and that could be a real turn-off for a woman who was attracted to danger. Maybe she'd found a more exciting partner. I thought about the skydiving video, and wondered who the man was. I saved my notes, turned off the computer, and walked down to my boat.

I love living at the marina. It's a community in the truest sense of the word. The day I moved aboard I received visits from several of my new neighbors who introduced themselves and pointed out their boats so I'd know where to find them if I needed anything. A woman who lived on a trawler across the dock from me said, "If you need to use a phone before yours is hooked up, feel free to come aboard anytime. I never lock the door." In all my years of renting apartments, houses, and duplexes in the Bay Area, I had never once had such an invitation.

Most of my neighbors who own sailboats live for the day they can take a break from work and go cruising. I just like knowing that if I decide this isn't the place for me anymore, I can untie my home and move on. It gives me a sense of freedom.

Although it seemed pointless to shower before going back to the *Fanny Pack*, I needed a psychological cleansing. The shower on board my boat doesn't have much water pressure, but it's convenient. When I was clean and dry, I dressed in jeans and a tee shirt and threw on a windbreaker to conceal the holster at the small of my back. I grabbed a fresh pack of cigarettes and made sure there was enough cash in my wallet to pay for information.

On the way to the parking lot I stopped in at my office and drew the Ruger out of its resting place under my desk. It slid smoothly into the Galco holster.

I arrived at the *Fanny Pack* at 7:37 p.m. There were no empty spaces in the lot, so I parked around the corner and walked back, holding my canister of pepper spray at the ready.

The whole strip club scene was different at night. There were more tables set up and they were closer together. Two women were dancing between tables, another was on the stage, and one was gyrating on a customer's lap. The dancer on stage looked barely old enough to drive. I reminded myself that the young women who worked in this establishment did so by choice. Unemployment was high, but they could probably have found office or retail jobs.

I planned to speak with Alfred Miner first, and then catch Candy before she went on at 8:00. Frank wasn't on duty, so I approached the bartender – female, Asian, five-five, long blonde hair, wearing a hot pink spandex bodysuit – and asked if Alfred was in. She silently pointed to the hallway with a two-inch French tipped talon.

I found Alfred Minor in his office. The door was open and the video monitors displayed several views of the club and one of a poorly lit hallway somewhere else in the building. Cigar smoke permeated the air. Normally I like the smell of cigars, but Alfred's was cheap and the tobacco odor was rank. I stood in the doorway unnoticed for a moment before knocking.

Alfred looked up at me with dark beady eyes, grinned, and said, "You look good, honey, but aren't you a little old for this kind of work?"

Fuck you, I thought, and smiled back at him.

"My name is Nicoli Hunter," I said. "I'm a private investigator looking into the death of one of your employees. Laura Howard?"

Alfred stopped smiling. "You're not with the police?" I shook my head. "What do you want to know?" he asked, rolling the cigar from one side of his mouth to the other.

"Whatever you can tell me about her. Who she was friendly with. Which customers she spent time with. Anyone you can think of who might have wanted her dead?"

He considered me for a moment, and then said, "I don't know who her friends were. The broads are always yakkin' in the dressin' room, but I rarely go in there. They take it off for the stiffs out front, but they get pissed if you walk in when they're naked.

"All the customers liked Laura, but she preferred the older gents. Maybe 'cause they got more money. I don't know anyone who wanted her dead. Certainly not me. She was a good draw. Now if that's all, I got a business to run."

"I need to talk to the dancers," I said. "Any objection?"

"Not if it don't interfere with their work. Come on. I'll take you to the dressing room." He winked and I shuddered.

Alfred walked me down the hall to the first door on the left. He knocked twice and yanked it open, revealing four women in various stages of undress, all of whom started yelling at once.

"Shut up a minute," he bellowed. "This here's a private dick." He grinned at his own joke. "She needs to talk to you about Laura, so be nice, but nobody misses a cue." With that he withdrew, leaving me standing in the open doorway.

Four voices simultaneously shouted, *"Shut the door!"*

I stepped inside and closed the door behind me.

"Hi," I said. "I'm Nicoli Hunter."

Group interviews are awkward under the best of circumstances, and with eight breasts of various shapes and sizes pointed at you it's difficult to concentrate. I'm also shy in the locker-room at the gym. I think this has something to do with my mother, the former nun, and modesty training. After I'd introduced myself, I asked each woman her name. I took out my notebook and jotted down a brief description of each dancer.

Bambi – Caucasian, early 20s, 5' 3", black hair, brown eyes, double D implants

Clarise – Caucasian, late teens, 5' 6", red hair, green contact lenses

Amanda – Mulatto, early 20s, 5'10", brown hair, blue eyes

Buffy – Caucasian, mid 20s, 5' 7", blonde with dark roots, blue eyes

I was relieved that at least three of the four didn't look as young up close as the women I'd seen dancing earlier.

They all claimed to have no knowledge of Laura's personal life and, of course, none of them had anything against her. No one had been close to her and the consensus was that Laura kept pretty much to herself. I asked if they had any idea who might have wanted her out of the way. They looked at each other and stopped talking.

"I just need to know if any of the customers or any of the other dancers had issues with Laura. It's a simple question."

Sometimes being rude gets a better response than being polite does. I have a carefully cultivated bitch persona, which I enjoy taking out of the closet on occasions such as this.

Buffy opened her mouth to speak, but at that moment the dressing room door opened and in walked a woman who *had* to be Candy. She was at least five-nine, even without the spiked heels, an Asian and Caucasian hybrid in her mid-twenties, with black hair down to her waist and inch-long jungle-red fingernails. She was dressed in a leopard-skin spandex unitard. She took in the scene at a glance and asked the logical question.

"You a cop?"

The other women had hastily gone back to applying make-up, turning away from me.

"No," I said. "I'm a PI investigating Laura's death. And you are?"

"My name's Candy," she said. "Can I see some ID?"

Talk about a bitch persona. I produced my private investigator's license and also handed her one of my cards. She set her black tote on a vacant dressing table and examined the license.

"Okay," she said. "I guess you're for real."

This woman unearthed something dark in my lizard brain. I disliked her more than I could justify. It wasn't because she was young, beautiful, and a sleazy bitch. It was because she was a young, beautiful, sleazy bitch, and she was talking *down* to me. I could only hope that if she looked like a middle-aged schoolteacher and talked down to me I'd have had an equally negative response. But this was no time for introspection. I unclenched my jaw and retrieved my license.

"I was asking if anyone knew who might have wanted Laura out of the way. Did you know her well?"

Candy sat down, crossed her legs, and lit a cigarette. I lit one too. Eventually she responded. "The only person in this joint who spent time with Laura is Frank. He's a bartender. You should talk to him."

"I'll do that. So you don't know of anyone with a grudge against Laura?"

"I didn't say that." She exhaled a smoke ring and glanced at the other women, who were pretending to ignore our conversation. "Everybody knows I threatened to scratch her eyes out if she didn't stay away from my regulars." She looked at me. "We all have our special customers, you know? Laura had no respect for that. She'd do a table dance for anyone, sometimes without being asked, even after I warned her to leave my guys alone. Tell you the truth, I'm glad she's dead."

I gave her points for honesty.

"What about the customers? Was there anyone who seemed hostile toward her?"

"Honey, the guys who come in here are horny, not hostile." That got a few nervous giggles from the other women. "I gotta go on in fifteen minutes. Are we done?"

I gave each woman a business card, thanked them, and left the dressing room, quickly closing the door behind me.

I went back to the bar and ordered a draft beer. I wasn't going to drink it, I just wanted to blend in. I asked the bartender the same questions and, after I gave her a twenty, got the same answers. She admitted there was a problem between Candy and Laura, but said she didn't think Candy was likely to become violent.

"She might break a nail or something. You know how much porcelain nails cost?"

I turned away from the bar and watched the dancers perform for about a minute, then I started watching the customers. The person I was looking for might be intelligent, but would not be well adjusted. I squinted, trying to see facial expressions through the smoke in the dark room. I didn't see anyone who looked like they could plan, much less execute, a crime that would baffle Bill Anderson and the RCPD forensics team. I set my beer on the bar and headed for the door.

Before stepping outside I took the pepper spray out of my purse. I walked cautiously to my car, watching every shadow. I made it to the car without incident and locked the doors once I was inside.

I decided to go back to the office and take a look at the pictures I'd taken of Anderson's murder book. I drove to the marina, my mind a whir of visual impressions I'd absorbed at the *Fanny Pack*. I needed another shower.

CHAPTER 7

I UNLOCKED THE OFFICE DOOR, turned on the computer, and resisted the urge to brew yet another pot of coffee. I plugged my digital camera into one of my USB drives and waited for the new photos to download. The pictures I'd taken weren't great. I'd been in too much of a hurry. But I could make out most of the words if I enlarged the view.

The crime scene report stated in cold clinical factoids that the body of a female Caucasian had been found behind a dumpster in a parking lot on Bay Road. The report listed the names of the patrol officers who had discovered the body and the address of the parking lot.

The victim had three stab wounds to the chest and there was a clear plastic bag secured over her head by a large blue rubber band imprinted with the word ORGANIC and the numbers 94060. *A zip code?* The victim had been wearing only a black leather miniskirt, which had been pushed up around her waist, and a pair of black ankle boots.

The victim's vehicle, a canary yellow Dodge Viper, was parked in the lot. It had been examined for physical evidence before being impounded. The only identifiable fingerprints in the Viper were those of the victim, who had been printed at the scene for the purpose of elimination. It was noted that the car was immaculate, as though it had recently been detailed.

Based on the condition of Laura's bedroom, this didn't strike me as out of character.

There were no weapons found at the scene.

As Detective Anderson had told me, the report mentioned that only a few unidentified partial prints and some smudges had been found on the plastic bag, and another partial print had been taken from the zipper pull of a black leather halter-top, which had been recovered from the dumpster.

I moved on to the pathology report.

No foreign hair or unusual fibers were found on the body. There was nothing under the fingernails, no defensive wounds on the hands or arms, and there was no indication that the victim had been restrained. Her genitalia had been pierced with two gold hoops sometime prior to the night of her death.

The rape kit swabs revealed traces of a spermicidal lubricant, which had been identified by the lab as particular to Trojan brand Supra condoms.

The three stab wounds to the chest were described in detail, and it was noted that they were inflicted postmortem and were not related to the cause of death. The cause of death had been suffocation – the plastic bag.

No wonder the police were restricting the information they shared with Laura's mother.

In addition to the three stab wounds, Laura had pre-mortem signs of bruising on the left side of her face.

I scanned back to the first page of the pathology report. No foreign pubic hair had been found. I wondered how that was possible. I was envisioning a hairless male when I thought of something that made me forget about pubic hair altogether. Laura was into risk. Some people find being deprived of oxygen erotic. I'd read about a few cases of accidental death due to auto-erotic asphyxiation. Often the victim is so intent on increasing the intensity of an orgasm with the use of some type of breath-stopping technique, that they lose consciousness before they can release whatever it is that's choking them. Maybe Laura *had* willingly allowed the killer to place the bag over her head. Maybe she had even asked him to do it. That would explain why Laura's prints weren't on the plastic bag. Her partner might simply have left it in place too long.

I've never studied medicine, but I understood enough of the report to know that Laura had not been drugged before she was murdered. Might she have had a moment of comprehension just prior to losing consciousness? Could it all have been a horrible accident? Maybe in the throes of passion her lover had mistaken Laura's jerks of asphyxiation for the spasms of orgasm. Perhaps the stab wounds had been an afterthought, to throw the police off track. Of course that wouldn't explain the bruise on her face or the fact that the same knife might have been used to kill a local librarian.

Laura had apparently driven herself to Bay Road and parked near a drugstore that was closed for the night. It seemed she had met or followed her lover to this rendezvous with one thing in mind, an assignation in a public place. Someone had brought along the plastic bag and the rubber band. Presumably these had been provided by Laura's partner, since her prints weren't on them. This raised another question. If the boyfriend had brought the bag, why weren't there any complete fingerprints on it? Had he tried to wipe them away after stabbing Laura, thus causing the smudges?

I wondered what was so appealing to a young woman with Laura's education and background about the sordid side of life. Maybe she was bored and wanted to experience something wild and out of control.

I typed up my notes of the evening's discoveries and expenses, and added my opinion about the plastic bag, then locked up the office and walked down the companionway. Any ramp that connects a dock to shore is called a companionway. In fact, anything that gets you from land to a dock or from the dock to a vessel is referred to as a companionway. During high tide the marina ramp is almost parallel to the shore, but at low tide it's so steep that if it wasn't corrugated you'd have to slide down on your butt.

I passed Elizabeth's trawler and continued down the dock, feeling a sense of warmth as I approached my home.

My Cheoy Lee is an ideal live-aboard vessel. It was built in 1980 and customized by the former owner, who passed away leaving it to his wife who, in turn, sold it to me for a song. Apparently he had died in the company of another woman. The wife was one of my first clients, but his infidelity was not why she hired me. She owned a local restaurant and was concerned about employee theft, so I installed some covert surveillance equipment for her. It was a coincidence that we neglected to tell her husband about the cameras, and that we happened to record his indiscretion with the hostess, and his subsequent heart attack. On the night of his death I sat with his wife as she watched that scene over and over again. Finally she said, "You wanna buy a boat?"

The Cheoy Lee's center cockpit pilothouse doubles as an enclosed front porch up on deck. It's also where the steering console is housed. From the pilothouse you descend into the galley, or kitchen, which is small enough that even I can keep it relatively clean. Forward of the galley is the main salon, where I spend most of my time. The aft stateroom, my bedroom, has a queen-size bunk set up against the bulkhead. The head, or bathroom, is equipped with a small tub and a stall shower.

I have only one plant on board, which I have tried numerous times to give away. When I got my license and was leaving the employ of Sam Pettigrew, the PI who trained me, he gave me the plant as a farewell gift. I've never seen another one like it. It resembles a miniature maple tree. The gift took me by surprise, since the closest thing to a display of affection from Sam prior to this had been a hundred-dollar bonus he'd slipped me when I completed twenty-two consecutive hours of surveillance. The plant is in a beautiful antique pot. I've tried to palm it off on my mom, my ex-husband, and a few of my friends. Boats are not a safe place for potted plants. When you're underway they tend to get tossed around and damaged. I trim it once a month to keep the size manageable, and I water it weekly. I also turn it every day so it gets even sunlight from the portholes in the galley, and in spite of the affection I feel for Sam, I resent like hell the time I spend taking care of it. I don't like being responsible for another living thing. Besides, if I kill the damned plant I'll be heartbroken.

The Cheoy Lee's Yanmar engine will run on anything from diesel fuel to bacon grease, an important feature if one intends to do any long distance cruising. The engine is housed under the pilothouse. There's a trap door in the pilothouse floor that opens directly into the engine compartment. This is convenient in the event you have engine trouble at sea.

My ex-husband Drew taught me how to sail. I'm not much of a swimmer and at first I was freaked out by all that water, but as I gradually became more confident, my fear of drowning diminished. Now I love the freedom of having a sailboat. It's ironic that my ex introduced me to a hobby that, after the divorce, became my lifestyle.

I showered on board again, made myself a green salad with canned tuna, and sat down to watch the evening news. For almost two weeks Laura Howard had been among the top local stories. The anchorperson stated that the police still had no one in custody. They showed pictures of the parking lot where Laura had been killed, then moved on to the murdered librarian who had been killed the week after Laura's death.

I was just about to change the channel when the anchor announced the discovery of an unidentified male homicide victim found tonight in a bank parking lot in Menlo Park.

Menlo Park. Less than three miles away from the marina, and less than a mile from where Laura had died. I shivered in spite of the balmy temperatures. *Too many murders too close to home*, I thought.

I picked up the remote and began searching for a mindless sitcom.

CHAPTER 8

ON FRIDAY MORNING I went to the gym and took a yoga class. Then I did my upper body workout with free weights and jogged on the treadmill until I felt the endorphins kick in. I showered, blew my hair dry, and drove back to the office where I munched on a week-old bagel while I made a list of what I needed to do to get the investigation rolling.

First I would e-mail CIS and request Laura's DMV records and any criminal records in San Mateo County. For sixty-five dollars any licensed PI can access DMV records and do a one-county search for arrests and convictions, plus a financial background. More than one county costs more than sixty-five dollars. It helps if you have the subject's driver's license or social security number. Otherwise you might get the wrong person's data.

I would call Laura's father at his office and schedule a time to speak with him in person, and I would call Kate and ask if she had Laura's private phone bills. Those hadn't been in her desk. If there was time, I would call Laura's Aunt Sylvia in L.A.

I set the list aside and took out Laura's bank statements. I started with the most recent statement and moved backward in time. Laura had thirty-three thousand dollars in her checking account. I considered how much of that income might have been from dancing and again wondered why she had lived with her parents. She could easily have afforded a rental house or an apartment.

Laura had been willing to pay the extra fee to have the bank return her cancelled checks each month, so I read the front and back of each one. When I got to April, I found what I was looking for. There was a check for twelve hundred dollars made out to the Sky Ranch on April eighteenth. On the back was a stamp indicating that it had been deposited at a Wells Fargo bank in Lompoc, California. I called information, wrote down the number, and dialed.

"Sky Ranch, Big Al speaking."

I assumed there must be a Little Al somewhere on the premises.

"Hi, Al," I said. "My name is Nicoli Hunter. I'm a PI in Redwood City and I'm doing background research for a woman whose daughter was recently killed. Can you tell me if you ever take snapshots of your skydiving clients before or after they make a jump?"

"Yeah, sometimes. We keep 'em here on the bulletin board."

"Are the pictures dated?"

"Usually."

I promised Al I'd mail him a check for fifty dollars if he'd send me any photos dated April 18th. Lompoc was over two hundred miles away and I didn't want to have to make the drive. To my relief, he agreed. As I set the receiver back in its cradle, I stared at the check. Why hadn't Laura used a credit card?

I called Derrick Howard at his office. Eventually I was connected with his assistant who seemed very professional in spite of her high-pitched, breathy voice. She asked my name and why I was calling.

"My name is Nicoli Hunter. I'm a private investigator and I've been retained by Mrs. Howard to look into the death of their daughter."

She put me on hold for a full minute, and then came back on the line and said that Mr. Howard was in a meeting. I asked how long she thought he would be, and she told me she really couldn't say. I left my office number.

Thirty minutes later Derrick Howard called me back. His tone was clipped and he sounded impatient.

"I'd like to come by and meet with you," I said. "It shouldn't take more than fifteen or twenty minutes. Is this morning convenient?"

"No, Ms. Hunter, it is not. I have a company to run, and frankly I don't understand why my wife insisted on hiring you."

I bristled. "Your wife hired me because she isn't satisfied with the results of the police investigation. I promise I'll take as little of your time as possible."

"All right," he huffed. "I'll give you a few minutes if you can be here by ten."

"Thank you." I hung up without saying good-bye.

I know some people convert grief into anger, but I reserve the kind of petulance Derrick Howard was exhibiting for close personal friends and relatives, and I think others should do the same. I dislike people who are rude. I make snap judgments about everyone I encounter, and based on my brief conversation with Derrick Howard, I determined that he was an asshole.

I've spent years studying psychology as a hobby. I've read everything from Freud to Jung, as well as the more recent schools of thought, and I pay close attention to other people's behavior as well as my own. When I feel threatened I become aggressive. I have an addictive personality and a penchant for self-doubt, consequently, I smoke in spite of the fact that I'm kind of a health nut. I've been married three times; once when I was still in high school, to get away from my parents, once when I was twenty-four, to do a favor for a friend who wanted to immigrate, and once for love. The most recent episode lasted four years. They were four good years, but Drew, my ex, wanted children, and I did not. When we decided to get a divorce I cried nonstop for two days. Then I realized I was better off. Drew and I loved each other, but we had very little in common. My self-esteem still took a beating, however. Drew has triplets now, which goes to show you should be careful what you wish for.

After Drew and I called it quits, I decided that was it for me. Who can honestly say they'll be with you until death, let alone love, honor, and cherish you that long? Most people don't know from one moment to the next what they want, so how can anyone claim to know what they'll want forty or fifty years in the future?

I'm happily single now, but I have to admit I sometimes yearn for male companionship, especially at night. I'm not opposed to having a relationship, I just don't want to make or accept any promises about living happily ever after.

My pet peeve is people who maneuver themselves into positions of power and then abuse that power. I've never been content, and I don't know how to relax. That's me in a nutshell.

I e-mailed CIS requesting the records search on Laura Howard, and then I checked my list and placed a call to Los Angeles.

Laura's Aunt Sylvia answered on the third ring, sounding like she'd been crying. It was nice to know someone in Laura's family was openly grieving.

"Hello?" she sniffled.

"Mrs. Davis?"

"Yes."

"This is Nicoli Hunter. Has Kate spoken with you about me?"

"Oh, yes. The detective, right? She said you might be calling. What can I do for you, dear?"

"I have a couple of questions about Laura. Is this a good time?"

"As good a time as any," she said, and blew her nose loudly near the receiver.

"When was the last time you spoke with her?" I began.

"About three weeks ago, I guess." She sniffled and sighed.

"Do you remember what you talked about?"

"About me, mostly. Laura was a good listener. Always interested in what was going on in my life. I'd told her I was signing up for salsa dance classes and she called to see if I'd gone through with it."

"Wow. So did you?"

"Oh, yes. The classes are wonderful. I've missed a couple since...you know."

"Of course. Did Laura happen to mention anyone she was dating?"

"Not that I recall, no."

"How did she seem to you?"

"You mean was she acting differently?"

"Yes. Did you notice anything out of the ordinary in her tone of voice? Did she seem unhappy, angry, depressed?"

"Actually she seemed a little more subdued than usual, but I couldn't tell you why."

"Okay. What can you tell me about the family?"

"Kate said I should tell you anything you wanted to know. You want to talk about Laura's relationship with her parents?"

"If you have the time."

"I have almost nothing *but* time," she said. "I recently retired."

"Oh really? What did you retire from?"

"I'm a clinical psychologist. Didn't Kate tell you? No, of course not. Why would she? I just assumed that was why you were asking me about the family."

"Kate didn't mention it, but I would like to hear your thoughts."

"You're very observant aren't you, dear? I suppose that's why you're an investigator. Laura was a very confused young woman. They spoiled her when she was little. Not enough discipline. No structure. They gave her anything she wanted without thinking about how that might affect her later in life. When Laura was twelve Derrick started his software company. Kate became involved with a couple of charities around that same time. So there was a change in the amount of attention they gave Laura. I think she may have felt abandoned...started acting out.

"When Laura was in high school Kate finally realized that she and Derrick had inadequate parenting skills. They took her to a psychiatrist, but that only made matters worse. She ran away from home when she was fourteen. The police brought her back three months later. She'd been living in a commune somewhere in Marin County. After that Laura's behavior deteriorated until she took that job dancing. It was the last straw for Kate. She seemed to give up on Laura after that."

"Wait. They *knew* Laura was an exotic dancer?"

"Oh yes. She made no effort to hide her occupation from Kate and Derrick."

However, Kate had hidden it from me. I wondered why.

"Derrick checked out when Laura was twelve," Sylvia continued. "I think he may have had a hard time dealing with her sexuality. Although, it's interesting to note that our father seemed to withdraw from Derrick when he was around that same age.

"Anyway, I tried to tell them Laura needed discipline when she was a toddler, but nobody listens to the aunt. So few people are qualified to be parents. The point is, Laura wasn't a bad person. She just needed guidance and structure. I'm probably telling you more than you need to know."

I couldn't write fast enough to keep up with Sylvia's commentary, so it took me a moment to realize she'd stopped talking.

"What? Oh no, this is exactly the kind of information I need. What happened when Laura was in high school?"

"She discovered boys. Started sneaking out at night. Coming home at dawn. Her grades suffered. Derrick caught her coming in early one morning. Kate told me about it later. She said that Derrick had called Laura a whore. The look on Laura's face when he said that just broke Kate's heart."

"Did you ever meet any of Laura's college boyfriends?"

"No, I never met him. Saw pictures of him though. Nice looking boy."

"She only dated one guy in college?"

"Yes. They were engaged."

"Do you remember his name?"

She thought for a moment before saying, "I'm sorry, I'm drawing a blank. I'm sure Kate and Derrick will remember though."

"So what happened? Why didn't they get married?"

"She broke it off. All she said to me about it was that he turned out not to be the one."

"What about female friends?" I asked.

"Laura didn't have many friends, male or female, because she didn't like herself very much. She thought there must be something wrong with anyone who wanted to spend time with her, poor child."

Sylvia and I talked for almost thirty minutes, then I thanked her for her time and her insights, and gave her my office number in case she thought of anything else that might help.

I shook the cramps out of my fingers and entered the notes I'd taken into Laura's case file. I needed to buy a telephone headset so I could type while I was listening.

I called Kate and, before I had a chance to say anything, she asked if I had decided to take the case. I realized that in my mind I was already committed.

"I still have a few things to check out before making that decision," I hedged.

Sometimes I need to say no before I can even think about saying yes. I asked if she'd be home for a while and she said she was on her way out, but that she'd be happy to wait for me, so I locked up the office and drove to Atherton.

Once again Kate answered the door herself. She was wearing white today. White slacks, an elegant white blouse, and a pair of taupe Ferragamo sandals. She looked flawless. Why should that annoy me? She invited me in and we sat facing each other in oversized armchairs in the living room.

"When I was going through Laura's desk," I began, "I didn't find any telephone bills. Is the phone in her room a private line?"

"Yes. I took care of the bills for her."

"Do you have the statements?"

She looked puzzled, but said nothing and left the room briefly. She came back with a single white envelope.

"I only have the latest one," she said. "After I pay them I throw them away. This just came yesterday."

I accepted the bill, minus the pay stub and envelope.

"What about her credit cards?"

"She had an American Express Platinum, but she almost never used it."

"Did you take care of those bills for her as well?" I asked.

"Yes."

Again she left the room, returning with a file folder of statements, which she handed to me. Now I knew why Laura had written a check to the Sky Ranch. For some reason she wanted to keep that part of her life private.

"There's one more thing I need to know, Kate. Why didn't you tell me that Laura was an exotic dancer?"

Kate flushed with embarrassment, and looked down at her feet before responding. "I was afraid if you knew... that you wouldn't respect her enough to take the case." She looked me in the eye and I saw the unspoken plea.

I nodded. "I'll call you tomorrow with my decision."

She silently ushered me to the door.

I drove back to the office and locked Laura's AMEX and phone bills in my growing file on the investigation. I was on my way back out when I thought to check my e-mail. Sure enough, among a few messages from my regular clients, I had a response from CIS. I scanned it quickly while it was printing. Laura had received three speeding tickets in the last twelve months. If her license had been suspended it wasn't mentioned in the report. I read further and discovered that she'd been arrested for solicitation in March, and that the charges had subsequently been dropped. *What the hell?*

I picked up the phone and called Kate, but I got the machine.

"Kate, it's Nicoli," I said. "I need you to call your attorney and ask him to request copies of Laura's criminal record from the Redwood City Police Department. I need to know more about her activities over the last year."

I left my office number, in case she'd misplaced it, then shut down the computer and locked up the office. It was time to meet Laura's father. I was *so* not looking forward to this.

CHAPTER 9

I ARRIVED AT INSIGHT SOFTWARE a few minutes early and cruised around the parking lot. The cars that occupied the lot looked expensive and almost half of them were SUVs. Considering the price of gas, the company must be doing well.

In the lobby I was greeted by a lovely black woman seated behind a U-shaped reception counter. She was wearing a headset and a form-fitting business suit. Her nametag read *Tanya*.

"May I help you?" she asked.

I handed her my card and said, "I have a ten o'clock appointment with Derrick Howard."

She pressed a few keys on her console, spoke softly into the headset, listened to the response, and said, "Mister Howard will be with you in a few minutes."

Tanya made me one of those visitor's badges that you stick to your lapel and that never stay put.

I seated myself on a couch near a huge rubber plant. While I was waiting I reviewed the notes I'd prepared for the interview and girded myself for the encounter.

Derrick Howard strode into the lobby at 10:07. He was at least six-two, slender but solid, and wore a pinstriped white shirt, a red power tie, and gray wool gabardine slacks. His hair was brown with some white around the temples and his features resembled a bird of prey – dark intense eyes and a beaky nose. He radiated a fierce intelligence. Many people feel intimidated when confronted by someone wealthy and powerful, but most people don't have a father who's a Cossack.

Derrick shook my hand as I introduced myself. His grip was firm and his hand was warm and dry. He smiled and apologized for keeping me waiting. Was this the same asshole I'd spoken with on the phone? Some individuals behave differently in person. They think they can get away with anything on the telephone because you can't see them. It's like the way people drive, but don't get me started on that.

Derrick escorted me down a series of hallways and up one flight of stairs to his office. When we were inside and he'd closed the door, his demeanor became frosty. Apparently the friendly act had been for the benefit of his employees.

His office was a corner suite with expansive windows. He seated himself behind an oversized mahogany desk. I took a seat on the other side of the desk and observed that my visitor's chair was about five inches lower than the executive swivel on which Derrick was perched. It's amazing the lengths to which some people will go to make others feel insignificant. I believe this is a holdover from childhood when we have no control over what happens to us. People have a fundamental need to believe they have command of their lives, and that often translates to control over others. In reality, all any of us can control is our own response to what happens.

I took out my notebook. "I understand Laura seldom brought friends home."

He shook his head. "Never."

"Did she talk about her friends, or any men she was dating?"

"No."

"Were you *aware* of any particular man she might have been seeing?"

"No."

"Did you know Laura enjoyed skydiving?"

He lifted an eyebrow. "What?"

"There was a videotape in her bedroom of Laura and a male companion skydiving."

"Really? I'd like to see that."

"I'll be sure to get it back to you. I was wondering if you have any idea who the man might be. He was tall, athletic, brown hair."

"No."

"Mr. Howard, were you close to your daughter?" Even taking what Sylvia had told me into account, I didn't want to assume anything.

"No, Ms. Hunter, I was not close to Laura. My business takes up most of my time. When she was a little girl things were different. We haven't been close since she was eleven or twelve. I'm sorry I can't be of more help to you."

Eleven or twelve. Puberty. Maybe Sylvia was onto something.

"Did you know Laura got three speeding tickets in the last year?"

The eyebrow popped up again. "No, I wasn't made aware of that," he said.

This was getting me nowhere. I chose not to bring up the solicitation arrest, the strip club, or the fiancé until I'd made a decision about taking the case.

"I may need to speak with you again," I said, handing him my card. "But I won't take any more of your time today."

He tucked my card in his breast pocket and said, "I'll walk you down."

We took a different staircase on the way out and passed a glass-walled computer lab full of men and women hovering over keyboards with large flat panel monitors. My eye was caught by a movie-star-handsome guy in his mid-thirties. Tall, wavy brown hair, nice build.

He must have felt me watching him, because he looked up and met my gaze. His eyes were dark and penetrating and as he stared at me I felt exposed, almost violated. There's no other way to describe it.

Derrick and I continued down the hall and he ushered me out a side door. I thanked him for seeing me and told him I'd be in touch.

Once I was outside I still couldn't shake off the visual encounter with the guy in the computer lab.

I walked to my car feeling unsettled. Laura's father showed no emotional response to the death of his daughter. Maybe he'd viewed her as an embarrassment or an inconvenience and was glad to be rid of her. Of course, he might just be a very private person. Maybe he was a seething cauldron of repressed emotion, ready to explode with the slightest additional pressure, and was just hiding it really well.

I wasn't sure what to do next, so I decided to take another look at my photos of Detective Anderson's binder. I drove back to the office and read the whole thing this time, start to finish. Then I lit a cigarette, picked up the phone, and called the *Fanny Pack*.

The phone rang seven times before someone picked up.

"*Fanny Pack*," said a male voice.

"Frank?"

"Yeah. Who's this?"

"Nikki Hunter. The PI, remember?"

"Oh, yeah," he said, without enthusiasm.

"Can you talk?"

"Why? Did you catch the guy?"

"Not yet, but I have another question about your relationship with Laura. You can answer yes or no."

"Okay."

"Did Laura ever ask you to choke her during sex, or to put anything around her neck?"

For about ten seconds I heard only music on the other end of the line. Then he whispered, "Are you *kidding* me? That's *sick*. Why would you *ask* me that?"

"I'm sorry, Frank. I'll talk to you later."

I hung up knowing I'd left him with an image that would haunt him. So what had I learned? That maybe it wasn't Laura's idea to put her head in a plastic bag. Maybe.

I took out the file folder of American Express bills and started going through them. The only items Laura routinely charged were expensive lingerie and garments from a shop called Bad Girls on Polk Street in San Francisco. Those were charges her mother had to have seen, and again I had the impression she was trying to antagonize her parents. When

I got to the April statement there was only one item on it for a Motel 6 in Lompoc on the eighteenth. I kept that one out and got the phone number from information.

The man who answered had a Middle Eastern accent and was difficult to understand. I asked if he kept records of his guests and what information was required before a room could be rented. He said everyone filled out a registration card with the usual information. I assumed that would include a name, address, telephone number, make and model of car, and vehicle license plate number. I asked him very politely to check his file for April 18, saying I'd gotten a bill from American Express for my daughter's Platinum card, with a charge for his motel on that date. I insisted that she had not been out of town that weekend. He was uncooperative.

It was beginning to look like I'd have to drive to Lompoc after all. I called the Sky Ranch again and asked for Big Al. He came on the line after a minute and told me he'd found three photos dated April 18. He hadn't mailed them yet, so I told him to hold onto them and asked for directions.

I stopped at the bank and deposited Kate's retainer, then I gassed up the 2002. I noted the mileage on the odometer so I could bill Kate for the trip, and hit the road.

As a rule I don't like long drives, but it was a clear day and the coast highway is scenic. While I was driving it occurred to me what a convoluted path I'd followed to get to where I was today. I grew up in South San Francisco and spent my formative years in the company of my cousin Aaron, an unruly kid with a talent for making mischief. Aaron was two years older than I was, and apparently this gave him a certain credibility with adults because he always convinced my parents that I was responsible for his crimes. I was often the recipient of punishments that should have been his, usually a spanking or being locked in my room without TV privileges.

Everyone's family is dysfunctional to some extent, but I like to think mine is unique. There was no physical expression of affection in our house. My parents did not hold hands, kiss each other, or embrace in my presence. They also didn't kiss or hug me. I would watch my friends interact with their families and wonder what was wrong with me. Everyone else was getting hugs and kisses. The only physical contact I remember is the regular spankings I received when I took the blame for Aaron's transgressions.

Although my dad spent time teaching me about guns and how to shoot, he did not play with me. He played, instead, with my cousin. He and Aaron used to run foot races in the back yard, but I was never invited to participate. I resented Aaron for this, but on some level I thought it was my fault, that because I was a girl I was unworthy.

Mom had been playing the piano since childhood, so when she was excommunicated and married my dad, she hung out her shingle and started taking in students. This allowed her to be at home so she could care for me while earning an income. Both of Aaron's parents worked, so Mom allowed her brother and his wife to park their devil child at our house.

I now understand that children are slaves to their survival instincts. When we feel threatened, we do whatever we think is necessary to protect ourselves. For Aaron, that meant blaming me for anything he'd done that turned out to be a punishable offense. At the age of four I received a particularly severe beating for one of Aaron's peccadilloes. I remember thinking at the time that I would never forgive him, or my parents.

Because of this ongoing torment, I developed a profound need to see that justice is done – a hunger for the bad guys to get what they have coming to them. On the other hand, as a distorted consequence of my obsession with justice, I began shoplifting when I was six. If my parents thought I was bad, I might as well be bad. My life is full of this kind of paradox.

Later, when I sold cosmetics, I graduated to stealing from my employer, till-tapping and taking merchandise home that I hadn't paid for. After a few years, my retail career segued into security. I was surprisingly good at spotting shoplifters and till tappers, and management decided that talent was more valuable to them than making a sales quota. Eventually I was promoted to a security management position for the chain of department stores.

When I accepted the management position I decided it was time to turn my life around. The fact that I'd had a miserable childhood didn't mean the world owed me anything. I mailed in anonymous cashier's checks until everything I'd stolen was paid for, or paid back. This took a while. I liked the security job, but I didn't find my true calling until I became a PI.

I believe the larcenous phase of my life contributes substantially to my ability to identify dishonest individuals today. It really does take a thief to catch a thief. In spite of the fact that I no longer rob anyone to satisfy my inner child, I have continued to live my life as though there is always something wrong and it's my job to fix it. Knowing this allows me to use the compulsion rather than allowing it to use me, most of the time, and it makes me very good at what I do.

Aaron became a criminal defense attorney. No doubt his childhood experiences also contribute to his success. We have an ambivalent relationship at best. I can't forget what a little shit he was as a child, and all he can remember of our time together is that when I was old enough to defend myself I started kicking his ass.

Almost three hours after leaving Redwood City I was on a dirt road leading to a vast field encircling two hangers and a number of small airplanes. I pulled into the unpaved parking area and looked around for signs of life. There were a few people smoking outside the hanger on my left, so I headed in that direction.

Inside, the hanger was partitioned into room-sized spaces. To the left of the entrance was an open dressing area where jumpsuits, helmets, and goggles were hung. Beyond this was a counter with a cash register and a few skydiving brochures scattered in asymmetrical piles. To the right was a seating area where several young people had gathered on hassocks and couches.

Behind the seating area was a small retail shop that appeared to stock all the paraphernalia associated with skydiving, and an office.

I spoke to a young woman positioned behind the cash register and she pointed out Big Al, who was giving a class to beginners. He was indeed big. I'd say about six-five and three hundred pounds, in his early thirties, Caucasian, brown hair, mustache and beard, brown eyes.

When Al inserted a disk into a DVD player and instructed his pupils to, "Pay attention and take notes," I approached and introduced myself.

Al gave me a warm, if slightly distracted smile, and shook my hand. His was calloused, warm, and dry. He asked me to wait a minute and went into the office, returning almost immediately with three Polaroid snapshots. I took a fifty-dollar bill out of my wallet and he gave me the photos. I fanned them out in my hands like playing cards and looked closely at each one.

The third picture took my breath away. Standing next to Laura, dressed in a brown jumpsuit similar to hers, was the man I'd seen in the glass-walled computer lab at InSight. I flipped the picture over. Only the date was on the back.

I looked up at Al, who said, "You okay? You look a little pale."

"This is really important. Do you have any records that would have this man's name?" I held up the photo.

Al scratched the back of his head and said, "There's the consent forms."

"Consent forms?"

"Yeah. Anybody goes up in a plane has to sign a waiver, you know, in case something happens, saying we're not responsible."

"You're kidding, right?"

"Come on, I'll show you."

The office was a disaster, with stacks of paperwork and file folders covering two desks, but Al knew right where to look. He approached one of two large file cabinets against the rear wall and opened the bottom drawer. Consent forms were grouped according to month and year. Finding April was a breeze. I decided to photocopy all the forms from the eighteenth, just to be safe. Al went back to his class, leaving me alone in the office while I did this. I tucked the copies and the photographs into my purse, and discreetly passed Al another fifty on my way out.

My knees felt weak as I crossed the field to the parking lot. Since this was my first murder investigation any little clue was likely to cause an adrenaline rush. I lit a cigarette and inhaled deeply, feeling the nicotine kick in. I was given my first cigarette when I was fourteen by my best friend in high school, Cher Costanza. It was a Salem. Now I smoke American Spirit Organics. I tell myself the lack of pesticides and additives makes them healthier than conventional cigarettes, but I know it's a rationalization. I smoke to dull down my feelings. I understand nicotine is an extremely addictive, user-friendly drug, and I'm equally aware that I need to quit depending on it. But not today.

I was too excited to drive, so I sat in my car and read the consent forms. Third from the bottom of the stack was a form signed by Laura, and directly beneath it was the consent form of Frederick Wulf, who lived in Menlo Park roughly two miles from the location where Laura had been killed. The hell with the Motel 6. I had what I needed.

CHAPTER 10

I called InSight on my cell and Tanya answered after three rings. Counting the number of times a telephone rings is a habit I picked up working for my mentor, Sam Pettigrew. In the PI business you have to document everything – the number of times a phone rings, the name and gender of the person who answers, the time, the date, everything they say, and everything you say – it all goes in the report.

I said, "Frederick Wulf, please."

"One moment, I'll see if he's in."

I quickly disconnected, my heart racing. I took some deep breaths and checked my rearview mirrors to make sure no one had been listening. I knew I was overreacting. Laura had gone skydiving with a good-looking guy who had an unnerving stare, and who worked for her father. That didn't mean anything. The fact that he lived within walking distance of where she was killed might mean something. My solar plexus was doing the samba. Sam taught me never to ignore my instincts. *Your body knows things your mind is clueless about, Nicoli.*

I lead-footed it back to Redwood City.

I arrived at the marina just after 5:00 and let myself into the office. I dropped my purse on the desk and rummaged through the office refrigerator looking for something to eat. All I found was a jar of dill pickles, some stale rice cakes, two bottles of mineral water, and a low-fat lactose free yogurt that I should have thrown out the previous week. I tossed the yogurt and ate one of the rice cakes at my desk.

I took the snapshots and consent form copies out of my purse. I needed to learn more about Frederick Wulf. The obvious source would be Derrick, but he might tell Fred I'd asked about him. I decided to return to InSight and follow him when he got off work. I washed down the rice cake with some water, then locked up the office and drove to Palo Alto.

I arrived at InSight at 5:23 and managed to find a parking space that gave me an angled view of both the front and side doors. I rolled down the windows, emptied the ashtray into a garbage bag, and began filling it up again.

At 5:35 Fred came out the side door. I slid down in my seat, trying to be invisible, and picked up my camera. I have the mini digital camera for quick jobs, like Anderson's binder, and a beautiful old Nikon with all the attachments that my mom gave me. I used the Nikon with a telephoto lens, allowing me to get a close-up of Fred's profile. He walked around the side of the building to a silver-blue Jaguar XJS convertible. As he was putting the top down I snapped a few more pictures, including one of his license plate.

I followed him as he slowly left the parking lot, staying about forty yards behind. On Highway 101 I closed the gap, but drove in the third lane while he took the first. Traffic was dense, making it easy for me to follow him without being obvious.

Fred took the Marsh Road/Atherton exit, made a left on Marsh, and a right on Bay, then another right onto a residential street. He pulled into the driveway of a small cottage. I parked at the end of the block and discreetly snapped a few more photos as he climbed out of the Jag and entered the cottage.

Laura had been killed on Bay Road in Redwood City and Fred lived in a cottage less than a block from Bay Road in Menlo Park. I don't believe in coincidence. I sat there thinking for a few minutes before digging my cell phone out of my purse and calling Elizabeth. She answered on the second ring.

"This is Elizabeth."

Elizabeth is always professional, even when answering her home phone.

"Are you doing anything tonight?"

"Hi, honey. Why do you ask?"

"I need you to watch someone for a couple of hours. I don't want to risk having him recognize my car, in case he sees it again later. If he goes out, I need you to follow him. Call me if he stops somewhere and I'll take over. Can you do it?"

"Is he dangerous?" she asked.

"I don't know yet. Maybe."

"What's the address?"

I read the address off the consent form, and gave her directions.

Elizabeth Gaultier is my best friend for many reasons, among them the fact that she seldom asks for favors, doesn't gossip, much, and she's always there when I need her. She's five feet and one half inch tall and about a hundred pounds. Her strawberry blonde hair, hazel eyes, and the scattering of freckles over the bridge of her nose make her look like an innocent but sexy waif. Her IQ would place her among the elite in Mensa if she were interested, which she isn't. Nobody calls her Liz or Betsy, at least not more than once. She manages a small scientific software firm in Sunnyvale. She's thirty-three years old, divorced, and has no children. Elizabeth collects acquaintances like crazy, but has only a few close friends. I consider myself fortunate to be one of them.

Nine minutes later her green VW Beetle pulled up behind me. I climbed over the 2002's gearshift and got out on the passenger side. I strolled casually back to her car, keeping my face turned away from Fred's cottage. The drapes in his front window were drawn, but there was no sense taking chances.

I got into the Beetle's front seat and slid down. I pointed out the cottage and the Jaguar, and gave her the digital camera and my cell phone. Elizabeth doesn't own a cell phone. She thinks they're a needless expense. I told her I'd be in my office waiting for her call. This wasn't the first time she'd covered for me on a surveillance, so there was no need for further instructions.

The shortest route to the marina took me past the parking lot where Laura had been killed. Making a last minute decision I pulled into the lot. A shiny new dumpster had replaced the one confiscated by the police. I got out of my car and walked around the dumpster. There was a rust-colored stain on the pavement. As I looked down at it I felt my eyes begin to fill. It could have been the frustration of working on a case that might be too much for me, or maybe compassion for a young woman whose life had ended tragically, despite the advantages she'd had since birth.

On the way home I made a quick stop at a Taco Bell for a low-fat Burrito Supreme, which I wolfed down while driving. I parked near the gated dock and hustled down to my boat where I changed into jeans, a tank top, and a windbreaker to cover the Ruger holstered at the small of my back. I washed my face and put on fresh lip gloss, then trotted up to my office to wait for Elizabeth's call.

The answering machine light was blinking when I got there. I pressed the play button. The message was from Kate, saying I could pick up a copy of Laura's criminal record at the RCPD any time, and that I should, once again, ask for Detective Anderson. Anderson was Crimes Against Persons, but he would have pulled all of Laura's records during the course of his investigation. I was not upset by the prospect of seeing him again.

As I sat at my desk waiting for Elizabeth to call, I thought about the case. What would I do if I discovered who had taken Laura's life, but couldn't prove it to the DA's satisfaction? My thoughts about Laura's death drifted to thoughts about death in general, and my family. These are subjects that are often on my mind.

Apart from the time we spent shooting at targets, the only happy memory I carry around about my dad is his view of superstition. When I was seven he told me our family was special because all bad luck was reversed for us. It was good luck to have a black cat cross our path, or to walk under a ladder. A broken mirror meant you could look forward to the next seven years. Because I believed him, Friday the thirteenth has always been a very good day for me.

My father was born in St Petersburg. His father, a Cossack, taught him how to kill with a miniature saber at the age of three. To hear him tell it, the Cossacks were more than just a band of Slavic horsemen, they were a bloodline of noble warriors. He once told me he'd changed his name when he arrived in the U.S. in order to avoid a Bolshevik hit squad. I didn't find this out until my early twenties, when I finally asked him why our name didn't sound Russian. He said he'd looked in his Russian/English dictionary and chosen Hunter because it was the closest word he could find to the translation of his family name, which he confided to me in hushed tones. He made me promise never to repeat it to anyone.

A few months later Dad disappeared, and I found myself hungry for the details of his life that I'd failed to ask about while he was around. I did some research on Cossacks and Bolsheviks, and it seemed to me that anyone on this so-called hit squad would have to be in his nineties, unless they were descendents of the original group.

I Googled the family name Dad had revealed to me and discovered a sixteenth-century Russian statesman and military leader with the same last name, who was also a cousin of the Tsar. I dug out Dad's old address book and wrote to his brother in Australia, but he never responded. Finally I called the director of the Russian Choir in Pebble Beach and said I was interested in learning more about my father's family. I told him my dad's full name, and he gasped, then went ballistic, shouting, *"One of them is still alive?"* I dropped the receiver in the cradle and jumped back, afraid he might come after me through the phone lines.

My father's disappearance is still a mystery. He took his little motorboat out on the Bay one morning and never came back. The Coast Guard found the boat, but he wasn't in it. Everyone assumed he had drowned, but Dad was a strong swimmer and his body was never found.

Maybe the Bolsheviks finally caught up with him, but I have my doubts. I half suspect that he had a mid-life crisis and decided to travel solo. I even thought I saw him once, from a distance, at the marina. I was so startled that without thinking I yelled, "*Dad*!" and started running in his direction. Whoever it was climbed into a red Thunderbird and sped away. I jumped in my little BMW and gave chase, following him all the way to the Marriott Hotel in San Mateo, where I lost him in the parking lot. Some detective.

My mother had learned to speak Russian when her order transferred her from Minnesota to a diocese in San Francisco where there was a large Russian community. When she arrived in the Bay Area, a naive young nun, she developed friendships with some of the gay men and women in her neighborhood, and began to question the Catholic doctrine condemning them. Over the next few years her disillusionment with the Church grew.

Mom was thirty when my father, having just arrived in San Francisco, found his way to the mission where she was serving the homeless two hot meals a day. Her knowledge of Russian gave her the opportunity to converse with him in his own language, and they spent long hours sharing their life stories.

When Dad found a job and rented himself an apartment, he invited Mom to dinner. She accepted, knowing she was treading on dangerous ground. After dinner he made an abrupt pass and she was easy prey, stumbling into her first sexual relationship.

The next day, in confession, Mom admitted breaking her vows. The clever priest convinced her to tell the mother superior, and she was promptly excommunicated. Hysterical with grief despite her disenchantment with the Church, she went to see my dad, and he immediately proposed. They had a civil ceremony at City Hall the following week. Mom didn't find out she was pregnant until after the wedding.

Elizabeth called at 7:35. "I'm at *The Wall* on Broadway in Redwood City. He just went inside. You want me to follow?"

"No. Just wait in your car and keep an eye on the Jag. Is he still driving the Jag?"

"Yes. I'm down the block, but I can see it from here."

"Okay. I'm on my way."

I locked up the office and jogged out to my car. *The Wall* is only two miles from the marina, but the traffic lights and stop signs slowed me down, and it took almost ten minutes to get there.

I spotted Elizabeth parked near the club and waved as I passed her car. I drove around the block a couple of times looking for a parking space, but I couldn't find one. I ended up in a bank lot almost two blocks away. I hustled back to Elizabeth's car and as I approached she got out of the VW and stretched.

"What's he wearing?" I asked.

"Brown slacks, brown loafers, brown polo shirt, tan leather jacket," she answered. "Color coordinated, but nice."

I thanked her, offered her five twenties for her time, which she somewhat grudgingly accepted, and refused to let her come inside with me.

"I don't want him to recognize you. I might need you to follow him again."

I collected my cell phone and camera, tucking them into my purse. After Elizabeth drove away, I took a deep breath and entered *The Wall.*

Chapter 11

The Wall is a rock club. On weekends they have live music and it's wall-to-wall people, hence the name. Since it was Friday night I had to fight my way to the bar and wedge myself between patrons to get the bartender's attention. It's illegal to carry concealed, even with a permit, while drinking alcohol in a public place. I'd been reluctant to leave my gun in the car but I didn't want to stand out, so soda water or coffee wouldn't do the trick. Taking my chances, I ordered a bottle of Guinness Stout, paid for it, and turned to see if I could locate Fred. It didn't take long. He was standing near the hallway leading to the restrooms, and he was watching me. So much for covert surveillance.

Fred was strikingly handsome. He was smiling and his gaze, once again, made me feel exposed. I fought the urge to check all my buttons and zippers. I smiled back at him and he began moving through the crowd in my direction. I quickly thought up a story about why he'd seen me with Derrick that morning.

When he reached the bar, he asked the expected question. "Didn't I see you at InSight earlier?" He had to shout to be heard over the music.

"I thought you looked familiar," I yelled. "The computer lab right?"

"Research and development. You come here often?"

Oh, please. "Just when I don't feel like being alone." Not that far from the truth. I'd been in the club once before, and I usually like being alone.

"You live around here?" he asked.

That was a tough one. Did I really want this guy to know where I lived? "San Mateo," I lied. "Off Hillsdale Boulevard. What about you?"

"Menlo Park. Buy you a drink?"

"Thanks, I'm still working on this one." I raised my bottle.

Fred was drinking something golden from a rocks glass. He ordered another from the bartender and we stood watching the band for a few minutes. I spotted a couple getting up to leave, and made a dash for their table. The band was going on a break. Fred joined me at the table, carrying his drink and two cocktail napkins. I don't normally like men who are compulsively neat, but I forced a smile as he sat down. The jukebox kicked in at a lower volume.

"My teeth were starting to vibrate," I said. "My name's Jennifer." I held out a hand. "My friends call me Jen."

His grip was firm and his hand was cool and dry. He'd been holding his glass in the other one. "Hello, Jen," he said. "You can call me Marc."

Okay, so I wasn't the only one obscuring my identity. "What is it that you do at InSight?"

"It's boring," he said, making it sound like a warning. "I write software programs."

"If you find it boring, why don't you do something else?"

"They pay me very well, and the benefits are good. Besides I have stock options to look after. There's something to be said for financial security, even if it doesn't make you happy. You ready for another Guinness?"

I looked down at my almost empty bottle. "Sure."

As I watched him weave his way to the bar I leaned back in my chair, comforted by the feel of the Ruger.

Fred returned with a fresh drink for himself and an open bottle of Guinness for me. I listen to the news and I know all about date rape drugs – odorless, colorless, tasteless, and incapacitating. *Never accept a drink you didn't watch being prepared or a bottle that is already open.* Fred raised his glass as if toasting something and the band resumed playing. I picked up the empty Guinness bottle, and as I was setting it aside I brushed my arm against the full one, knocking it into his lap. He jumped up and gave me a look that unmistakably conveyed his displeasure. I shrugged apologetically.

Fred cut a path to the men's restroom. I set my purse in a dry patch on top of the table, took the two Guinness bottles to the bar, and asked for a towel. After I'd mopped up the spill I ordered myself another.

Fred was back a few minutes later, with a huge wet spot on his trousers. He downed his drink in one swallow and told me he was going home to change clothes. He invited me to join him.

I let my jaw drop and he quickly assured me that once he had changed we would find someplace quiet to have a drink. That sounded good to me.

When we were outside I told Fred I'd follow him and asked where he was parked and what he was driving. He pointed out the Jaguar. I told him I was driving a green BMW. He waited in his car until I pulled up behind him and then took off at lightspeed. I managed to keep up.

We arrived at Fred's front door in less than five minutes. I quickly locked my car and followed him inside.

The cottage was charming. It had an open-beam redwood ceiling, a fireplace in the living room, and a spacious kitchen. Fred didn't offer me a tour, but went directly to the bedroom saying he'd be right back. I really couldn't blame him. His pants were soaked.

While he was in the bedroom I scanned the living room and then went into the kitchen. I found some junk mail in the kitchen wastebasket and a phone bill addressed to Frederick M. Wulf. Maybe his middle name was Marc.

I was going through his refrigerator when he came out of the bedroom.

"Thirsty?" he asked.

"No, just nosy. You can learn a lot about a person from the contents of their refrigerator." I smiled sweetly, but my heart was pounding. I *hate* getting caught in the act.

"And what have you discovered about me?"

"You're a victim of organized thinking," I said. "All your labels are facing forward." I pointed into the open refrigerator. "You probably don't procrastinate. None of your dairy is expired. You eat organic vegetables, and you like hot mustard." I closed the door. "I haven't checked the freezer yet."

He laughed. It was a nice laugh, but it made me feel endangered, like a mouse cornered by a hungry cat.

"Where to now?" I asked.

"We can go to the Brass Rail in Palo Alto. It's usually pretty quiet. Or we can stay here and have a drink."

I thought about that for a minute. I really wanted a chance to search the place, but I wasn't likely to have the opportunity unless he left me alone in the house. "I didn't see any beer in the fridge," I said, opening the door to double check.

"No beer. I have single malt scotch, Kettle One vodka, and a very nice French Bordeaux."

"Hard liquor puts me to sleep and wine gives me a headache."

It's true. My body doesn't tolerate most sugars. Whenever I eat sweets or drink wine or whiskey, I get a headache and stiff joints the next day. If I'm feeling self-destructive I drink Jose Cuervo Especial or Bombay Sapphire. When I'm really down on myself I eat chocolate.

"The market's only a block away," he said. "Guinness Stout?"

"That would be great, but I hate for you to go to so much trouble."

"It's no trouble. I'll be back before you have time to inventory the freezer. Would you like anything else? Maybe some cheese and crackers?"

"That would be great," I said. The more time he spent shopping, the longer I'd have to search his house.

I followed him into the living room and before he could get out the door I asked how he felt about cigarette smoke.

"I have no feelings about it whatsoever," he said. "There's an ashtray in the kitchen cabinet to the left of the sink."

As soon as he was out the door I popped back into the kitchen and found the ashtray. I lit a cigarette, leaving it in the ashtray on the coffee table.

I looked out a crack in the living room drapes to make sure the Jag was gone, and then dashed into the bedroom. There was no window, so I flipped on the overhead light and started going through drawers.

Fred preferred dark-colored Dolce & Gabbana cotton briefs, and wore a medium. His socks were neatly paired, the blacks and colors separated from the whites. Sweaters were in the bottom drawers, all neatly folded. I slid my hand into and under each drawer, feeling around for anything out of place. There was nothing.

In the closet I found shirts on the left, trousers in the middle, and jackets on the right. On the floor the dress shoes were on the left and the athletic shoes on the right, all lined up, toes pointing toward the back. It reminded me of Laura's closet. I wondered if she had ever visited Fred at home.

There was a file box on the overhead shelf. I stood on my tiptoes and took it down. The box contained bank statements, PG&E bills, phone bills, water bills, a copy of his lease for the cottage, and yes, his middle name was Marcus. There was also an envelope from an Alice Wulf in Santa Barbara. I read the one page letter. Alice was apparently Fred's mother and she was requesting a visit, or at least a phone call, from her son. Fred didn't strike me as the dutiful son type, so Alice was probably out of luck.

In the back of the box was a folder containing his paycheck stubs from InSight. He was doing pretty well for himself. I pocketed one from early in the year. I could use his social security number to run a background check.

I was about to put the box back on the shelf when I spotted a videocassette behind where the box had been sitting. I pulled over a straight-backed chair and climbed up to retrieve it. It was a Fuji cassette and the case wasn't labeled, just like the one I'd found in Laura's bedroom. I put the tape back where I'd found it and replaced the box on the shelf.

I took a quick look in the bathroom. There was a twelve-pack of Trojans in the medicine cabinet. I picked up the box and read the label. They were Supra spermicidal prelubricated condoms. *Holy shit!* I had read about these in Laura's pathology report.

I ran to the living room and peeked outside. No Jag. I grabbed the Cyber-shot out of my purse, returned to the bathroom, and snapped a few shots of the medicine chest contents. In addition to the condoms there was a bottle of Tylenol, Pearl Drops tooth polish, and Scope mouthwash, all with their labels facing forward. I resisted the urge to turn one of them sideways. Before leaving the room I lifted the toilet tank lid, and checked the tub and shower, but found nothing else incriminating.

I stepped back into the living room and dropped the camera into my purse. I puffed on my cigarette, scattered the ashes around in the ashtray, and stubbed out the butt.

On to the freezer. Nothing notable there except Fred's obvious compulsion for order. There were two packages of organic peas and two of organic corn. They were neatly stacked with the labels aligned, corn on top of corn, and peas on top of peas. This guy was too tightly wrapped to be emotionally stable and should seek professional help.

There was a knife rack next to the gas range with each knife in its slot, and there was a long whetstone with a handle, also in a slot. None of the knives in the rack had sharp little spikes soldered to the hilt.

Under the sink I found carefully organized cleaning supplies, a lined trash receptacle, and two recycling bins, one for glass and one for plastic.

I figured my time was about up, so I returned to the living room and peeked out the window just as Fred/Marc drove up. I plunked myself down on the sofa, picked up a copy of Fortune magazine, and tried to look relaxed. I sat there while Fred unlocked the door and let himself in, hoping the extra few seconds would give my heart time to slow.

"Sorry to take so long," he said. "There was only one cashier." He pulled a bottle of Guinness out of the six-pack and handed it to me as he walked into the kitchen. "Would you like a glass?"

"Sure," I said, following him.

He set the bag on the counter and took a pilsner glass out of an overhead cabinet. Then he went to the freezer, scooped up some ice cubes, dropped them into the glass, and added a splash of tap water, swirling it around until the glass was frosty. He emptied the glass into the sink, dried it carefully, and set it on the counter. I found a bottle opener in the silverware drawer, popped the top, and half filled the glass.

"I hope you like Brie," he said, taking a box of water crackers out of his shopping bag.

Brie always makes me feel a little lightheaded. Probably a mold allergy. I said nothing. He placed the Brie on a dinner plate, removed a carving knife from the rack, and sliced the wheel so that each piece of cheese would fit on top of a cracker. Then he neatly surrounded the cheese with the bland little disks of wheat.

"You've done this before," I said.

"Once or twice." He smiled. "Let's go into the living room. Do you like jazz?"

"Generally. What have you got in mind?"

"How about Miles Davis?"

"Great," I said. "There are so many definitions of jazz. One can never be too careful."

Fred chuckled softly. He chose a CD and slipped it into the system. The volume was low. He disappeared into the kitchen, returning a minute later with a rocks glass containing three fingers of light golden liquid - probably the single malt. He positioned himself a few feet from me on the couch, turned to face me, took a sip of his drink, and said, "So, how long have you been a PI?"

I almost horked Guinness out my nose.

"Two years next month," I sputtered. "How did you know?"

"I asked Derrick about you." He was smiling, enjoying the game.

I was embarrassed and pissed off. "Why didn't you say something earlier?"

"I was curious, you know, to find out if you were checking me out as a prospect, or as a suspect."

I considered the implications. He'd left me alone in his house, so either he didn't have anything to hide, he'd hidden it well, or he was playing for higher stakes than I was.

"Is your name really Jennifer?" he asked.

"It's Nicoli. How long had you been seeing Laura?"

"A few months. Am I a suspect?" His eyes shone with the kind of light I used to see in my cousin Aaron's when he pulled the wings off a moth.

"Why would you think that?" I asked. "Does her father know you were dating?"

"No, and I'd prefer to keep it that way. I don't know how he'd react and I'm not ready to leave InSight just yet."

The age difference between Fred and Laura couldn't have been more than ten or eleven years. I didn't think he had reason to worry.

"I can't promise anything," I said.

His face darkened. "How did you know where to find me tonight?" he asked.

"Coincidence," I said. "My office is in Redwood City. I worked late and felt like having a drink. What made you ask Derrick about me?"

"I like the way you look," his eyes grazed my body, "and I liked the way you looked at me."

I felt that sense of violation again. This was getting old.

"Let's get the obvious questions out of the way," I said, fighting the urge to scoot away from him on the couch. "Where were you the night Laura was killed?"

He didn't flinch and he didn't hesitate. "I was home," he said. "Alone."

"How did you two meet?"

"We met in the parking lot at InSight. She drove down to see her father one day and he was busy. I just happened along at the right moment. She asked if I'd like to join her for lunch and that was the beginning of a short-lived but vigorous relationship."

I felt myself react to his choice of words. The woman he'd been sleeping with had been brutally murdered and he chose to characterize the affair as *vigorous*.

"How often did you see each other?"

"A couple times a week. I even went to see her dance once. She was good."

"Do you know if she was seeing anyone else?"

"I didn't ask, and she didn't say."

I picked up a water cracker. "So what *can* you tell me about Laura?"

His eyes narrowed slightly. "How did you find out we were dating?"

"I found a skydiving video in her bedroom."

He looked surprised at first, and then irritated. "Laura was spoiled," he said, "but she was beautiful and fun to be with. She was pissed off at her parents and determined to do anything she could to get their attention. It's not uncommon. She was bored, like the children of wealthy parents often are. It must be exciting being a private investigator. What made you decide on that as a career?"

I ate another cracker while I considered my answer. "I wanted to track down and punish bad guys, but I didn't want to be a cop," I said. "It's not as glamorous as it sounds."

"No?" He looked intrigued.

"Most investigations are routine and the majority of surveillance time is spent sitting and waiting. What made you decide to write software?"

"It pays well. Why didn't you want to be a cop?"

I looked at him. "I don't like being told what to do. I think I'll be going." I set my glass on the coffee table and stood. "You've been a good sport about all this. May I call you if I think of any other questions?"

"Absolutely," he said. He was on his feet, his hand resting on my arm. "How about dinner tomorrow night?"

I tried not to shrink away from his touch. "Why don't you give me your number and I'll let you know in the morning."

He took out a business card and wrote his home number on the back, and then he asked for mine. I reluctantly gave him one of my cards, but did not volunteer my home number.

As soon as I was out the front door I heard him throw the dead bolt. Maybe a little paranoid? I could feel his eyes on my back as I walked to my car.

CHAPTER 12

WHEN I GOT BACK to the marina I hurried down to Elizabeth's boat. I needed to talk this through with someone objective. The trawler lights were on and the door was open. I leaned over the handrail and knocked on a window. A moment later Elizabeth appeared in the doorway.

"How'd it go?" she asked.

"I need to talk."

It was a warm night so Elizabeth came outside, followed by K.C., her huge orange tabby cat. We all sat down on her dock steps.

"He spotted me as soon as I went inside and bought me a Guinness. When he gave it to me the bottle was already open, so I spilled it in his lap. He invited me to his place and after changing his clothes he left me alone in the house while he went out for beer and Brie. I tossed the place. Then he came back and asked me how long I'd been a PI."

"Oh my *God*!" she said. "Tell me about the case. Why were we following him?"

I told her the whole story. She'd read the newspaper accounts of Laura's death, and caught the nightly news updates, but neither had covered the details.

"Hideous," she said, when I'd finished. "How did he know you were a PI?"

"After I left InSight he talked to Derrick about me. Anyway, I asked him some questions and he seemed to answer candidly, but I found a box of condoms in his medicine chest and they were the same kind I read about in Laura's pathology report. Did you get a look at his eyes?"

"No. Why?"

"They're really intense. He asked me to have dinner with him tomorrow night."

"Well, *that's* interesting."

"Yeah."

"What did you say?"

"I told him I'd let him know in the morning."

"Nicoli Maxine Hunter. Tell me you didn't give him your phone number?"

"Don't get excited. I gave him my business card."

"You're an idiot."

"He knows I'm a PI and I'm in the phone book. Besides, I really don't have any reason to suspect him, apart from the fact that he dated Laura, and he lives so close to where she was killed … and the condoms. But that could be, you know, coincidence."

"You don't believe in coincidence."

"You're right. I don't. I was thinking you could check out his house while we're at dinner."

"Excuse me?"

"I'll pay you. Fifty an hour, same as before. Look for a knife with two spikes on the hilt. If you find it don't touch it, just take a couple pictures of it. One up close and one from a distance so you get some of the room in the frame." I pulled the Cyber-shot out of my purse and handed it to her. "Go through the videotapes and DVDs in the living room and see what's on each one. There's a VHS tape behind the file box on the shelf in the bedroom closet. If it's a skydiving video don't bother to fast forward through the whole thing, I already have a copy. And check the flue in the fireplace.

"He has a laptop computer on a desk near the living room window. If the computer is turned on take a look at his files. See what he has in the *My Pictures* folder. Oh, and there's a small garage."

"*Wait* a minute! How will I get in? And what if the neighbors see me? They might have one of those neighborhood watch things."

She was hooked. I could see it in her eyes.

"It's a quiet neighborhood," I said, "I didn't see anyone looking out their windows when I was there tonight. I'll tell him I can't meet him until late, say nine or nine-thirty. That way anyone who's going out will be out, and the ones who are staying in will be inside with their drapes closed. You can park a few blocks away. Wear dark clothes. Something you would wear to go jogging. There's probably a side door into the garage. I know there's a door between the garage and the kitchen. I have a set of lock picks I can lend you. I'll show you how to use them tomorrow."

"What if I find the knife? We won't be able to go to the police and tell them how I found it."

"I'll tell Detective Anderson I was interviewing Fred at his home because I found out he was dating Laura, and I just happened to see a knife like the one he described to me."

"And you think, based on that, he'll be able to get a search warrant?"

"I don't know. Will you do it?"

"Of *course* I'll do it. But if I get arrested you'd better pay my bail, and I mean immediately. If I have to spend even one night in jail our friendship is over."

"Great!"

I kissed Elizabeth on the cheek, ruffled K.C.'s silky ears, and sauntered off to my boat.

While I was eating dinner I scribbled notes about the day's events. When I had everything documented to my satisfaction, I closed the hatch and fell into bed. My mind wouldn't stop working, so I picked up one of Lois Greiman's Christina McMullen novels from the headboard and read until I dozed off.

Chapter 13

NIGHTMARES ABOUT SERIAL KILLERS plagued my sleep and when my alarm went off at 6:00 on Saturday morning I felt like I needed another four hours. I had a sense of foreboding, but chalked it up to a restless night and dragged myself out of bed.

I started a pot of coffee and turned on the news. According to Channel 36, the temperature would be in the eighties today and the sky would remain clear. The sun was already streaming through my portlights.

I filled a mug with coffee, added lactose-free milk, and lit a cigarette. After my second cup I began to perk up a little. My thoughts returned to the previous night and I began to wonder if involving Elizabeth was a such a good idea. She was right. It was risky and good friends are hard to find. I was having serious second thoughts when the boat swayed and someone knocked on my pilothouse door. I snatched up a terry cloth robe to cover the tee shirt I'd slept in, and opened the hatch.

Elizabeth was standing on deck, her eyes bright with excitement.

"Are you going to show me how to use those lock picks?"

I trudged up the steps and opened the door, squinting in the sunlight. "It's Saturday," I whined. "Don't you ever sleep in?"

"Come *on!*" she said, flapping her arms. "Finish your coffee, take a shower, and cheer up! I'll be back in an hour."

She bounced off the boat and I went back inside.

After my third cup of coffee I was fully awake. I grabbed my shower bag, a towel, and a handful of dog biscuits, and headed for the marina facilities.

The restrooms are about a hundred and twenty-five yards from where my boat is docked. I paced it off before I chose the slip. It's a nice walk. The only time I resent it is in the winter when it's cold, raining, or windy. Besides, if I don't mind the lack of water pressure, I can always shower on board.

I said good morning to a couple of my neighbors who were outside varnishing their brightwork. I inhaled the marina smells as I walked; sawdust and wet varnish, salt water and seaweed, diesel fuel, last night's barbecued chicken, and the pungent odor of someone's overflowing holding tank. Along the way I stopped to visit with Hobbs, Denali, Rocky, Rasputin, and D'Artagnon, a few of the marina dogs.

The marina culture wouldn't be the same without the dogs. Hobbs is a big goofy yellow Lab who loves being hugged. If you're one of his people, his whole body will wag when he sees you. He lives aboard a sailboat with two humans, Will and Leslie, and is easily bored. He takes frequent, unescorted walks around the marina in search of something to do. If he head-butts your hatch in the middle of the night and you don't let him in, he'll snub you the next day.

Denali also resides with Will and Leslie. She's a brindle Lab around fourteen years old, and she's a singer. When she sees a friend approaching she howls with delight, and I'm often inspired to howl along.

Rocky is part Golden Retriever and part Chow. He's starting to gray around the muzzle and he's very affectionate, dopey, and unpredictable. He's also obsessed with tennis balls. On hot days he's been known to drop one of his balls in the water, and then follow it in. Fortunately he's a good swimmer.

Rasputin is an English Setter and is extremely well behaved apart from his penchant for licking faces. He loves to carry things around in his mouth. He can hold up to six small dog biscuits before he's forced to begin chewing, and he picks up garbage of all descriptions from the marina grounds, just to have something to carry.

Last, but far from least, is D'Artagnon, the self-appointed marina watchdog. He's a black Labrador Retriever, frequent visitor of those who feed him treats, and a glutton for affection. He lives with Kirk and Jonathan, father and son, on a Bluewater 42. I have a soft spot in my heart for this guy. His tail is crooked where it was broken when he was a puppy, he's always hungry, and he is never satisfied that you love him enough.

As I made my rounds I gave each dog two biscuits and scratched behind their ears. It's one of my morning rituals. I love dogs, but I resolved never to own one again after my two-year-old English Mastiff jumped a six-foot fence and tracked my scent onto the freeway. I tell my friends it's too much responsibility for me, that I want to be able to travel without attachments, but the truth is I don't have the emotional courage to endure another loss.

Elizabeth came back at 7:30. She knocked on the open pilothouse door and I shouted for her to come in. I was cleaning my revolver at the galley counter, so she sat down and watched. The Ruger SP101 is a stainless steel five-shot .357 magnum with a two-inch barrel. It's built like a hammer. It will never break down.

When I finished, I handed her the unloaded gun. "I want you to take this with you tonight."

She held it carefully, her eyes wide. "No way am I carrying this," she said.

"You probably won't need it, but I'll feel better if you have it with you. Just put it in your pocket."

"It weighs a *ton*!"

"Is it too heavy for you? Okay. Let's go shopping."

We took my car and stopped at the 1-Hour-Photo on El Camino, so I could drop off the film from my Nikon, then drove on to Heinz's Gun Shop in San Carlos. Heinz opens at 8:00 a.m., even on Saturdays. I bought my first handgun from him when I was working for Sam Pettigrew.

Heinz is about five-eight and a hundred and seventy pounds with a full head of silver hair and steely blue eyes set in a craggy face that you can tell was once handsome, even though he's now older than dirt.

I escorted Elizabeth to a display of used handguns, but it was clear she was in unfamiliar territory. I asked Heinz if I could look at a used matt black Glock twenty-six he had in the display case. It was a small 9mm composite frame that only weighed about twenty ounces, but held a ten-round magazine plus one in the chamber.

Elizabeth took the gun and I showed her how to sight it. She held it at arm's length for a minute, and she was okay with the weight, so we grabbed earplugs, goggles, and a box of ammo, and went back to Heinz's indoor firing range.

I gave Elizabeth a lecture on handgun safety as I loaded the magazine, pointing out the lack of an external manual safety on the gun. It's the only thing I don't like about Glocks. The safety guard is part of the trigger mechanism, so if anything trips the safety accidentally the gun can easily go off. A lot of cops have shot themselves in the foot by failing to keep their fingers out of the trigger guard on the draw. This is also why it's unsafe to carry a Glock in your purse.

Elizabeth listened attentively and watched every move I made. When I had the mag loaded I showed her how to insert it into the gun and how to pull back the slide to chamber a round. I fired a few shots at a paper silhouette target while she watched. Then I handed her the gun and stood back. Elizabeth emptied the magazine, set the gun down, and took off her goggles.

"Wow," she said, in a throaty voice. "What a *rush*."

"How does it feel in your hand?" I stepped forward and squinted at the target. She'd actually come close to the 10X a couple of times. 10X is center body mass on a silhouette target.

"It's a handful," she said, "but I think I can control it."

"Good. Reload the magazine."

I watched as Elizabeth pushed the mag release and then clumsily pressed bullets into the magazine one at a time. This was not going to be a problem, it was just an unfamiliar process. The problem came when she tried to reinsert the mag into the gun. She placed it in the handle of the Glock and gently pushed upward. I think she was expecting it to snap into place. When it didn't, she looked at me, bewildered.

"You have to jam it up in there," I said. "Pull it back out a little, then give it a good shove."

After a couple of tries she had it. She pulled back the slide and emptied the magazine into the target again. This time she got a round in the 10X and whooped like a teenager.

We returned to the front counter and I wrote Heinz a check. I presented my PI license and my concealed carry permit. Heinz and I go way back. He had me fill out the forms for the two-week waiting period, then carefully wrapped the Glock, three magazines, and two boxes of 9mm parabellum ammo, and put them in the bottom of a bag below the counter, which he topped with a hunting vest I would later return.

When we were back in the car Elizabeth gave me an open-mouthed stare.

"What?" I asked.

"Isn't there a two-week waiting period? Will he get in trouble?"

"Are you going to tell anyone?"

"Of course not!"

"Did anyone else see him do it?"

"There was only one other guy in there and he was on the other side of the store."

"So what's the problem?"

"You must be a good customer."

"I buy all my guns and ammo from Heinz, and I listen to his stories about being a Hitler Youth. He likes me."

Elizabeth hugged the bag all the way back to the marina.

We walked down to my boat and I tossed the vest in the pilothouse and placed the bag with the Glock and ammo in my dinghy. I keep the dinghy inflated year round in case one of my neighbors is having a party and I don't feel like walking or driving. It's a big marina.

"You need more target practice," I said.

I checked my trash and found three empty plastic water bottles and a diet root beer can. I dug my fanny pack holster out of the stateroom locker. I wanted the Glock secured while we were bouncing around on the water.

We got into the dinghy and I showed Elizabeth how the gun fit into the holster, reminding her not to put her finger inside the trigger guard unless she was ready to fire. I strapped on the fanny pack and we motored out to the slough.

I am not by nature a violent person. Although I grew up target shooting with my dad, he only taught me how to use a long gun. I learned to shoot a handgun much later in life at the insistence of Sam Pettigrew. Sam used to take me to the range once a week. He also helped me get my concealed-carry permit. He knew the right people at the Sheriff's Department. Sam doesn't believe in taking unnecessary risks. *Pepper spray just pisses some people off, Nicoli,* he used to say. *You need something with stopping power.*

At first, handling any type of pistol creeped me out. It seemed so much more personal than a rifle. If I ever had to shoot someone in self-defense, I wanted to be as far away from the part of the gun where the bullet came out as possible. But the more time I spent practicing at the range and at home cleaning my little Ruger, the more confident I became.

Elizabeth had a good eye and, in spite of her concern about breaking a nail, she was comfortable with the Glock in about an hour. Her wrists were sore and the palm of her hand was red, but she had a self-satisfied smirk on her face. We took the dinghy back to the marina and I taught her how to clean the gun.

At 10:30 I dug out my lock picks. Time for lesson number two. I keep several locksets stowed in my galley settee. I showed Elizabeth how the internal mechanism worked on each type of lock, and again she proved to be a quick study. After the first few tries she could open a standard lock in less than a minute. Sometimes it pays to have a high IQ.

I called Fred and told him we were on for dinner and he asked what kind of food I liked. I said any place with a salad bar would be fine with me. He suggested the Chart House in Half Moon Bay. That would be about a thirty-minute drive.

"Perfect," I said. "Why don't I meet you at your house at nine?"

He agreed, saying nothing about the fact that San Mateo, where I had told him I lived, was between his house and Half Moon Bay.

Elizabeth and I left the Glock on her trawler and walked up to The Diving Pelican, the marina restaurant. Over lunch we discussed the layout of Fred's house. I drew her a diagram on a paper napkin and made notes of what to check in each room. I felt confident now that she had the skills and information necessary to conduct a successful search.

Chapter 14

After lunch I stopped by the office and called the Redwood City Police Department, hoping to get my hands on Laura's criminal arrest records, but Detective Anderson wasn't in. It was Saturday, after all.

I went to the gym and spent half an hour on the treadmill and twenty minutes on the StairMaster, then used the Nautilus machines and the free weights. I pushed myself to lift more weight than usual and the endorphins did their job. I felt great.

That afternoon I colored the white streaks in my hair with some temporary stuff that shampoos out, and painted my nails with clear polish. I considered shopping for a new outfit and realized I was behaving like this was a real date. I decided, instead, to take a power nap.

When I got up I made coffee, and when it was ready I filled a thermal mug and walked up to the office. As I was unlocking the door I remembered I had Anderson's cell number. I found his card in my wallet and dialed. He answered on the second ring. He'd been working an assault case and was now in his office. He said he'd been expecting my call.

Ten minutes later Detective Anderson met me in the RCPD lobby. He was carrying a manila folder, and he smiled when he saw me.

"You do something different with your hair?" he asked.

"Just colored it," I said, blushing.

"Looks good."

My body responded to the compliment. My ears felt hot and my stomach growled.

He escorted me into the same interview room we'd used before. This time we both sat down at the table. I opened the folder and looked at the file. Laura had been arrested for solicitation while working at the *Fanny Pack*. The next day the charges had been dropped.

"What's the story?" I asked, holding up the arrest report. "Do you know any of the details?"

"Some. When I was assigned the homicide I pulled her criminal record and called McCarthy, the arresting officer. He said he'd been undercover at the club because there was a prostitution ring operating out of there. Laura did a table dance for him without being asked and whispered in his ear that she'd blow his mind for five hundred bucks. He Mirandized her and hauled her in. Which was stupid if you think about it, since he was supposed to be undercover. Later, when her attorney showed up, she told him that she'd known McCarthy was a Vice cop and that she wanted the customers to see her being arrested because it would increase her tips. Apparently she'd only been dancing there for a few weeks and hadn't developed a following yet. She had no priors, so the charges were dropped."

"Sounds like another way to aggravate her parents," I said. "It also sounds like she had a good attorney."

Anderson's eyes shifted away from mine. He didn't respond to my comment about the attorney.

"I searched Laura's room yesterday and I didn't find any birth control," I said. "No pills, no diaphragm, no condoms, no sponges. Did your people remove anything?"

"We didn't find anything related to birth control in her room. Her purse was found in her car. It had two condoms in it, but they weren't Trojan Supras."

He stared at me with a furrowed brow, as though he was trying to figure something out. I started to feel uncomfortable, so I turned back to the file. I read everything on Laura's arrest and took some notes, but nothing was sinking in. There was too much tension in the room.

Eventually I handed the folder back to him, thanked him for his time, and asked if I could call if I had any more questions. He said he'd be happy to help any way he could, but he didn't sound happy.

Driving back to the office I thought about the encounter, trying to work out what had caused Anderson's mood to change. He'd gotten chilly when I mentioned Laura's attorney. I made a mental note to ask Kate for the lawyer's name and contact info.

So far my only real suspect was Frederick Marcus Wulf. Fred was bright, bored with his job, handsome, and charming. He seemed to have a sense of humor and didn't intimidate easily. He was organized to the point of being anal, but didn't mind leaving a snoop like me alone in his house. He might be one of those macho types who repress their emotions, causing everyone else to think they don't have any. Motive? Maybe Laura was threatening to tell her father about their relationship. That would be consistent with her previous behavior – trying to embarrass her parents. I didn't think Fred being a little older was the issue. The fact that Fred was using Laura for sex might annoy her father. It would be enough to upset most fathers, especially when added to the fact that Fred worked for him. Some parents would take that as a sign of disrespect.

Fred, like Laura, seemed to be chasing an adrenaline rush. Was it possible he'd killed her for sport, or had they been experimenting with erotic oxygen deprivation and it just got out of control?

I itemized my expenses and added my notes on the solicitation bust to Laura's file. I remembered I hadn't told Kate I would take the case, so I called her and gave her the news. She thanked me, sounding relieved.

"Are you making any progress?" she asked.

"It's too soon to tell, but I'll send you a report next week."

I stopped at Elizabeth's boat on the way to my own. She was watching TV and ironing with the door open. K.C. was curled up on deck. He stretched and opened an eye at me as I climbed the dock steps, then closed it again.

"Do you remember how to get to Fred's house?" I asked Elizabeth.

"Of course," she said, setting the iron down. "I'm really nervous."

"If you have any trouble getting in, or if the neighbors look suspicious, just forget the whole thing, okay?"

"Okay."

"Want me to stop by when I get home?"

"*Duh!*"

I continued down the dock to my boat, stopping briefly to scratch behind D'Artagnon's ears and under his chin. He wagged his tail in a circular motion like a propeller, and licked my nose.

CHAPTER 15

At 8:15 I CHANGED into black jeans, a black silk tank, tan leather boots, and my camel hair blazer. I tucked the Ruger into my small-of-the-back holster, checked the mirror, and added lip gloss and mascara.

Elizabeth was sitting outside on her dock steps as I approached her trawler. She was looking very athletic, wearing spandex shorts, a tee shirt, running shoes, and a terrycloth headband. My fanny pack holster was strapped around her waist.

"I was hoping I'd catch you on your way out," she said. "What time do you want me to get there?"

"Nine forty-five. We should be gone by nine-thirty. You'll see my car out in front. If you see the Jag, just keep walking. Why don't you take my cell phone so I can call you before we leave the restaurant?" I dug the Nokia out of my purse and handed it to her. "Are you okay with this?"

"Yes. No. What if I get caught? I mean, if one of the neighbors sees me and calls the police, what should I say?"

"Don't say anything. Just ask for your phone call. Call my machine at the office. I'll check my messages as soon as I get home. Don't worry. Everything's going to be fine." Famous last words.

"You think?"

"Absolutely. Park a couple blocks away. Maybe in the Marsh Manor lot on Bay. Jog the last block as you're approaching the house. Look around to make sure no one's paying attention to you, run up to the side gate, and let yourself in. Once you're through the gate you won't be visible from the street."

"Okay." She brightened a little. "I can do this. Be careful."

"You too."

As I walked to my car I thought again about calling the whole thing off, but then we might never know. I got in the BMW and drove to Menlo Park, arriving at Fred's house ten minutes early. I sat there looking around the neighborhood. I didn't see anyone peering out their front windows. Most of the drapes in the surrounding houses were closed.

I got out of my car, slammed the door hard, and did a quick spin, checking to see if anyone responded to the noise. No one did. Not even Fred.

I approached his door and knocked. The peephole went dark for a beat and then Fred slid back the deadbolt and opened the door. He wore a pair of navy-blue wool gabardine slacks with a crimson V-neck cashmere sweater, and he was holding an empty rocks glass.

"Wow, you look great!" I said.

His eyes glowed with satisfaction. "So do you," he said. "Come in."

"Sorry I'm early. It's a bad habit I picked up at birth."

He chuckled. I usually like men who laugh at my jokes.

"You want a Guinness?" he asked.

"Sure. What time is our reservation?"

I followed him into the kitchen and he handed me a bottle of stout, which I opened myself.

"Nine forty-five. We have plenty of time. I called the Chart House this afternoon and they're socked in with fog, so I thought we'd go to the Garden Grill instead. They have a great salad bar."

The Garden Grill was in Menlo Park, five minutes from Fred's house, and they didn't have a salad bar. I knew the owner, Jessica James, and had been a regular since it opened. Also, the proximity increased the risk for Elizabeth.

"I *love* the fog," I said, "And I was really looking forward to a walk on the beach after dinner." I hate people who wheedle, but I am not above doing it myself.

"Really? Well if you're sure, I'll give them a call and see when they can seat us."

His phone was in the kitchen. I perched on the arm of the sofa so I could eavesdrop.

He made the call, requested a table for two, and then said, "Thank you," and hung up.

"They can seat us at nine fifteen," he said. "We'd better get going."

"Great!" I exhaled, realizing I'd been holding my breath.

I ditched my half full Guinness bottle in the kitchen sink and headed for the front door, then glanced over my shoulder and saw Fred stride to the sink. He emptied and rinsed the bottle, then dried it and placed it in the recycling bin. More than a little compulsive. No matter what happened with the case, we wouldn't be seeing each other for long.

The winding road to Half Moon Bay makes me nervous under the best of circumstances and Fred took the turns at fifty-five miles an hour. Going around some of those curves at a high speed is just stupid. I thought he might be trying to scare me until I remembered that he and Laura shared a penchant for risk-taking. Maybe that was why they had been attracted to each other.

When we arrived at the coast the first thing I noticed was the complete absence of fog.

"It must have cleared up since this afternoon," he said, reading my thoughts.

We pulled into the Chart House parking lot at 9:17, and were lucky enough to find a vacant space. When we entered the restaurant we were seated immediately, although most of the tables in the dining area were occupied. If I didn't do something to slow the evening down we'd be back at Fred's cottage too early for Elizabeth to complete her search. I decided to have an appetizer, an entrée, and the salad bar, to give her enough time. So much for my diet.

I ordered oysters on the half shell, and Fred ordered the same. Our waiter, Stephan, offered beverages, and I chose a mineral water while Fred ordered Glenlivit. Stephan gave us menus after listing the evening's specials, and I took my time reading about each entree, trying to determine which items would take the longest to prepare. I decided on the lobster Thermidor, a spinach soufflé, and the salad bar.

Stephan served our oysters and when he took my dinner order a polite smile spread over his face, no doubt envisioning a healthy tip. I'd have to insist on paying that myself. Fred ordered the poached salmon with wild rice.

After Stephan left we both focused on our oysters. They were fresh, firm, plump, free of grit, and properly chilled. *Very* good. Anyone who enjoys oysters doesn't want to be distracted while eating them. We were silent until all the shells were empty. Then I looked across the table at my dinner companion.

"So, Marc… Do you want me to keep calling you Marc, or do you prefer Fred?"

"I'm thinking of changing my first name to Marcus," he said. "Fred sounds so banal."

"Okay, Marc," I smiled, trying to be disarming. "Tell me about yourself. Where did you grow up?"

No sense procrastinating. I wanted a full psychological profile on this guy and he would either cooperate or he wouldn't.

"Southern California," he said. "My father was a minister and Mom taught high school English."

I felt a twinge of sympathy. I knew first hand how hard it was to live with a religious parent.

"Are they both still alive?"

"My mother is. My father passed away last year."

"I'm sorry. Was he ill?"

"Adrenal insufficiency."

I considered for a moment what might cause someone's adrenal glands to fail.

"Does your mom still live in Southern California?"

"Santa Barbara. What about you? Were you raised around here?"

"Born and raised in San Jose," I lied. I didn't want this guy getting any ideas about paying my mom a visit. "I think I'll go get my salad," I said, putting an abrupt end to any conversation about my family.

I managed to waste five minutes circling the salad bar, dishing up a small portion of each item. I like to try everything, even if I can't tell what it is by looking at it. When I got back to the table Fred was on his second scotch.

"I love a good salad bar," I said. "So many choices."

"It looks like you chose everything." He was smiling, but his tone was condescending.

I picked at my salad, not wanting my reactions to become sluggish from overeating. I'd nibbled away a third of it when our entrees were served. The spinach soufflé was moist and light as a feather, and the lobster Thermidor was to die for.

"Tell me about the skydiving," I said.

"We only did that together once. Laura said she liked the free-fall, but after the chute was open it became tedious because you had the same view all the way down. I think she just went along to introduce me to a new thrill. She'd become bored with it after her first solo jump."

"Solo jump?"

"That's when you jump out of the plane alone. Your first jump has to be in tandem with an instructor. You're strapped into a double harness together."

"So that time on the video wasn't your first jump?"

"Oh no, it was my first."

"And they let you jump alone?"

I could guess why, but I wanted to hear it anyway.

"Laura paid them triple the usual rate for both of us so they would let me jump without an instructor. They could have lost their license, but she was very persuasive. She said she wanted me to fully experience the free-fall, so they rushed me through the beginners' class, and up we went."

"How was it?" I asked.

"It was exhilarating. If you've never tried it, you really should. But Laura was right, once your parachute opens and you've seen the view, the rest is monotonous."

After dinner I ordered coffee and requested a doggy bag for what was left of my lobster. It was 10:55. I excused myself, and went to the ladies' restroom. There was a pay phone in the hallway. Elizabeth answered on the first ring.

"It's me," I whispered. "Is everything okay?"

"Tough locks. And you didn't tell me there was a chain on the kitchen door. I haven't found the knife. I'm trying to put everything back exactly where it was and that's slowing me down. Are you on your way?"

"We're done eating. I'll try to talk him into a walk on the beach, but we might be back in the next twenty minutes. Do what you can, and get out in fifteen."

"Okay."

"Elizabeth?"

"Yeah."

"Thanks."

"No sweat."

I used the facilities, washed my hands, put on fresh lip gloss, powdered my nose and forehead, and strolled back to the table. Fred had already paid the check and left a cash tip. My doggy bag was waiting.

"Listen," I said, "I've made a pig of myself. The least I can do is take care of the tip."

"That's not necessary," he said, getting up.

"Please. I feel guilty."

"Fine."

He collected his cash and I placed a twenty on the table.

When we were outside I asked if he was up for a walk on the beach. He looked at me for a long moment, his expression neutral, then he looked down at his shoes and, finally, said, "Why not?"

There was very little light on the beach, just the glow cast by the lights from the restaurant and the adjacent parking lot. We carefully picked our way down the hillside to the sand. I lit a cigarette and moved toward the water.

"How's the investigation into Laura's murder coming along?" he asked.

I was impressed that he could make a question like that sound so casual, like, *How's your cat? How's that pesky murder investigation going?*

"Slowly. Did you know she'd been arrested for solicitation?"

"She told me about that. Thought it was a great joke. So, any suspects?"

"Several."

I was glad he couldn't see my face in the dark.

We walked along the beach for about twenty minutes, and then walked back up to the car. During all this time alone with me in the dark Fred never made a pass or even attempted to put his arm around my shoulder. I was relieved, but also curious about what was going on in that big brain of his.

We drove back to Menlo Park and he invited me in, offering a nightcap, but I said I was tired. The next thing I knew he had his arms around my waist and was pressing his lips to mine. He slipped his tongue between my teeth and I was so surprised I forgot to struggle. A jolt of electricity coursed through my body, striking all those seldom-used erogenous zones. Then he released me, stepped back, and said, "Goodnight, Nicoli."

I got into my car and waved as I drove off. There was no doubt he'd felt the revolver at the small of my back. I spent the trip home wondering about the kiss. It was exciting and a little unnerving, and it did *not* leave me wanting more. It had effectively thrown me off balance, for a minute anyway. Was this guy genuinely interested in me, or just looking for the next conquest? Was he checking to see what that bulge at the small of my back was? Did he intentionally keep his hands off me all evening so the kiss at the end of the night would be a shock? Was he dating me just to keep track of where I was in the investigation? Was I reading too much into everything he said and did? Probably. I wondered if Laura had questioned his motives before getting involved with him.

When I arrived back at the marina I locked the BMW and inched slowly down the steep companionway. It was low tide and my boots didn't have rubber soles. Elizabeth was seated on her dock steps waiting for me, her usual glass of Kahlua, vodka, and milk in one hand, my cell phone in the other.

"I thought you'd *never* get here! Come inside. Did you have a good time?"

"Not bad. Scary driver. Kind of charming. Good kisser. Enough small talk. What did you find in his house?" I followed her into the trawler.

"Nothing," she said. "What do you mean good kisser? I thought your interest in this guy was purely professional." She slid the door closed behind us.

"It is. He kissed me, I didn't kiss him. Nothing, huh?"

"Nope. Sorry. After you called I fast-forwarded through that videotape. It was what you said. Just some people skydiving. The computer wasn't turned on, by the way. I took a quick look around the garage. There were some shelves I couldn't reach, and there was no ladder. There wasn't time to drag a chair out from the house because I still had to reinsert the chain lock on the kitchen door from the outside. That's not easy, you know. I did notice how clean and organized everything was, even in the garage. What is he, some kind of neat freak?"

"Totally. Thanks, Elizabeth. How's your pulse?" I pulled seven twenties out of my wallet.

"Almost back to normal." She accepted the cash. "I probably won't sleep much tonight, but it was fun, as soon as it was over anyway."

She handed me the phone and took my camera out of her pocket. I dropped both into my purse. She reached under one of the settee cushions and pulled out the Glock, still in the fanny pack holster. I slipped that into my purse as well. I slid the door open and stepped outside, then stopped and turned back.

"Listen, I have to go to that strip club again tomorrow night. I know you have to work on Monday, but we can leave early. I really don't want to go in there alone again."

"I've always wanted to go to a strip joint!"

I gave her a hug. "I'm glad you're my friend. See you tomorrow."

On board my boat I dropped my purse on the stateroom floor, and turned on the evening news. While I watched I stripped off my clothes, and crawled into bed. I slept for about twenty minutes before my subconscious woke me up. I found the notepad and pen I keep on the headboard and made a list.

1. Laura's former fiancé's reaction to her career choice

2. Derrick's reaction to his daughter's solicitation arrest

3. Who will inherit the Howard fortune, now that Laura's dead?

Having exhausted my imagination, I nodded off again and slept soundly.

CHAPTER 16

ON SUNDAY MORNING, after two cups of coffee and a warm shower, I felt pretty good. I moseyed up to the office, turned on the computer, and opened Laura's file.

I called Kate and Derrick at home. Kate answered after three rings. I asked if I could stop by around 10:00. She checked with Derrick and said that would be fine.

I called Detective Anderson on his cell.

"Anderson." He sounded annoyed.

"It's Nikki Hunter. Do you have any off-duty time available?"

I could hear the wheels turning as he wondered why I was asking.

"I might be free tonight," he finally said. His tone of voice had softened.

"I'm working until about 8:30," I said. "Can you meet me at my office?"

"I should be able to do that."

I was smiling when I hung up the phone.

I tried calling the *Fanny Pack* to find out if Frank and Candy were working that night, but there was no answer, so I dialed Sylvia in Los Angeles. She answered on the fourth ring, sounding groggy.

"Sylvia, it's Nicoli Hunter. Did I wake you?"

She was silent until her memory kicked-in. "Oh yes, the private investigator. Any suspects yet, dear?"

"Not really. I'm going to see Kate and Derrick this morning and I wanted to talk to you first. I need to know about the family's money."

"You mean in relation to Laura?"

"And in general."

"Well, Laura was about to inherit a substantial sum. When our parents died they left half of their money to Laura and the other half to her brother Rod. My husband and I never had children."

What the fuck?

"I didn't know there was a brother. Kate told me Laura was an only child."

"Well, I suppose to Kate she *was* an only child. Rod is Derrick's son from a previous marriage."

"Oh. Can you tell me about the provisions of the will? How much money are we talking about?"

"Laura would have inherited five million dollars on her twenty-fifth birthday, plus the interest, of course. It's been in a money market account for a few years. I guess now that she's gone the money either reverts to Derrick and me, or to Rod."

"Where does Rod live? Has he already collected his portion of the inheritance?"

"Yes, he received his shortly after their death, when he turned twenty-five. He lives in San Francisco. At least he used to. I haven't spoken with him in years. We were never very close. Rod's a strange one. Raised by his mother."

Like that could be any worse than being raised by Derrick.

"Do you have an address and a phone number?"

"Just a minute, dear." I heard a drawer open and close, then she came back on the line. "Are you ready?"

"Yes."

"He used to live in Diamond Heights," she said. "I don't know if this is current."

She read me an address and telephone number, and I copied them down. I thanked Sylvia and ended the call.

I dug out the photocopy I'd made of Kate's check and sent an e-mail to CIS requesting a financial background on the Howards. A checking account number is sufficient for this type of research.

Before I left for Atherton I totaled my hours and the running list of expenses, subtracted Kate's initial deposit, and printed an invoice. I took the Ruger out of my purse and slid it back into the Velcro holster under my lap drawer. I still had the Glock in the fanny pack holster which was in my oversized purse. I probably didn't even need to carry a gun, but because it was my first homicide investigation I was feeling insecure. Of course if I needed to draw the Glock in a hurry, getting it out of the fanny pack would slow me down. I had a Triple K pistol purse with a built in holster stowed somewhere on the boat. I decided I had enough time to switch bags before my meeting with the Howards.

I found the pistol purse in the stateroom locker and transferred the contents of my bag, securing the Glock in the holster compartment. If I wore the purse on my left hip with the shoulder strap across my chest, I could cross-draw with my right hand while holding the purse in place with my left. I tried it a couple of times and the action was smooth enough.

I was still angry with Kate for not telling me about Laura's half brother Rod so I broke the speed limit all the way to Atherton. It's a short drive, but I generally avoid breaking the law because I hate the humiliation of getting caught. While I was driving I went over what I would say to Kate and Derrick, imagining how they might react to being reprimanded by the hired help.

There were two late model 5 Series BMWs in the driveway when I arrived. My little Bimmer is over twenty years old, but I take good care of it. I parked behind one of the sedans, patted my dashboard affectionately, and got out of the car.

I knocked on the front door, which was promptly answered by a middle-aged woman wearing a black dress and a white apron.

"I'm Nicoli Hunter," I said. "I have an appointment with the Howards."

She was looking right at me, but I had the feeling she didn't understand what I had said. After an awkward moment, Kate walked up behind the woman and said something in Spanish. The woman nodded and walked away.

"Sorry about that. Celia's English isn't very good. Please, come in."

Kate escorted me into the living room, where Derrick was reading the Wall Street Journal. I admire people who can read the Wall Street Journal and not fall asleep after the first paragraph.

"Ms. Hunter." Derrick stood up and offered his hand. I shook it reluctantly. "Please sit down," he said, gesturing to the elegant sectional on which he had been seated. "What can we do for you?"

"You can start by telling me about Rod and his relationship with Laura." I paused for dramatic effect. "Then you can tell me about the inheritance."

Derrick glanced at Kate. "Rod and Laura didn't see much of each other," he said. "There's really nothing to tell about their relationship. How did you find out about the inheritance?"

"That doesn't matter. What *does* matter is the fact that neither of you mentioned it to me. Surely you must know that five million dollars plus interest provides a significant motive. Who gets all that money now that Laura's out of the picture?"

Kate visibly cringed at my choice of words before responding. "Half of the money will go to Rod, and the other half will be divided between Derrick and his sister, Sylvia."

"And the reason neither of you chose to mention this to me?"

Kate fielded that one as well. "I didn't think it was pertinent. Rod has already inherited five million, so he can't possibly need the money enough to harm Laura, and we would never hurt our own daughter."

I considered what she had said about Rod. *He can't possibly need the money enough to harm Laura.* What if he *did* need the money enough? She also didn't say anything about whether she and Derrick, or Sylvia for that matter, could use the money.

"I'd like to get a copy of the will," I said. "And I'd like to speak with your attorney. I'll need his name and phone number."

They were both silent for a moment, then Kate said, "Of course," and left the room.

When she was gone I turned to Derrick who was looking at me as though I was a bug under a microscope. His eyes seemed empty and at the same time calculating, disconnected from what was going on around him, but observing everything with detached interest. That visible indifference pissed me off, since his daughter had so recently been butchered.

"I understand Laura was arrested for solicitation," I said, watching for a change in those emotionless eyes.

He darted a glance in the direction Kate had gone. "Who told you that?" he asked, still watching for Kate.

"I ran a background check," I lied, not wanting to get Anderson in trouble for showing me the file.

"Kate doesn't know anything about that, and I'd prefer to keep it that way."

"Okay. I'll come by your office tomorrow and we can discuss it in private."

Derrick crossed his legs and gently shook the wrinkles out of his newspaper.

Kate returned a moment later and handed me a slip of paper on which she had written the name Gerald Kuhlman and a phone number with a 415 area code. The name meant nothing to me.

"Did Laura date anyone special while she was in college?" I asked. Sylvia had told me Laura was engaged, but I didn't want to tip my hand. They had intentionally hidden Rod and the inheritance from me and I wanted to see if I could catch them in another lie.

Kate and Derrick looked at each other. "Only Charles," she said.

"Last name?"

"Spencer. Charles Spencer. We were very disappointed when Laura broke off their engagement. He was such a nice boy."

"Did she tell you why she stopped seeing him?"

"She said he was predictable, whatever that means."

"Do you know where Charles is living now?"

"He used to live in Palo Alto," Kate answered. She glanced at Derrick. "We haven't seen him recently."

"Do you have any of Laura's college yearbooks, or a picture of Charles?"

"Laura never bought the yearbooks." Kate looked down at her hands, clearly ashamed that her daughter hadn't purchased her college annuals, as if that decision alone reflected all her failings as a mother.

"What about a photograph?"

She looked at Derrick again. When he ignored her, she looked back at me and shook her head.

"Anything else you'd like to tell me?"

Kate said nothing and Derrick didn't look up from his paper.

"Okay. Thank you for your time." I fumbled in my purse for the bill I'd printed up and handed it to Kate. "You can mail me a check. I'll show myself out."

I left, satisfied that I'd made my displeasure known in every possible way. Since I was already in Atherton I decided to swing by Stanford University, just a few miles further south, to see if the library was open on Sunday. After driving around the campus, lost, for twenty minutes, I accidentally happened upon the library. It was a large ornate building and, luckily, it was open.

I located the reference desk and asked to see the annuals for the years when Laura had attended. The young man behind the counter looked put out, but he went and got them for me and plunked them down on the desk.

"These can't leave the library," he said.

"Thank you," I replied grudgingly.

I took the yearbooks to a table and opened the most recent one. Charles Spencer wasn't hard to find. He was the class valedictorian, for one thing. He was also in the chess club, on the football team, and was heavily involved in theater arts. His picture was all over the place. I even found a shot of Charles and Laura seated on a hillside. The caption read *most likely to get married.* Ouch. He was a good-looking guy with a muscular build. I wondered when Laura had decided he was predictable.

I made photocopies of three of the better pictures of Charles, including the one with Laura in it, then I carried the books back to the reference desk and asked the clerk where I could get a mailing list of alumni.

"You'll have to talk to Administration about that," he said.

I thanked him again and walked out to my car. I managed to find my way out of the campus maze without getting lost this time, and drove north to the 1-Hour-Photo. I collected my pictures of Fred and looked them over before driving back to the office. He was very photogenic, and I had a good shot of his license plate from the InSight parking lot. Feeling pleased with myself, I took out my little notebook and wrote myself a reminder to have CIS run a criminal background on Fred. I should have done that already. I'd had his social security number since Friday night.

All of a sudden I had suspects coming out of my ears. When I got back to the office I listed them all in Laura's file, just in case I developed amnesia. When the list was complete I considered taking a drive to San Francisco and surprising Derrick's son, Rod, but I didn't feel like making the trip for nothing, so I called. The phone rang four times before the voice-mail kicked in.

"You've reached the home of Rod Howard. If you leave a message, I'll get back to you."

I waited for the beep, then left my name and number, not mentioning why I was calling. No sense tipping him off if Derrick hadn't already done that.

I was feeling tired, irritable, and hungry. I walked across the marina to The Diving Pelican and ordered the roast turkey special. I finished most of it, then went down to Elizabeth's trawler to see if she was home. She wasn't. I shuffled the rest of the way to my boat and collapsed. Turkey always makes me sleepy.

An hour later I woke up, called my office machine, and retrieved my messages. Rod had returned my call. His father had told him who I was. He said he'd be home until 6:00 p.m. It was 2:00. He hadn't left his phone number.

I dug through my purse looking for my notebook, but after emptying everything out onto the bunk I remembered I'd left it on my desk. I put on sunglasses and made the trek back up to the office.

All the marina dogs were inside hiding from the heat. As I passed Elizabeth's boat I noticed her door was still closed. Probably shopping.

When I reached the office I listened to Rod's message again. He sounded impatient. A family trait? I located my notebook and found the number, dialed it, and waited while the phone rang four times.

"Rod Howard."

"This is Nicoli Hunter," I said. "I got your voice-mail message. If you're going to be home for a while I'd like to speak with you in person. I can be there in about forty-five minutes." If traffic was light I could make it in thirty.

"You mean today? Can't we just talk on the phone?"

It's easier to tell if someone is lying in person.

"I have some pictures I need to show you." I anticipated his next suggestion. "They're too dark to fax."

"Oh, I suppose," he sighed. "Do you know how to get to Diamond Heights?"

"Two-eighty to San Jose Avenue, left on Dolores, and left on Twenty-ninth?"

"Yes. Then turn right on Diamond and park. I'm at the corner of Twenty-eighth and Diamond, on the right. You have the address?"

I read him the address Sylvia had given me and he confirmed that it was correct.

"I'll see you in forty-five minutes," he huffed, and hung up.

I could picture him glaring at the phone with his father's eyes.

CHAPTER 17

THE DRIVE TO SAN FRANCISCO went swiftly and I was there by 2:40. Parking was something else altogether. I drove slowly around the block, and finally settled for a spot under a tree full of sparrows that my little Bimmer would just fit into. The car needed to be washed anyway.

I squeezed into the space, locked the car, and walked the half block to Rod's address. It was a two-story gray bungalow with white trim. The houses on either side of Rod's were identical to his, except for the color. The one on the left was a pale peach, also with white trim, and the house on the right was white with green trim. There was a fence around his tiny front yard, and a locked gate at the entrance to a walkway that led into a small courtyard.

I pressed Rod's buzzer, looking up at the second-story windows. After a few moments the gate emitted a high-pitched whine and I pushed my way through. On the other side of the courtyard was a concrete stairway leading up to the front door. The door was red and the brass knocker was shaped like a bull's head with a ring through its nose. I was halfway up the steps when the door opened.

Rod Howard was indeed a younger version of his father, with slightly more delicate features. His nose was hooked, his lips were thin, and he was over six feet tall. His eyes were hawk-like and his pupils were dilated. I reached out to shake his hand and, after a moment's hesitation, he responded. His was cold and damp, his grip firm, but twitchy.

"Nicoli Hunter," I said. "Thank you for seeing me on such short notice."

"Come in," he said, sounding exasperated. "Would you like coffee? I just made a pot."

"That would be great. Thanks."

"Cream or sugar?"

"Do you have any lactose-free milk?"

"No."

"Then regular milk will be fine. No sugar, thanks."

My reaction to lactose in small doses is mild. I just get a little phlegmy. Unfortunately, this does nothing to diminish my craving for dairy.

Rod went into the kitchen to get the coffee and I wandered into the living room. The furnishings were modern and sparse. Everything was neutral in color. The carpet was light beige, the leather sofa was cream-colored, and the lithographs on the walls were black and white with red accents.

There was a fireplace against the rear wall that looked like it had never been used. There were no ashes, anywhere. A stereo system dominated the front wall under a plate glass window facing the street. To the right of the living room, also at the front of the house, was a dining alcove containing a large flat panel TV, a cherry wood table, and six matching chairs. The kitchen was between the dining alcove and the front hallway.

Rod came out carrying a tray with two steaming mugs, napkins, and a small pitcher of milk. He set the tray on the dining room table. I chose a cup and added milk. I tried a tentative sip. The coffee was hot, fragrant, and robust.

"Excellent."

"I grind the beans myself," he said, and smiled briefly.

"I can tell."

After I'd finished half the cup I reluctantly set it down on a napkin and took out the pictures I'd copied from the yearbook. I spread them on the table. Rod looked at them as he sipped his coffee and picked up the one of Laura and Charles together.

"God she was beautiful. When was this taken?"

"It's from her last year in college. Do you recognize the man?"

He looked more closely, then said, "No. Is this Charlie? I never met him."

"Yes," I said. "It's Charles Spencer. Did Laura talk to you about him?"

"She mentioned him occasionally. We didn't really see that much of each other. She'd mostly just call. Sometimes come up for the weekend when Dad and Kate were getting her down."

He set the picture back on the table and clenched his jaw, causing the muscles to bunch. Something was making this guy edgy. It could be my presence, or it could be whatever made his pupils remain dilated in the bright sunlight coming through the picture windows. Probably it was a combination of the two.

"I don't suppose you have any idea where Charles lives."

"No."

"What did Laura say about him?"

"When they first got together she thought he was wonderful, but after a couple of years she told me he was rigid and controlling." His right eye twitched, and he pressed a finger to his temple.

"Did you talk to her after they split up?"

"No more than usual. Why?"

"I'm curious about how Charles handled the breakup."

"Now that you mention it, she did say he wouldn't let go. He kept showing up at the house, even when she wasn't there. He asked Kate to try and talk some sense into her, as if that would do any good."

"Was Laura afraid of him?" I asked.

"I don't think so. Do you think *he* killed Laura?"

"I haven't even met him. Did you get the feeling from your talks with Laura that he was capable of violence?"

"Well, she said he was a jock, and you know how they are."

I assumed Rod hadn't done well in sports. Time to stop beating around the bush. "I understand you'll be getting half of Laura's inheritance."

"That's right, and Dad and Aunt Sylvia will get the rest."

"How do you feel about that?"

"Oh my *God*, what a *question*! How would *you* feel if you lost a sibling and then inherited a few million dollars?"

"I don't know," I said. "I guess I'd feel guilty."

"Well, that's how I feel. I've got a load of laundry to put in the dryer. I'll be right back."

He stalked down the hall toward the rear of the house and went out through a back door.

I listened to his footsteps descending the stairs. When I couldn't hear them anymore I made a quick tippy-toe tour of the house. Office, bedroom, and bathroom in the back. Nothing much of interest in the office. Art books on the bedroom shelves. The bathroom was pristine. Only prescription drugs in the medicine cabinet.

On my way back to the living room I spotted a leather shoulder bag on the hall table opposite the front door. I held my breath, listening intently, and when I didn't hear approaching footsteps I took a chance. Digging into the bag I quickly located his wallet, found his driver's license, and memorized the number. I replaced the wallet and dashed back into the dining room just as Rod came up the stairs. I picked up my cup and tried to slow my breathing, repeating the license number in my head.

He came out through the kitchen, looked into his cup and said, "You want more coffee?"

"Please."

I made a note of his driver's license number while he was getting the coffee.

Rod seemed even twitchier now than he had before. I wondered if he might have supplied Laura with the crank Frank said she had used.

"Can you think of anyone who might have wanted Laura out of the way?"

"What makes you think it was someone she knew?"

"I don't know. Just a hunch, I guess. Any ideas?"

It didn't seem appropriate to discuss the absence of defensive wounds with Rod, or to mention the fact that Laura'd had sex just prior to her death. I *hoped* it had been someone she knew. If she'd turned to prostitution and had been killed by one of her clients, the odds against finding her murderer were even higher.

"Laura was beautiful and smart," he said, "and sometimes tactless. I suppose it could have been someone who was jealous of her. But if you really want my opinion, I think our father deserves a second look. He molested Laura when she was a child, you know. She told me about it one night when she'd had too much to drink. Maybe he couldn't handle her displaying her beautiful body for all those strangers every night."

Holy shit!

"What about you?" I asked, my mind racing in disgusting directions.

"I beg your pardon?"

"Did your father molest you?" It was a reasonable question. I had read that pedophiles are often attracted to both male and female children.

"Oh. No. Not that I recall anyway," he said. "Although that would explain a lot." He gazed out the window and his eyes lost focus.

"Do you know if Laura told anyone else about this?"

With an effort Rod pulled his attention back to me. "I don't think she even remembered telling me," he said, and sipped his coffee. "She'd recently started therapy with a woman she said was both a psychologist and a Shaman. During one of their sessions her childhood memories started to surface. Poor kid had no idea how to deal with it. That's why she came up here for a visit. She needed to get out of the house and process the information. You know...that's the last time I saw her." He frowned, and sipped more coffee.

"And you believed her?"

"Yes. She was drunk, but she described what she'd remembered in detail, and the particulars convinced me."

I wanted to know about the particulars, but I couldn't bring myself to ask.

"Did you ever confront your father about it?"

He coughed out a laugh. "You haven't spent much time with Dad, have you? He's not a man you casually confront. Besides, I wouldn't want to risk being disinherited. That wife of his isn't much better. She's addicted to tranquilizers. I have no idea why Laura chose to live with them. What a misery that must have been for her."

It was time for me to go. I'd leave Rod to ponder whether or not he'd also repressed childhood memories too traumatic to cope with.

I took out a business card. "Do you remember where you were the night Laura was killed?" I asked, holding out the card.

Rod's face flushed and the veins in his temples bulged. "I was here," he said. "Alone."

I thanked him for his time and since he hadn't taken my card from me, I placed it on the table. I asked him to call if he thought of anything else I should know, and I let myself out, the hair on the back of my neck prickling.

Chapter 18

DRIVING BACK TO REDWOOD CITY I replayed the Rod Howard interview in my mind. I didn't like Rod, but that was no reason to assume he'd kill his own sister for half of a measly five million dollar inheritance, plus interest. The way he'd casually brought up the issue of molestation, implicating his father, gave me something to think about. I half suspected he'd done that to divert attention away from himself. Maybe the combination of the money and his desire to point the finger at his dad made him a suspect, but I didn't get a killer vibe from Rod. I would run financial and criminal backgrounds on him, and then decide if he was worth a closer look.

I wanted to suspect Fred/Marc, but the only incriminating item in his house was the box of condoms.

Derrick was annoying enough that I almost hoped he was guilty of something for which he could be incarcerated. I'd pay him a visit at his office tomorrow and see how worked-up he got discussing Laura's solicitation arrest.

Charles was looking good too. Rigid, uptight, not willing to let go after Laura ended the relationship, and a jock. Definitely in the running. I'd have to track him down.

When I got back to the office I hauled out my Palo Alto phone book. It's a little known fact that private investigators keep stacks of telephone directories in their offices for occasions such as this. Not everything can be found online. There were six Charles Spencers listed in the city of Palo Alto. I called the first one and got an answering machine. I left my name and number, and dialed the second. A man who sounded at least a hundred answered on the third ring.

"Is this Charles Spencer?" I asked.

"Yes."

"Charles Senior or Charles Junior?"

"What?"

"Sorry. I must have the wrong number."

The next was answered by a cheerful woman who sounded like she was in her twenties.

"Is this the home of Charles Spencer?" I asked.

"Yes, it is," she chirped.

"Is he there?"

"Not at the moment. May I take a message?"

"Actually, I'm trying to organize a reunion and I'm not sure I have the right number. Did Charles go to Stanford?"

"Why yes, he did! Who's this?"

Oops. It hadn't occurred to me she might have been in the same class. Now I was stuck.

"My name is Nicoli Hunter." When you're stuck, you're stuck.

"Nicoli. I don't remember any Nicoli, but it's a big campus."

"What's your name?"

"Ashley. I used to be Ashley Drake. Now, of course, I'm Ashley Spencer."

"Ashley, why don't you give me your address and I'll send you all the information."

"Excellent! I *love* reunions."

She gave me an address on Emerson Street in Palo Alto.

"When is it going to be?" she asked.

"Sorry? Oh, the reunion. Not for a couple of months. I'll get this information packet right out to you."

I hung up before she could ask any more questions. I'd get up early tomorrow and follow Charles to work.

I typed an e-mail to CIS requesting a standard background check on Frederick Marcus Wulf, based on his social security number, and asking for DMV, financial, and criminal records on Rod Howard in San Mateo, San Francisco, and Santa Clara Counties.

After sending the e-mail I checked my watch. I had time to do my grocery shopping before meeting up with Elizabeth. I drove to Whole Foods and loaded the basics into my cart; tuna, lettuce, avocado, broccoli, carrots, raw sunflower seeds, peanut butter, organic Kona coffee, spring water, and dog biscuits. I snacked on the sunflower seeds driving back to the marina.

As I was walking down the companionway Elizabeth appeared in her open doorway, said, "Wait a minute," and disappeared back inside.

Because Elizabeth's boat is at the bottom of the ramp, she has learned to recognize familiar footsteps. I reached her trawler and set my groceries on the dock steps.

She returned a moment later, brandishing two new pairs of size four-and-a-half shoes. The first looked like tiny black combat boots, but stylish, and the second were teal and purple reef runners.

"Very nice," I said.

"What should I wear tonight?"

I was relieved that she'd remembered.

"Whatever you're comfortable in. It's a dive. The employees dress in spandex or nothing at all."

"Okay, casual. Sevenish?"

"Perfect."

I walked to my boat and put away the groceries, then sat down in the main salon, put my feet up on the settee, and drank one of the bottles of water. That's when I remembered I was meeting Detective Anderson after Elizabeth and I got back from the *Fanny Pack*. It was almost 6:00. *Crap!* I grabbed a towel and my shower bag, and sprinted up to the marina facilities.

When I was squeaky clean I took a long appraising look in the mirror and decided I needed to get more sleep. I'm one of those unfortunate individuals who need at least eight hours a night in order to be at my best. I gelled, scrunched, and dried my curls, then hurried back down to my boat.

I put on the same outfit I'd worn the night before, minus the high-heeled boots. I slipped on my Eccos instead. People who live aboard learn to minimize, particularly in the area of wardrobe. There isn't room for duplication, so we generally have only the essentials. Otherwise we end up with boxes of clothes we don't even remember we own in storage.

I checked the Glock's magazine and pulled the slide back to make sure a round was chambered. I slipped it back into my purse holster, noting with satisfaction its compact profile.

I applied some ruby-red lip gloss and just a dab of Must de Cartier, my signature scent. Then I loaded my pockets with dog biscuits and strolled over to Elizabeth's. I stopped along the way to feed D'Artagnon the biscuits, reminding him what a good dog he was. When he'd swallowed the last bite, he leaned his forehead up against mine, sighed, and wagged his tail.

As I continued down the dock, I noticed a petite brunette perched on the steps of Elizabeth's trawler. She was wearing a floral print mini-dress and a pair of tiny black combat boots. I did a double take.

"What do you think?" she said.

"I almost didn't recognize you. What's the idea?"

"In case any of the people we talk to tonight is a psycho-killer, I don't want them to be able to recognize me. I borrowed this from Lily. Does it look real?" she asked, patting her head.

"Yes. You look great, but I like you better as a strawberry blonde."

"Thank you, sweetie. Are we ready to go?"

"In a minute. I want to brief you on what we're looking for."

"Can't we do that in the car?" she asked.

"I guess so."

We arrived at the *Fanny Pack* at 7:13. I'd forgotten to call and ask if Frank and Candy worked on Sundays. Too late now. I pulled into the last available space in the parking lot.

Elizabeth stopped just inside the door, the way I had on my first visit.

"Oh my God," she said.

I gave her a gentle shove and we walked toward the bar. Frank was on duty.

"Hi, Frank," I said, as we sat down.

He squinted at me through the cigarette smoke, smiled, pointed at me, and said, "The PI, right?"

"Right. This is my friend, Lisa."

Elizabeth reached across the bar and shook his hand. *Unbelievable.* He gave her a big smile.

"Coffee?" he asked, glancing in my direction. Before I could answer he'd filled a cup and was concentrating on Elizabeth again. "And what can I get for *you?*" he said, leaning forward.

Apparently Frank thought this was a social visit. Elizabeth ordered a tall Mudslide. Frank prepared the drink with a flourish, filled a tall rocks glass, placed two straws in it, and set the chocolaty concoction in front of Elizabeth expectantly. He had made a rapid recovery since our last conversation.

She took a sip. "Wow!" she exclaimed.

"Too strong?" Frank asked.

"Oh no. It's perfect," she giggled.

I decided to break up the party. "Frank, I need to show you some pictures."

He turned to me, looking a little surprised that I was still there. I pulled the yearbook photocopies of Charles out of my bag, along with the Polaroid shot of Fred and Laura from the Sky Ranch, and one of the pictures I'd taken of Fred at InSight. I placed them on the bar and he looked at each one.

"Well, he looks kind of familiar," he said, pointing to the photo of Fred next to his Jaguar, "But I see so many people in here, and it's always dark. I'm not sure."

"That's okay," I said. "Were you working the night Laura was arrested?"

"No, but I sure heard about it. It was all anybody could talk about. Candy was royally pissed off, but she's always pissed about something."

"What about Alfred?" I asked.

"He thought Laura was cool for not telling the cops about the rooms upstairs when she got busted." He realized what he'd said, blanched, and started washing glasses.

"It's okay Frank. I'm a PI, not the police."

"Oh, yeah. I guess everybody knows what goes on up there anyway. Laura was never part of that, though."

"So she knew the guy was a cop?" I asked.

"That's what she said."

"How?"

He thought about it for a minute. "I'm not sure."

"Okay. Thank you, Frank. You've been great."

I put a twenty on the bar as Frank made his rounds, checking on the other customers. Elizabeth was watching a lap dance.

"Elizabeth," I said. She didn't seem to hear me. *"Elizabeth,"* I said, louder this time. I finally had to grab her arm and give her a shake to get her attention.

She was so startled she almost fell off her barstool. "*What!*"

"Let's go talk to the dancers." I pointed to the hallway.

"What?" she repeated.

The music wasn't that loud. I think she was in shock. As we moved away from the bar Frank told Elizabeth he'd keep her drink cold for her and she grinned like an idiot.

Alfred's door was closed, but I could smell the cigar smoke. If he was watching his monitors he already knew we were there. We continued down the hall and I knocked on the dressing room door. Almost a minute passed before it was opened a crack. Buffy peered out at us. I reminded her who I was and asked if we could come in. She looked puzzled, but stepped back, allowing us to enter.

Candy was seated at her dressing table, putting on make-up. She gave us a sideways glance, and then looked back into the mirror. There was one woman present whom I hadn't met before, a tall willowy brunette. I decided to try the group interview thing again. I pulled the pictures out of my bag.

"Does anyone recognize either of these guys?" I asked, as I spread the pictures across an unoccupied vanity table.

Buffy and the woman I hadn't met before came over. They both looked stoned, and I spotted a tiny charred wad of aluminum foil on Buffy's make-up table.

Neither of them recognized Charles or Fred. I walked the pictures over to Candy.

"How you doin', Candy?"

"Fine. You?" She made eye contact with me in the mirror.

"Not so good. I need your help."

When in doubt, ask for help, that's my motto. It got her attention. She selected the picture of Charles and Laura, and placed a long red fingernail on the image of Charles.

"If this is him he's older now, less hair, but he's still built nice. He used to come in once or twice a week. Stayed in the back, in the shadows."

Shazam!

"Was this when Laura was working?" I asked.

"Yeah."

"Tell me about Laura's arrest. I understand she propositioned a Vice cop."

"Yeah, the bitch. With all my regulars watchin' too."

"How did she know he was Vice?" I asked.

"Well, that's the funny thing. I was on stage when it happened. She walked right up to this guy's table like she knew him. He didn't request a table dance. I checked."

"So it looked like she'd met him before?"

"Sort of." She gave me back the photocopy. "I gotta go on."

"Thanks," I said to her back as she sashayed toward the door.

I turned to the other dancers and handed out business cards again. I asked if any of them knew how Laura had found out the officer who'd arrested her was Vice. No one said a word. They just looked at each other and shook their heads.

I collected Elizabeth, who was hovering near the door, and we went down the hall to Alfred's office. His door was open now, but he wasn't inside. We were turning back toward the bar when we heard a toilet flush and Alfred sauntered out of the men's room, puffing on a stogy.

"Hey, Alfred," I said.

He looked me up and down, making my skin crawl, then turned his attention to Elizabeth. A lecherous smile spread over his face. "You lookin' for work?"

Elizabeth's mouth dropped open and she looked at me, a stunned expression on her face.

"She's with me," I said. "Nicoli Hunter, PI, remember?"

Alfred tore his eyes away from Elizabeth. "Oh, yeah. What do you want?"

"I just need to show you a couple of pictures. Won't take a minute."

"Okay," he grumbled. "Come on in."

We sat, even though he hadn't offered. Elizabeth seemed mesmerized by the closed-circuit video monitors. I handed Alfred the pictures of Charles and Fred. He looked them over, and said, "So?"

"Have you seen either man before?"

"Nope. But that don't mean they ain't customers. I spend most of my time in the office and you can't really make out faces on these things." He gestured toward the monitors.

"Okay. Tell me what happened when Laura was arrested."

"You heard about that, huh? It was no big deal. She was new, and she propositioned this guy from Vice. When she got arrested I was sure she'd blow the whistle on my little operation, but she kept her mouth shut like a good girl. After that I asked her if she wanted to work upstairs between sets, but she wasn't interested. You sure you aren't lookin' for work?" he asked Elizabeth.

"No, but thank you for asking."

Elizabeth is polite under the most unusual circumstances.

I gathered up the pictures and we went back to the bar. Elizabeth wanted to finish her drink. It was 8:02 and I was meeting Anderson at 8:30. I toyed with the idea of leaving her there, but decided that wouldn't be kosher, even if Frank was more than capable of watching out for her.

I let them flirt with each other for another ten minutes while I watched Candy make love to a pole on stage. When

I finally pointed to my watch, indicating it was time to go, Elizabeth looked disappointed. We said goodnight to Frank and he told Elizabeth what days and hours he worked, and asked her to come back. She giggled again.

When we were outside and the door had closed behind us I said, "Cradle robber."

"He's not *that* young," she countered. "Besides, it's flattering when a younger man is attracted to you."

We were in the parking lot walking toward my car when I heard the crunch of gravel behind us. I cast a casual glance over my shoulder as a stocky man wielding a knife stepped out from behind an SUV. He was dressed all in black and wearing a ski mask. It was much too hot for a ski mask. I reached for the Glock, but before I could draw the gun Elizabeth kicked him in the balls and then slammed him in the face with her shoulder bag. He dropped the knife and fell to his knees, and we ran like hell.

We made it to the BMW and turned to look back. The man was still doubled over, but he was on his feet limping in our direction, and he'd retrieved his knife. We jumped in the Bimmer and I almost ran the guy over trying to get out of the parking lot.

Later, when the adrenaline wore off, I kicked myself for not yanking up his mask before running away. In fact, I could have held him at gunpoint while Elizabeth called the police. You know what they say about hindsight. Besides, would I have shot him if he'd tried to get away before the police arrived? Probably not. It wasn't worth it.

"Jesus Christ," Elizabeth said, pulling off her wig and scratching her scalp.

"Are you okay?" I asked.

"I'm fine. That's never happened to me before. It was kind of exciting." She checked the toe of her new boot for scuff marks.

"Almost getting mugged, and who knows what else, is not exciting. It's life threatening!"

She was enjoying this far too much. I was still trembling.

I've had one or two close calls in my career as a PI. The most frightening incident involved an unfaithful husband I was tailing, who was six-four and over three hundred pounds. This was back when I worked for Sam Pettigrew. We were double-tailing the guy because we had the time and it's safer that way. One car stays close to the subject for a while and then drops back when the other car comes forward. We stayed in communication by cell phone. I was driving the green 2002, which I have to admit is easy to spot. These days I rent a Toyota or a Honda when I want to be inconspicuous.

The subject pulled into a strip mall and I parked nearby. He got out of his car and I got out of mine and walked over to a pay phone so I could watch him without looking out of place. He lit a cigarette and walked right up to me. I pretended to be talking on the phone and turned my back to him. He tapped me on the shoulder and I half turned, saying I'd be done with the phone in a minute. He jerked the receiver out of my hand, slammed it down in the cradle, and placed one hand on either side of the booth, trapping me between his huge arms.

"Why are you *following* me?" he bellowed.

I turned to face him and felt a surge of anger I was about to unleash with a fist to his windpipe when Sam appeared on his right. Sam is black and just under six feet tall. He was in his early sixties at the time, and weighed about two-fifty. I held myself in check long enough to see what he was going to do. What he did was yell at me.

"*There* you are!" he shouted. "Where the hell have you been? 'Scuse me fella." He nudged the subject out of the way. "I've been waiting here for two *hours*!"

"I was just trying to call you," I whined.

"Well, come on then," he said, reaching around King Kong and taking my arm. "That's the last time I trust you to be on time."

Sam escorted me into the nearest bar, bought me a Guinness, and talked me down.

"It happens, Nicoli," he said. "If someone has a guilty conscience they expect to be followed. Sometimes they spot you. Can't be helped."

It's the only time I remember Sam being gentle. He's gruff and abrasive by nature.

"You think he wanted our purses?" Elizabeth asked, interrupting my thoughts.

"I don't know."

I rolled down my window and lit a cigarette. I hoped it was just a random mugging. I wasn't crazy about the idea of being attacked by someone who knew me.

I checked the rearview mirror. No one appeared to be following us, but I got on the freeway just in case. I took the Whipple Avenue exit and pulled into a car dealership on Bair Island Road, turned off my lights, and waited to see who passed by.

Less than a minute after we parked a jeep drove by, turning in at the marina. About thirty seconds later a VW Rabbit passed, followed by a Mercedes sedan. The Mercedes pulled into the car dealership and the VW passed the marina, apparently going someplace farther down the road. Bair Island is a dead end. Anyone going back to town or to the freeway would have to drive past us.

The car dealership was still open and one of the salesmen approached the 2002. I leaned out my open window and told him we were having an argument about whether or not we could afford a new car, and he left us alone.

The next car to go by was Bill Anderson's red Mustang. I pointed it out to Elizabeth. "My date," I said.

After that, we sat in silence, trying not to jump out of our skin.

Five minutes later the jeep came back out. The windows were slightly tinted so I didn't get a good look at the driver, but I could see enough to know it was a man. I wrote down the license plate number.

Chapter 19

Detective Anderson was waiting outside my office when I arrived. He sniffed the air around me and said, "You smell a little smoky, but nice."

"Thank you, I think. Sorry I'm late." I fumbled with my keys. "My friend and I got mugged coming out of the *Fanny Pack*."

He took hold of my shoulders, spun me around so I was facing him, and looked me over.

"Are you all right?" he asked. "I *told* you to be careful! What happened? Did you call the station?"

"One question at a time, please."

I found the right key and unlocked the office. We went inside and I flipped on the lights.

"We're both fine. Unbeknownst to me, my friend Elizabeth is an expert kick-boxer and purse-wielder. She knocked the guy down and we ran for the car. I think he followed us though. Can you check a license plate number for me?"

He hesitated, probably wondering if I knew the RCPD could lose access to the DMV network if it was discovered civilians were being given confidential information.

"Maybe," he said.

Close enough. I dug my notebook out of my purse and read him the plate number I'd copied off the jeep. He grimaced slightly as he wrote it down.

I unlocked my Pendaflex drawer and slipped the photographs and yearbook pictures into Laura's file, then glanced at my answering machine. No messages.

I took a deep breath and made eye contact. "You feel like a beer?" I asked.

"Sounds good."

We drove to Otto's again, in Bill's Mustang. He held the door open for me when we entered the restaurant, and I smiled. I'm not one of those women who is offended by this type of behavior. I think it's sweet. I hold doors open for people all the time.

There was one unoccupied booth in the lounge. I sat while he went to the bar. He came back with our drinks and after a few sips of Guinness I began to relax.

"How well do you know Jack McCarthy?" I asked.

"Why?"

"No one can tell me how Laura knew he was Vice before she propositioned him."

"She told her attorney she knew he was a cop. That doesn't make it true."

He was right about that. Although some people can just tell. I can spot a cop from fifty paces.

"What about the attorney?" I said. "What can you tell me about Gerald Kuhlman?"

Bill looked out the window and took a sip of his beer.

"You can talk about the investigation, but you can't talk about the attorney?" I snapped. The adrenaline rush was burning off and I was moving from fear into anger.

"I don't know anything firsthand," he replied. "And I don't repeat gossip."

I stared at him, saying nothing, for about a minute. A minute is a long time to stare at someone in silence.

Finally he relented. "I've heard he's politically connected. When he makes a request it always filters down the chain of command. I don't know from how high. I do know it makes my boss very edgy."

"Thank you," I said, and let the subject drop.

I filled him in on everything I'd uncovered so far – the fiancé who'd refused to let go and who may have been stalking Laura, the half-brother, and the inheritance. Since he'd trusted me with the info about Kuhlman, I even told him what Rod had said about Derrick molesting Laura when she was a child. He started taking notes. I told him about Fred Marcus Wulf and the Supra condoms I'd found in his medicine chest. I didn't have a motive for him, but he'd been dating Laura and I believed she'd known her killer.

"You've been busy," he said. "I assume you know there's been another murder."

"You mean the man in the bank parking lot? I heard about that on the news. Is there a connection? Same knife again?"

"Possibly. The puncture marks were there. The male victim was a hairdresser. Andrew McConnell. So we have two women, different types and ages, and one man, all Caucasian. In each case a knife was involved and all three appear to have been killed where the bodies were found, outdoors, in public places."

"Do you think there's a chance the librarian and the hairdresser might have been killed to cover up a personal motive for killing Laura?"

"It's feasible. Although that might make more sense if she hadn't been the first victim. There were no defensive wounds found on Andrew McConnell or on Laura, though McConnell was stabbed in the back, so he wouldn't have seen it coming. The librarian, Barbara Herbert, was kind of beat up. Some of her teeth were chipped from being pushed face first into a brick wall. All three victims had just had intercourse, and in each case their companion used a Trojan Supra condom." He waited for my reaction.

"Wait," I said. "Andrew McConnell's companion used a condom? Are you saying McConnell was gay?"

"Or bisexual."

If there was one killer, that meant we were dealing with either a bisexual man or a woman packing a dildo. That might explain the absence of foreign pubic hair on the victims. I tried to picture Charles the jock having sex with another man, and then did the same with Rod, Derrick, and Fred/Marc. The next image to invade my consciousness was Candy in a strap-on. Not all that unlikely if you thought about it. I didn't want to think about it.

"Nicoli?"

"Hmm?" I turned to face him. "Call me Nikki."

"Okay, Nikki. What are you thinking?"

"Oh...I was just trying to picture it."

His laugh was warm and contagious.

After we finished our drinks, Bill drove me back to the marina. He walked me from the parking lot to my office and gave me a lecture about being more careful. I unlocked the door and turned to face him. I had an impulse to kiss him, but I managed to control myself. I shook his hand instead.

"Lock this behind me," he said.

I locked the door and watched him round the corner, then turned to my desk. I had two new voice-mail messages. The first call was from Marc, a.k.a. Fred, saying he'd had a good time the previous night and asking if we could do it again next Friday. I made a note to call him back. The second call was a whispered message from Buffy.

"Hi. This is Buffy, from the *Fanny Pack*. I couldn't say anything in front of the others, but I know how Laura found out that guy was a Vice cop. I told her. I knew him from before. I just meant to warn her, you know, so she wouldn't do anything to get herself in trouble. Anyway, I thought you should know. Don't tell Candy, okay?"

I sat at my desk thinking about what Buffy might have done that caused her path to cross McCarthy's. Then I remembered I wasn't getting paid to investigate Buffy's lifestyle.

I checked my e-mail. The financial background on the Howards had come in from CIS. There was also a soft copy of an invoice. I printed the file and the invoice, set the invoice aside, and read the report. It was confusing at first. Assets were listed in many forms, including Derrick's stock in his own company and its current market value. Finally I got to the liquid assets column. That didn't look so good. If you took away their property, the company, and their stock portfolio, they were only worth a little over seven hundred thousand. Hard to believe, considering their lifestyle.

Could Derrick have killed his own daughter, or paid someone else to kill her? He was controlling and abrasive, and possibly a pedophile, but he didn't strike me as the type of person who would kill for money. Of course, half of Laura's inheritance was probably more than four million with the accrued interest, and it did appear Derrick was low on cash.

I lit a cigarette and opened the computer file on the case. It took me almost an hour to enter all the new information and I was yawning by the time I'd finished. I copied the updated file onto a flash drive and tucked it into my purse. Then I shut down the computer, locked the office, and headed for my boat.

Before I reached the bottom of the companionway Elizabeth's door slid open and she poked her head out.

"You just getting home?" she asked.

"I've been up in the office for a while."

She came outside and perched on her dock steps. "What did you find out from Detective Anderson?"

"Can I tell you tomorrow? I'm beat."

Elizabeth's face fell, so I sat down and gave her a quick summary. When I had finished, she sat quietly for a moment, and then said, "What do you think?"

"I don't know. It's hard to picture Laura's father having the imagination to pull it off. Did I tell you Laura's half brother said Derrick molested her when she was a child?"

Elizabeth tilted her head to one side. "No. You forgot to mention that." She said this with some degree of sarcasm.

Elizabeth is originally from New Orleans, where her mother still lives. During her first year of college she worked evenings and weekends answering a suicide hotline. She was unsuccessful dissuading one teenage girl, who had been repeatedly raped by her father, from taking her own life. The girl hung herself while Elizabeth listened on the phone. A coworker called 911 while Elizabeth tried frantically to get the girl back on the line, but the EMTs were too late. She takes incest issues very seriously.

"I have no way of knowing if he's telling the truth," I said.

"You don't think she told anyone else?"

"It's not something you just bring up in casual conversation, is it? Besides, according to Rod she'd just started recovering the memories in therapy."

"There are support groups, but they're extremely protective. They'd never confirm whether or not she was a member. Suppose we assume Rod is telling the truth. How does he know? Did he see this happen?"

"He says Laura got drunk one night and spilled the whole story. She apparently described what happened in a way that convinced him."

"*Ugh*."

"Yeah. So if it's true, it might make Derrick a suspect if he thought of Laura as his property, and, you know, she was taking it off for the unwashed masses. But I don't trust Rod not to make the whole thing up. I'm waiting for a background report on him. That reminds me, I have to be up early to follow Charles to work tomorrow. I gotta go."

"Okay. Sweet dreams, honey."

After a much-needed hug from Elizabeth, I trudged down the dock to my boat, tossed my clothes on the stateroom floor, set the alarm for 5:00 a.m., and climbed into bed.

Chapter 20

My Dream Machine began playing acoustic guitar music at 5:00, but it didn't wake me until 5:20. I struggled into a sitting position, punched off the CD, and threw back the covers. I needed coffee. I started a pot, extra strong, washed my face, lit a cigarette, and waited for the coffee to finish dripping.

I downed the first twenty-ounce pot and it wasn't enough, so I made another and got dressed. I carried my insulated mug up to the office where I'd left Charles Spencer's address. It was already 5:50. Traffic on Highway 101 is heavy after 5:30 on weekdays. I located the address and hustled out to the parking lot.

I was on the freeway heading south by 6:00 a.m. I took the Embarcadero Road exit and turned right on Emerson. I found the Spencers' gingerbread house easily, and parked down the street. I finished my coffee and realized that I needed a bathroom. It's inappropriate to relieve yourself behind a bush in the residential section of Palo Alto, so I hoped Charles was an early riser.

At 7:33 Charles Spencer opened his front door and stepped out onto the porch. Candy was right, he hadn't changed much since college. He was still in good shape but he had a little less hair. A young woman, Ashley, I presumed, was right on his heels, looking fetching in a pink jogging suit. She was blonde, slender, and perky, and bore a noticeable resemblance to Laura. She kissed him good-bye at the car and watched him drive away, waving and smiling.

I waited a beat and then followed Charles, who drove into downtown Palo Alto and made a right on University Avenue. He pulled into an underground garage. I parked on the street and waited, impatiently. Charles came out a minute later, walked half a block, and entered Hubner & Ross, a stock brokerage.

I got out of the car and hightailed it to 525 University, the only high-rise on the block, hoping it would be unlocked at this hour. It was. I took the elevator to the second floor and found a ladies' restroom.

A few minutes later, feeling much more composed, I walked into the underground garage where Charles had left his car, and wrote down his plate number. Maybe I could get Detective Anderson to run it for me. I'd need his driver's license number in order to request a background check.

I walked back up to the street and entered Hubner & Ross. In spite of my jeans and tee shirt, the young receptionist greeted me with a sunny smile.

"Hi," I said. "I'm Sarah Jenkins. Is Charles Spencer in yet?" I didn't want to tip Charles off in case one of the Howards had told him about me.

"Yes. Is he expecting you?"

"No, but I only need a few minutes."

She looked curious, but didn't ask any more questions. She called Charles on the intercom and asked if he had time to see a Ms. Jenkins. She hung up the phone and said, "He'll be right out."

Charles stepped out of a rear office, looked at me quizzically, and extended his hand. I shook it. It was warm and dry and his grip was almost painfully firm. He held on a moment longer than was appropriate while standing a little too close.

"I'm Charles Spencer," he said.

"Nicoli Hunter, Mr. Spencer. I wonder if we could speak privately for a few minutes."

He shot a glance at the receptionist, who shrugged. Without another word he escorted me down the hall to his office. It was small and had no windows, but it had a door, which he closed. He offered me a chair and sat down behind his desk.

"What's this about, Ms. Hunter?"

"I'm a private investigator. I was hired by Kate Howard to look into the murder of her daughter, Laura."

Sometimes it pays to be blunt. Charles recoiled as though he'd seen a rattlesnake perched on his desk. All the color went out of his face, except for his cheeks, which turned red. How was that even possible?

"I assumed you knew she was dead."

"I read about it in the paper," he said. "Why do you want to talk to me? I haven't seen Laura in ages." His hands were spread, palms down, on top of his desk, and he was tilting himself back in his chair, apparently in an effort to distance himself from me.

"It's routine," I said. "I'm talking to everyone who knew her."

That seemed to relax him a little. He let the front wheels of his chair touch the ground, and his color returned to normal.

"I understand you handle Kate and Derrick's investments." I was fishing, of course. They had told me nothing of the kind. In fact, Kate had said they hadn't seen Charles recently.

"That's right," he said.

Bingo!

"Is it a sizable portfolio?"

"Well, it's not small."

"When was the last time you saw Laura?"

Charles turned two-tone again, just for an instant.

"I haven't seen Laura in over a year. Not since we broke up."

Lying sack-of-shit.

"Charles, I took some of your yearbook pictures to the *Fanny Pack*. I know you went to see her dance, frequently."

Now his whole face turned purple and he shuddered. Could an aneurysm be far behind?

"I think you'd better leave," he said, standing abruptly and pointing stiff-armed at the door.

"Okay, but I have more questions." I held out one of my cards. "Maybe we can schedule a time that's more convenient for you."

He didn't move, so I put the card on his desk and backed out of his office.

Standing on the sidewalk in front of the brokerage, I lit a cigarette and thought about the interview. It didn't seem likely that someone as volatile as Charles could murder anyone without leaving an evidence trail. He might strangle Laura with his bare hands in a fit of rage, but it would be done without stealth. That was assuming he was even capable of such a brutal act. He was probably just afraid I'd tell his wife that he'd been spending time at a strip joint.

I walked back to my car and called Derrick. I got the receptionist and then Derrick's admin, who said he would be in meetings all day.

"Please tell Mr. Howard that if I don't hear from him within thirty minutes, I'll discuss the matter in question with Mrs. Howard." I gave her my cell number.

My phone rang before I made it the three blocks to the freeway. I let it ring a few times before answering. I was feeling vindictive.

"Nicoli Hunter," I said, in my most professional voice.

"I don't appreciate being threatened, Ms. Hunter," said Derrick.

"And I don't appreciate being lied to. I'd like to speak with you in person this morning. I'm already in Palo Alto. I can be there in ten minutes."

He didn't say anything for a moment and I imagined steam coming out of his ears. Then he said, "You'll have to get here quickly. I have back-to-back meetings all day."

"On my way."

When I arrived, Tanya, the receptionist, called Derrick's admin, then looked at me apprehensively as she issued a visitor's badge. Derrick came out to get me two minutes later. We walked up to his office in silence. He closed the door and sat down behind his desk. I stayed on my feet this time.

"I imagine you've heard from Charles by now," I began. "I'd like to know why you and your wife chose to tell me you hadn't seen him recently when he handles your stock portfolio."

"If you must know," he said, "we'd already spoken about it before you asked. We decided Charles would never hurt Laura, so there was no reason to involve him. Besides, we really haven't seen him recently. He handles our transactions by telephone and e-mail."

"You decided? Like you decided there was no reason to tell me about Rod and the inheritance? Just how much interest does five million dollars accrue in four years?"

He stared at me levelly, his face expressionless.

"You'll have to forgive me," I said. "I'm used to dealing with clients who want me to find the truth. When a client lies to me, it makes me suspicious. Let's talk about Laura's solicitation arrest. How did you manage to keep it from Kate?"

He sighed impatiently. "When Laura was arrested she called our attorney and Gerald called me. I asked him not to mention it to Kate, and told him to arrange for Laura's release on the condition that she wouldn't mention it to Kate."

"So you blackmailed your own daughter before getting her out of jail."

"I will not tolerate being judged by an employee," he said, with absolute calm.

"Let's get something straight, Derrick. I don't work for you. Your wife hired me to look into Laura's murder, so technically *she* is my client, but I work for myself. I am no one's employee. Is that clear?"

Derrick said nothing.

"Were you aware that Laura got herself arrested intentionally?"

"No," he said. "I knew she was angry, but …" he let the thought go unfinished.

"That's why she took the job at the *Fanny Pack*, isn't it? Because she was angry with you, and with Kate."

"I suppose so, yes." Hardly a confession, but as close as I was likely to get.

"Why didn't you talk to her? You could have gone into family therapy."

"Do you have children, Ms. Hunter?"

"I don't even have a dog," I said, though why I'd volunteered that information was beyond me.

He glanced at his watch and stood up. "I have a meeting to get to."

I decided to leave quietly. I followed him to the door and he held it open for me.

"Can you show yourself out?" he asked.

"Of course. Thank you for your time."

He nodded and closed the door behind me. I took the back stairs and stopped by Research and Development. Fred was there, but he was concentrating on what he was doing. What he was doing was bending over the shoulder of a twenty-something redhead who was seated at a computer. He was leaning on her desk with one hand, and the other hand was resting on her shoulder. I smiled to myself and kept walking.

Chapter 21

When I got back to the office I called Bill Anderson on his cell, knowing incoming calls to the PD were automatically recorded.

"It's Nikki," I said, when he answered. "I need a DL number." I read him Charles Spencer's license plate number.

He didn't comment one way or the other, but he did ask if I was free for lunch.

"What time?" I asked.

"One o'clock? I've got some things to tie up here."

"Okay."

"I'll meet you at your office."

"That'll work. I'll pick something up. You have any menu preferences?"

"Surprise me," he said.

I could tell from his voice that he was smiling, and so was I. I called Bennett, the owner of The Diving Pelican, and ordered roast turkey and top sirloin sandwiches to go. Then I called Sylvia. She answered on the second ring.

"Sylvia, it's Nicoli. How are you doing?"

"Oh hello, dear. I'm all right. How's the investigation coming along?"

"I need your help again. I keep hearing from third parties about Kate and Derrick's attorney, Gerald Kuhlman. Can you tell me anything about him?"

"Oh, yes. I know Gerry. He and Derrick went to Harvard together. I even went out with him a couple of times. I think one of the reasons he moved his practice to San Francisco was so he could be closer to Derrick. They've grown apart over the years, though, both being so busy. I understand Gerry has himself quite an empire now. Derrick tells me some of his clients are politically significant."

"Wow," I said, half to myself. Her description of Kuhlman jibed with what Bill Anderson had told me. "Sounds like a good person to know."

"Yes, I suppose he is."

"Thanks for the info, Sylvia. I'd be lost without you."

"No, you wouldn't, but it's nice to hear anyway. Call me if you need anything else."

I liked Sylvia and she was a great source of information. I'd have to send her a thank you card when the investigation was concluded.

I started updating Laura's file and while I was typing I remembered that I had yet to examine her most recent phone bill. I located the statement Kate had given me and scanned it quickly, then began highlighting the numbers she'd called more than once. I recognized Sylvia's number, having just called her. There was a number in San Francisco that Laura had called three times. I checked my notes and found it was Rod's. There was one in Menlo Park that she'd called four times. I checked the consent form from The Sky Ranch. It was Fred's number. No big surprise there. The calls to Fred were short, each less than three minutes. The last one was at 6:00 p.m. on the night she was killed. Maybe making plans to meet up later in the drugstore parking lot. The calls to Rod were longer. I wondered what they had talked about.

I glanced at my e-mail and saw that I'd received one with attachments from CIS. It was the background I'd requested on Rod Howard. The first attachment showed me that he had two parking tickets in San Francisco in the current year, and that two years ago he'd been convicted of possession of an illegal substance. He'd been fined and placed on probation for six months. The report didn't list what the substance was, but it was a safe bet that Rod had at least one expensive habit.

I opened the next attachment - his financial background. A *very* expensive habit. Apparently Rod had burned through his inheritance and piled up some vicious debts. His car wasn't paid for, he owed back taxes, and his house was mortgaged. I wrote a check to CIS and put it with my outgoing mail. Money well spent.

I decided to give Gerald Kuhlman a call and see if he was willing to meet with me. I found the paper on which Kate had written his number, and dialed. The phone rang twice before being answered by a receptionist who sounded mechanically poised.

"Kuhlman, Ross, and Bassett. How may I direct your call?"

I gave her my name and asked for Gerry Kuhlman. She requested that I hold. A moment later I was transferred to another woman.

"Mr. Kuhlman's office," said a silky alto voice.

"My name is Nicoli Hunter. I was referred by Derrick Howard. I wonder if I might speak with Mr. Kuhlman."

"What is this regarding?"

"I'm a private investigator. I was hired by the Howards to look into their daughter's murder."

She considered that briefly and then said, "One moment, please." When she came back on the line she told me that Mr. Kuhlman couldn't be disturbed just now. I wondered how she'd found that out without disturbing him. She asked specifically what I wanted to speak with him about and I told her I wanted to discuss Laura's criminal record and the disbursement of her inheritance. She took my phone number, asked me to spell my first and last names, and said she would give Mr. Kuhlman the message. I was sure she would. I was equally sure Kuhlman would speak with Derrick before calling me back.

I checked my watch and hurried down to the boat to freshen up before lunch. I was looking forward to seeing Detective Bill Anderson. I changed into a pair of cargo shorts and a Hawaiian shirt, and put on fresh lip gloss, then walked across the marina to The Diving Pelican to pick up the sandwiches I'd ordered. I took a minute to chat with Bennett, the owner; a short, solidly built man I've known since moving aboard. He's outwardly cantankerous, but always has a smile for me.

Anderson arrived at my office at 1:15. He knocked on the open door and I motioned him in.

"Another five minutes and I would have eaten both of these myself," I said.

"Sorry. I got hung up."

"Hungry?"

"Starved. What have we got?"

"We have roast turkey and top sirloin. Take your pick."

"Wow, tough choice. Can we split 'em both?"

A man after my own heart. I set out paper plates and napkins, and got two bottles of mineral water and the jar of dill pickles out of the fridge. We ate and drank quietly for about ten minutes, and it was nice. If you're comfortable being silent with someone it implies a degree of compatibility.

When we were finished eating, Bill wiped his mouth with a napkin, then dug in his pants pocket and pulled out a folded piece of white paper. He handed it to me. Typed on the page was the name Ralph Hearn, an address on San Mateo Drive, and a phone number. Underneath that was an eight-digit number.

Anderson said, "The guy who owns the jeep is a PI and he does *not* have a good reputation. He's been in trouble with the law more than once. Frankly, I'm surprised he still has his license."

"What kind of trouble?"

"Breaking and entering. Aggravated assault."

"So you're saying someone hired another PI to assault me?"

"You don't know for sure this is the guy."

"You're right, I don't. Maybe I'll pay Mr. Hearn a visit."

"That could be dangerous. Besides, even if it is him, he won't tell you who he's working for."

"It can't hurt to ask." I looked at the paper he'd given me. "What's this?" I said, pointing to the number typed under Hearn's address. "Is this the driver's license number for Charles Spencer?"

He nodded.

"You married?"

"Nope." He showed me the great smile with the crinkles around the eyes.

"Attached or involved?" I asked.

Another smile, wider this time. "Nope. You?"

"Nope. Why are the fingernails on your right hand longer than the ones on your left?" I'd been dying to know.

"I play the guitar," he responded.

That I was not expecting, and it was a pleasant surprise. It's not often you find someone creative in law enforcement, or any government position for that matter. Or maybe that's just my prejudice talking.

"I used to play the piano," I said. "How about dinner sometime?"

"I'd like that," he said. "Wednesday?"

"Wednesday works for me."

"Meet you here at eight?"

"Okay," I said. "And thanks for the info." I waved the page he'd given me like a flag.

"Don't mention it," he muttered, "please."

He got up and started toward the door, then turned back to me. "You aren't flirting with me just to get DMV information are you?"

The look on my face must have spoken volumes.

"Sorry," he said hastily. "See you Wednesday." He waved over his shoulder as he went out the door.

I sat at my desk feeling perplexed for a few minutes before picking up the phone and calling Hearn's number. It rang four times.

"Hearn Investigations," said a gravelly male voice.

"Is this Mr. Hearn?"

"Who wants to know?"

Odd question.

"My name is Bernice Rhodes. I need someone to follow my husband."

"Well, then, I'm your man."

I was willing to bet he was. We made an appointment for 3:00 that afternoon.

Before leaving the office I sent an e-mail to CIS, requesting a background check including credit history on Charles Spencer.

Chapter 22

San Mateo is about ten miles north of Redwood City. It's a conservative, middle-class town, primarily residential, but like all cities, it has a dark side. I parked around the corner from Hearn's office, locked the car, and walked back, pepper spray in hand. A jeep like the one I'd seen the night before was parked on the street. I checked the license plate and felt my stomach clench. It was a match.

The office was a tacky storefront, the windows filmed with soot and streaked from the last rain. The front door was unlocked, so I opened it and stepped inside.

The outer office was furnished with a metal desk, a brown vinyl couch, and a glass coffee table covered with magazines and fingerprints. Cigar smoke hung in the air.

Ralph Hearn stepped out of a dark hallway. His salt and pepper hair was greasy. He was stocky and in his mid fifties. He looked shorter than the guy Elizabeth and I had encountered at the *Fanny Pack*, but holding a weapon makes everyone look bigger. There was an angry welt on his forehead.

It took a moment before recognition registered on his face, then his mouth opened, but no sound came out.

"Mr. Hearn?"

"What are you doing here?" he finally said.

"My name is Nicoli Hunter. I think you know why I'm here."

He was silent, but I decided to wait him out. After a moment he said, "I don't know what you're talking about. I'm expecting a client. If you'd like to make an appointment..."

"I'm your three o'clock," I said. "I wanted to make sure you were here when I dropped by."

He looked cornered at first, and then resigned. "Come on back," he sighed.

I followed him into a small office at the back of the suite. He removed some file folders from the visitor's chair and I sat down.

The wall behind Hearn's desk displayed his framed business license and some enlargements of him golfing, as well as a poster of what appeared to be a younger, trimmer Hearn in the boxing ring. There was an ashtray in the middle of his desk the size of a dinner plate, filled with cigar and cigarette butts. The desk was piled high with case files. The telephone receiver was coated with a yellowish film and the carpet hadn't been vacuumed in decades. If he was expecting a client he certainly hadn't made an effort to tidy up, or maybe he had.

I scanned the files on his desk, looking for a familiar name. He saw what I was doing and snatched a folder out of the pile, placing it in his lap drawer, which he locked.

He fished a cigar butt out of the ashtray, lit it, and said, "All right, Nikki. What do you want?"

"Call me Nicoli," I said. "I want to know who hired you." Nothing like putting your cards on the table.

He stared at me with hard eyes. "I can't help you," he said.

"Look, Ralph, we're both professionals," I stretched a point. "I understand client confidentiality, but I'm investigating a murder at the moment and apparently someone wants me to stop. If your client turns out to be the killer, you could be charged as an accessory." I was making this up, of course, but it sounded like a plausible threat.

He shook his head. "I can't help you," he repeated.

"Your choice. Your cover's blown either way. I'll make a point of telling everyone involved in the investigation that I spotted you the first time you tailed me. Maybe I'll even call some local TV stations and newspapers, and tell them about the attempted assault. It might make an amusing human interest story. Local PI turns thug. I promise I won't make you look good."

That got his attention. "Wait a minute," he sputtered. "You wouldn't really do that, would you?"

"If you tell me who hired you I promise not to confront them with that information, and you can even keep following me if you want to. Just don't expect it to be easy."

"I need time to think about this," he said, stubbing out what was left of his cigar.

"I'll call you tomorrow," I said.

I got up and left. He didn't bother walking me to the door.

Ralph Hearn was a sleaze, but I could understand his hesitation. A PI never reveals who the client is to the subject.

I drove back to my office, hoping the background on Charles had come in. He seemed emotionally unstable and that worried me.

I checked my e-mail, but there was nothing from CIS.

I updated my case notes, adding the interview with Ralph Hearn, and then reread the entire file again. As I read my notes about Fred, I realized I hadn't returned his call. I looked up his work number and dialed. When we were connected I told him I'd be happy to have dinner with him on Friday night. My treat. I said I'd meet him at the Garden Grill at 8:00. He sounded pleased.

CHAPTER 23

THE BACKGROUND REPORTS ON both Fred and Charles came in Tuesday morning. Charles had no criminal record and appeared to be doing quite well in the stock market. He'd joined Hubner and Ross the year he graduated from Stanford and had purchased his house later the same year. He'd married Ashley only six months ago – perhaps when he'd finally given up hope of a reconciliation with Laura.

Fred, on the other hand, had an indecent exposure conviction from last year. Probably just a nude sunbathing thing, but it piqued my curiosity. I remembered him saying his father had died recently. I had an unbidden image of Fred pissing on his father's grave. Too bad I couldn't ask him about the arrest without tipping my hand.

I called Ralph Hearn a little after 10:00, got his answering machine, and left a message saying he had until noon, and then I planned to make good on my threat. Whenever possible, I do what I say I'm going to do.

I had reached a point in the investigation where I felt stalled. I pulled out some other case files and typed up reports and invoices, paid some bills, and then walked across the street to the mailbox, sending off the reports, the invoices, and the checks I'd written.

I walked back to the office and tidied up my desk, hoping that an organized environment would help me focus. I brewed a fresh pot of Kona and filled a mug, topping it with milk. I sipped the fragrant brew, and plodded back to my desk. Taking the flash drive containing Laura's file out of my bag, I inserted it in the computer, and saved the updated version yet again, then dropped the drive back into my purse. I lit a cigarette and reread the file, hoping lightning would strike and I'd have some amazing new insight into the case.

When I was finished, I decided I needed to look into the lives of the other two victims, Barbara Herbert and Andrew McConnell. I dug through a stack of old newspapers until I located the stories. Good thing I'd put off recycling.

I read the articles and discovered that Barbara had been employed by the Redwood City Public Library on Middlefield Road, and Andrew had practiced his art at the Mane Line salon on Jefferson. I called the salon to schedule an appointment. When the receptionist asked which stylist I wanted, I asked which of them had been there the longest.

She said, "That would be Kurt."

Kurt had an opening the next day at 2:30.

I locked up the office and drove to the Library. When I entered the lobby there were two employees assisting customers who were checking out books, and a third behind a small metal desk. I approached the one at the desk, an Asian male in his late twenties with thick glasses and shoulder length hair.

He smiled and said, "May I help you?"

"My name is Nicoli Hunter. I'm a private investigator looking into a murder that took place here in Redwood City. Did you know Barbara Herbert?"

His face froze. "How do I know you're not another reporter?"

I handed him my PI license and he took a moment to examine it, then returned it to me and said, "What do you want to know?"

"Did she work up front here with you?"

"No, Barbara worked the reference desk." He nodded toward the back of the library.

"Were you close?"

"Not really. We were friendly, but we didn't see each other socially."

"What hours did she work?"

"Twelve to nine. Same as me."

"Were you aware of anyone special she was dating, or any close friends she might have had?"

"You know, the police already asked us all these questions. I didn't see her with anyone, but that doesn't mean she wasn't dating, it just means I don't know. She and Betsy were pretty close. Betsy's in reference too."

"Okay. Thanks."

I handed him a business card, asking him to call if he thought of anything that might help. He glanced at the card and tucked it in his shirt pocket.

I walked back to the reference desk and found two women seated at computer terminals. Both were occupied at the moment. I waited in line and observed them as they worked. One was slender, Caucasian, and in her late forties, with graying mousy-brown hair cut in a pageboy. She wore rimless glasses and was dressed like a Laura Ashley catalog model. The other was in her twenties, heavy set, possibly Samoan or Hawaiian, with a vast quantity of wavy black hair. She wore a white blouse tucked into a royal blue skirt. I was betting the older woman was Betsy. They both finished with the people they were assisting and looked up at me. I approached the older of the two.

"Are you Betsy?" I asked.

She smiled and pointed to the other woman, who said, "I'm Betsy. Can I help you?"

So I was wrong. I'm a PI, not a psychic.

"Hi," I said. "My name is Nicoli Hunter." I shook her hand. It was soft and her grip was gentle. She had puppy dog eyes and a sweet smile. "I'm a private investigator," I continued. "I understand you and Barbara were friends. I was hoping we could talk."

The smile disappeared and her eyes filled with tears. "I don't understand," she said.

"Can I take you to lunch, or meet you outside when you get off work tonight?"

"I go to lunch at three," she sniffled.

I asked her where she'd like to eat and she said, "Max's." It's an all-you-can-eat buffet-style restaurant on El Camino with a world-class salad bar.

I said I'd be back at 3:00, thanked Betsy, and shook her hand again, which was now slightly damp.

I drove over to Max's and paid for two meals and beverages in advance, so Betsy and I wouldn't have to waste time standing in line. I pocketed the receipts and spent the next hour browsing the mystery section at Barnes & Noble.

At 2:50 I drove back to the library. I waited in the lobby, not wanting Betsy to feel rushed. At 2:58 I saw her go into the ladies' restroom. A few minutes later she joined me in the lobby. We walked to my car and made the drive to Max's in awkward silence.

Once we had piled our plates with food and were seated, I let her take a few bites before asking my first question.

"Did you and Barbara spend a lot of time together?"

"You mean outside of work?" she mumbled, her mouth full. I nodded. "I wouldn't say a lot. But some. We were friends, even though we were totally different."

"How do you mean?" I asked.

"Well, Barb was kind of eccentric, but she was secretive about it. She didn't think people would accept her if they knew what she was really like. The funny thing is, everybody could see right through her, and we all liked her anyway."

"Eccentric in what way?"

"Well, I guess she wouldn't mind me telling you under the circumstances. Barb had an active fantasy life. She lived in books a lot of the time. Loved romance novels and murder mysteries. Sometimes she would pretend she was a character from one of the books she was reading. She'd change her hair and the way she dressed to look like the character."

"How long had you known her?" I asked.

"Three years. Since I started working at the library."

"Betsy, I need to know who Barbara was dating. I know this is difficult for you, but the thing is, I'm sorry, but the thing is she had sex right before she was killed." Betsy's fork stopped halfway to her mouth. "Her companion used a condom," I continued, "and the police think it might have been someone she knew. There was no evidence to indicate the gender of her partner, so it actually could have been a man or a woman."

I waited for her reaction. She took a bite of macaroni salad, chewed slowly, swallowed, and said, "I've been thinking about it a lot since the police came and questioned all of us. I think she was seeing someone. I only saw her with him once and she didn't talk to me about him, which made me a little suspicious. Barb was circumspect about her fantasy life, but if she had a date she'd get so excited she'd tell me every detail about the guy. She didn't go out very often."

"Can you describe the man you saw her with?"

"Not really. The only thing I remember is that he was tall and good-looking."

"Did you notice his hair color? If he had a beard or a mustache? Height? Weight? Anything?" I was desperate for something that would identify one of my suspects.

"I don't remember if he had a beard, but I don't think so. It was dark when I saw him. He met her after work one night, but he didn't come inside. He was waiting in the parking lot. I was walking out to my car and I saw them talking. I waved, but Barb didn't see me. Then they got into their cars and she followed him out of the lot. I asked her about it the next day and she said it was no big deal, just a date. She seemed kind of embarrassed."

"Do you think you would recognize him if you saw a picture?"

"Oh, I don't know. It was pretty dark."

"What was he driving?"

"I was afraid you were going to ask me that. I don't notice cars and I had no reason to pay special attention. All I can tell you is that it looked expensive and it was a light color."

Derrick drove a black BMW. I'd seen Charles driving a white Taurus wagon, but there was probably something else in his garage. Fred Wulf drove a silver blue Jaguar XJS. I'd have to ask him if he spent much time at the library.

"What else can you tell me about Barbara?"

"She was a great person. Very open-minded. She didn't judge people, if you know what I mean. And she was shy, especially with men. She didn't have much of a life really. She liked working at the library because it gave her more time to read than a conventional job would. She loved to read. I think she found the adventure she was looking for in books because she was afraid to look for it in real life."

Betsy paused to eat.

I considered what I knew about Laura, automatically comparing it to what she was telling me about Barbara. Laura certainly couldn't be called shy, but the part about looking for adventure fit. I remembered the romance novel on her bedside table – something else they had in common.

Betsy and I finished our lunch and I drove her back to the library. She accepted one of my business cards and said she would call if she thought of anything else.

I checked my watch, and realized I had time to do some of the work I'd been putting off since taking the Howard case. I stopped by the office and opened the Excel workbook where I keep my master schedule, made a list of the customers I'd been neglecting, stuffed some survey forms into my purse, and left the office.

Most of my work involves bar and restaurant surveillance. The owners of these establishments pay me to observe how their employees perform when they don't know they're being watched. I drink and dine at their expense, and report in obsessive detail on everything that happens from the moment I enter until I leave. I evaluate customer service, attitude, and quality of cuisine, and I watch for till-tapping and other types of theft. Occasionally I install covert security cameras, viewing the discs in my office after hours.

I sit in on termination interviews when someone has been caught stealing and needs to be let go with as little fuss as possible. I'm there to convince them that they're lucky the police haven't been called, although it's rare for an employer to file charges. Time is money, and the general consensus is that it isn't worth the trouble. Catching dirt-bag chefs in the act of pilfering seafood is not what I envisioned when I got my PI license, but it pays the bills.

There are seven restaurants and eleven nightclubs in the San Francisco Bay Area for which I provide 'shopping' services on a regular basis. Many of them expect biweekly reports and I'd been too busy to take care of them since accepting the Howard case.

I'd planned to cover at least three establishments that night, but by the time I'd finished the first dinner survey I was exhausted. I managed a half-assed bar survey in downtown Palo Alto, and decided to call it a night.

Chapter 24

I had called Ralph Hearn's office at 4:30 on Tuesday afternoon, and I tried again on Wednesday morning. Both times I got his voicemail. I didn't bother leaving messages. He'd obviously made his decision. Although I hadn't seen his jeep around, nor had I spotted anyone else following me.

True to my word I called Derrick Howard at InSight, then Kate Howard at home, and Charles Spencer at his office. I informed each of them that a PI from San Mateo had been following me, and I mentioned Hearn by name. I asked them each if they had hired him. Kate was stunned, Derrick was impatient, and Charles hung up on me. It didn't matter. I'd done what I set out to do. I got Rod Howard's answering machine and left him a detailed message about Hearn. I would tell Fred/Marc over dinner on Friday. I wanted to watch his reaction.

At 2:00, I drove to the Mane Line hair salon for my 2:30 appointment. I asked the receptionist, a teenager with spiky purple hair, to point Kurt out to me so I could watch him work.

At first glance he looked more like a beach bum than a hair stylist. If you got past the first impression, however, you might notice that he had a very good haircut. He was just over six feet tall, with a barrel chest and a beer gut. His hair was reddish brown and artfully layered. His complexion was ruddy and his nose showed signs of alcohol abuse. He had a neatly trimmed beard and mustache, both of which were starting to show some white, and he wore shorts, flip-flops, and a tank top. I started having second thoughts about letting him cut my hair. I wanted to look nice for my dinner with Detective Anderson.

I turned my attention to the woman seated at Kurt's station. His hands guided the scissors deftly, almost gracefully, through her hair, and when he was finished she looked amazing. He'd given her a bi-level cut with the front short and coifed around her face, and the back long, ending in a point between her shoulder blades. He handed her a mirror and turned the chair so she could look at the back. The customer tossed her hair, checked both views in the mirror, and squealed with delight. She kissed Kurt on the cheek and gave him a cash tip before leaving.

Kurt stuffed the bill in his pocket and picked up his blow dryer to clean off the chair. He then swept up the hair on the floor and a moment later walked to the reception desk and said something to the purple-haired imp. She pointed at me and Kurt approached, smiling.

"Are you Nicoli?"

"Call me Nikki," I said.

Kurt and I shook hands. His was warm, slightly damp, and callused. He escorted me to his station.

"What are we doing today?" he asked.

"It's a graduated layer cut, but I think it needs to be cleaned up a little. What do you think?"

He looked at me in the mirror, inserted his fingers beneath my curls, and shook, then watched them settle back into place.

"I think you'd look great with a slightly shorter cut and some highlights."

I can't tell you how many hairdressers have said those very words to me, and my reaction is always the same. "I'm not interested in highlights and I like the length. In fact I'd rather you didn't take more than half an inch off the bottom." *Oops*. I'd forgotten I needed information from this guy.

"Okay," he said, with a shrug. "Let's get you shampooed."

Kurt had wonderful hands. He not only shampooed and conditioned my hair, he massaged my scalp while he was doing it, and all of this without getting any water in my eyes or ears. I was considering changing hairdressers even before seeing what he did with the cut, or maybe I'd just come in for shampoos.

He wrapped a towel around my head and led me back to his station where he draped me in a vinyl cape. He ran a wide-toothed comb through my hair to get the tangles out, then picked up his blow dryer and attached a diffuser.

"I'm just going to dry it a little so I can watch what the curl does," he said.

Most hairdressers cut curly hair the same way they cut straight hair. They make everything symmetrical, and when your hair dries and curls up, it looks uneven. Kurt knew what he was doing.

"How long have you been cutting hair?" I asked.

"Two years."

My mouth dropped open.

"I know," he said, "not very long. But I have a knack, and I learn fast."

"What did you do before?"

"I was an electrician."

I like to think nothing surprises me.

"What made you decide to become a hair stylist?"

"That's a long story. Let's just say I was ready for a change."

"Wait a minute," I said. "When I called, I asked for the person who had been here the longest."

"That's me. It used to be Andrew, but he's gone. All these other people are new."

"Is Andrew the man who was killed?"

That went over like a lead balloon. Kurt turned off the blow dryer and set it down, then picked up his scissors.

"Yeah," he said.

Clearly he didn't want to talk about it, but I forged ahead.

"How long had he been here?"

"Nine years, but he'd been cutting hair for twenty."

"Wow. He must have been good."

"He was the best. He used to cut my hair."

"What kind of a person was he?"

Kurt locked eyes with me in the mirror and all of a sudden I was afraid of what he might do with those scissors.

"Why all the questions?" he asked. "Are you a reporter?"

"No, I'm not a reporter."

"Morbid curiosity?"

"I'm a private investigator." I swiveled the chair around to face him and lowered my voice. "I'm looking into the Laura Howard murder and I think there may be a connection between Andrew's death and hers. If I could find out more about Andrew, maybe I could put it together."

"If there's a connection why aren't the police looking into it?"

"I don't know. Maybe they are."

"What do you want to know?" He turned my chair back around and continued trimming my hair.

"I'm interested in the people Andrew was involved with during the last few months of his life."

"Men or women?" he asked, watching my face.

"Both," I said.

"Well, there was this one guy. I saw Andrew cut his hair a couple of times, and I think they were dating. I base that assumption on body language, and the fact that Andrew seemed flustered around him."

"What did he look like?"

"He was tall and sharp-looking, but he seemed pretty full-of-himself. Very GQ."

A perfect description of Fred.

"If I brought in some pictures do you think you could identify him?"

"Sure. It's not the kind of face you forget."

"Was he dating any women?" I asked.

"Not that I know of."

After that we were silent until Kurt set down his scissors, added some hair gel, and scrunched up my curls. He handed me a mirror and spun the chair so I could look at the back.

"Wow. It looks great! Listen, the police would be really pissed-off if any of this leaked to the press."

"Don't worry."

"Thanks, Kurt." I handed him a twenty.

He looked at the bill and said, "You pay at the front counter."

"I know," I said. "This is for you. Best haircut I've had in years. Can I come back tomorrow with the pictures?"

"Sure. I'll be here at ten."

He removed the vinyl cape and I went to pay the receptionist. My heart was pounding. I'd never felt this charged-up working on an investigation before. I had found a possible connection between the murders *and* I'd found a new hairdresser! I was having a very good day.

I returned to the marina and took a quick shower on board the boat to get rid of the prickly little hairs that had fallen down my collar. I dressed in my regular uniform of shorts and a lightweight blouse, and trotted up the dock.

As soon as I unlocked the office I noticed my answering machine light was blinking. I pressed the play button and was glad to hear Detective Bill Anderson's voice. The message was short, simply saying that we needed to talk before dinner. I hoped he wasn't going to cancel.

I dialed his number and got voice-mail. I left a message, then booted up the computer and added the interview with Kurt to my file on Laura. I entered the haircut and tip on my expense spreadsheet. It was a legitimate expense. Once again I updated the flash drive I was carrying in my purse. Okay, so maybe I'm a little obsessive. Sue me.

I pulled Laura's file folder out of my Pendaflex drawer and removed the picture of her with Fred Wulf in skydiving gear, the picture of Fred next to his Jaguar, and two of the pictures of Charles Spencer I'd copied from the yearbook. I placed them in an envelope, which I tucked into my bag.

Bill called me back at 4:30 and asked if he could stop by the office. There was something he wanted to talk to me about in person.

"Sure," I said.

I hastily tidied up, which meant organizing the files on my desk into neat stacks and emptying the ashtray. I went into the bathroom and checked my image in the mirror, added lip gloss, and fluffed up my new haircut.

Bill was on my doorstep ten minutes later. He knocked before entering the office and closed the door behind him. His face looked grim.

"Hi," I said, standing to greet him and taking in his solemn demeanor. "What's wrong?"

"Tell me what happened with Ralph Hearn." Not even a hello.

"Why? What's going on?"

"Just tell me what happened."

"Okay. I called and made an appointment with Hearn right after you left on Monday. I gave him a fake name and told him I wanted my husband followed, you know, to make sure he'd be there. Then I showed up for the appointment at three. It took him a second, but he recognized me. He asked what I was doing there, said he was expecting a client. I told him I was his three o'clock and eventually he invited me back to his private office.

"I asked him who had hired him. He refused to say, of course. I said if he didn't tell me, I'd inform everyone involved in the case that I'd spotted him on Sunday night, and I threatened to go to the media about the attempted mugging." I blushed at the memory. "Now tell me what the hell is going on."

"Did you leave a message on his answering machine yesterday morning?"

I thought for a moment. "Yes, I did. He never got back to me. How did you know about that?"

"What did you mean when you said he had until noon or you'd make good on your threat?"

"Just what I told you. That if he wouldn't say who'd hired him, I'd tell everyone involved in the case that I'd spotted him following me. Has Hearn filed a complaint against me or something?"

"He's dead, Nikki."

The impact of his words knocked the wind out of me and I sank into my chair. "Oh, fuck."

"His body was found this morning. His landlord went in to collect the rent. The San Mateo County Sheriff's Department listened to your voicemail message. I heard about it through the grapevine and gave them a call."

"What are you telling me? He had a heart attack or something?"

Hearn had looked like he had high blood pressure. *Please let it be natural causes.*

"He was murdered."

I felt a chill run the length of my body. "How?"

"I'll tell you in a minute. This is serious, Nikki. You left the man a threatening message and within twenty-four hours he was dead."

"You don't think I'm a suspect do you? I told you what my message was about."

"It doesn't matter what I think. It's not my case. But I want you to tell me everything you did after you made that call, right up to this morning around eight."

My mouth dropped open. Then I sucked it up, lit a cigarette, and said, "Fine." I quickly ran through the last two days in my head before continuing. "After I left the message for Hearn I was here typing reports and invoices and paying bills. I walked to the mail box across the street. I walked back here and straightened up the office, made some coffee, and updated the flash drive with the Laura Howard file on it. Then I reread the file one more time and decided I needed to talk to friends of Barbara Herbert and Andrew McConnell.

"I found some newspaper articles about their murders. I made an appointment with a hairdresser named Kurt at the Main Line where McConnell worked, and then I drove to the Library. I spoke with a couple of employees, and took one of them to lunch. Her name was Betsy. Her lunch break wasn't until three so I spent some time at the Barnes and Noble while I was waiting. I was there from about two until a little before three. Then I picked Betsy up at the library and we had lunch at Max's. She told me Barbara had been seeing someone, but she couldn't really describe him. After lunch I drove her back to work, gave her a business card, and asked her to call if she thought of anything else I should know.

"When I got back here I called Hearn's office again, and got his voicemail again. I didn't leave a message. I did a couple of bar and restaurant surveys last night, and was home in bed by ten.

"This morning I called Hearn again, got the voicemail again, and didn't leave a message. I decided he was a lost cause, so I made good on my promise and called Derrick and Kate Howard, and Charles Spencer, and left a message for Rod Howard. I was going to talk to Fred Wulf about it in person on Friday. We're having dinner.

"At about two I drove to the Mane Line hair salon. At approximately two-thirty I got this beautiful haircut and had a conversation with the hairdresser, Kurt, who was a friend of McConnell's. Turns out he'd been dating someone who sounds a lot like Fred Wulf, so I asked if I could bring him some photos to look at. I have pictures of Charles and Fred both, and I was hoping he could ID the guy McConnell was seeing.

"When I left the salon I came back here and took a shower. Then I opened the office and got your message. Now tell me how the fuck he was killed."

Bill squinted at me for a minute, probably assessing my stability before making his decision.

"With a garrote made of heavy-test fish wire and a pair of home-made grips. There was a taser burn on his neck. Time of death hasn't been established yet."

I put my head between my knees and tried to breathe. Bill came over to the desk and laid his hand on my back.

"You okay?"

"I don't know yet." I stayed down.

"Sorry to be so blunt."

"It's okay. Just give me a minute."

When the room stopped spinning I slowly sat up, lit another cigarette, and inhaled deeply.

"Did they find a case file with my name on it in his desk?"

"No. Nothing in the office with your name on it, except that message you left on his machine."

"So I'm a suspect?"

"A person of interest, yes. You should probably give the Sheriff's Department a call before they come looking for you. Ask for Detective Dietrich."

"He was killed because of me, wasn't he." It wasn't a question.

"I wouldn't jump to any conclusions. There's no evidence to indicate that."

"Yes, there is. He had a file on me. When I was in his office I started reading the labels on his file folders and he grabbed one and locked it in his desk, in the lap drawer. If they didn't find that file, the odds are he was killed by someone who didn't want me to find out they had hired him. What about his computer? Has anyone gone through his computer files?"

"Not yet."

"Jesus. You know any good bodyguards?"

"If you're serious, I could recommend a couple of people."

"Why don't you give me their names and numbers?"

He wrote down three names and phone numbers, saying all of them were police officers who did some moonlighting as bouncers or bodyguards.

"I gotta get back to the station," he said, reluctantly. "Can we have dinner tomorrow night instead of tonight?"

"Sure. Eight o'clock?"

"I'll meet you here." He started toward the door.

"Bill…do you mind if I call you Bill?"

He turned back to me. "Yeah," he said. "I mean no."

"Thanks for telling me in person."

"No problem. See you tomorrow."

CHAPTER 25

I PUT OUT MY CIGARETTE, took a deep breath, and called the San Mateo County Sheriff's Department. I asked for Detective Dietrich and was promptly connected.

"Dietrich." It was a woman's voice.

"Is this Detective Dietrich?" I asked.

"Yeah. Can I help you?"

"This is Nicoli Hunter."

She was silent for a moment, and then said, "The Nicoli Hunter who left a voice-mail message for Ralph Hearn yesterday?"

"That's me. I just spoke with Detective Anderson here in Redwood City. He suggested I give you a call."

"Would you be willing to come in so I can ask you a few questions?"

"I'd really rather answer them over the phone, if you don't mind."

She thought about that. "I'd prefer to discuss this matter in person, Ms. Hunter. And the sooner the better."

I couldn't really blame her. In her place, I'd want to watch my suspect's reactions too.

"Of course. I can be there in fifteen minutes. Will that work for you?"

"Yeah. That'll work. You know how to get here?"

"I think so. Are you in the County Center building?"

"Yep. See you in fifteen."

She hung up without another word.

County Center is off Middlefield Road in Redwood City. Not all that far from the marina. I could be there in five minutes, but needed the extra time to make photocopies of my receipts from my lunch with Betsy and my bar and restaurant surveys from last night, in case Dietrich needed to be convinced of my whereabouts.

I stuffed the photocopies in my purse, locked the office, and trudged out to the parking lot feeling guilty for my small role in Hearn's death. I never should have told him I was investigating a homicide. I'd been too eager to badger the name of his client out of him. I really hate feeling guilty. Hearn was a low life, but he didn't deserve to die.

I pulled into the County Center lot, collected my purse, and locked the 2002. Just because there were a lot of cops around didn't mean my sweet little ride would be safe.

In the lobby I used an internal phone to dial Dietrich's extension. She said she'd be right out, and I shuddered with anticipation. I'd never been a murder suspect before, or even a person of interest.

Dietrich marched into the lobby only seconds after I'd hung up the counter phone. She was about five-three and a hundred and twenty pounds of muscle dressed in khakis and a navy polo shirt. Her short dark curls framed an oval face unadorned by make-up. She looked about my age, but the wrinkles between her eyebrows had been deepened by years of frowning. In her line of work, that made perfect sense.

She held out her hand as she approached, "Ms. Hunter. Thank you for coming in."

"Not a problem." I took the proffered hand and she briefly crushed my fingers.

"Follow me, please."

Dietrich escorted me through a series of corridors and into a small interrogation room. When she'd closed the door and flipped a counter switch, she said, almost as an afterthought, "You don't mind if I record this, do you?"

Clearly the recording had already begun.

"Not at all."

Dietrich announced her name and mine and the time and date, then wasted no time getting down to business.

"Your voicemail message to Mr. Hearn yesterday was a little cryptic. What did you mean when you said he had until noon," she glanced at some notes in front of her, "and then you planned to make good on your threat?"

"He'd been hired to follow me," I said. "I assume you know I'm also a PI?"

"Anderson told me."

I described the attempted assault at the *Fanny Pack,* and repeated the story of my encounter with Hearn in his office, including my threat to reveal his incompetence to my primary suspects, and to go to the newspapers and radio stations.

She listened without comment until I had finished, then said, "Let me get this straight. When you said he had until noon, all you meant was that if you didn't hear from him who his client was by noon yesterday, you would tell some people that you knew he had been following you, and then go to the press and tell them he had attempted to assault you?"

"That's right."

"And did you do those things?"

"Yes. Well, I didn't go to the press, but I called several people and told them I'd spotted him following me."

"Who, exactly?"

"Laura Howard's parents, her half-brother Rod, and her former fiancé, Charles Spencer."

She asked me for their phone numbers and addresses, and I gave them to her.

"Can you tell me where you were between five and ten p.m. last night?"

"I was doing bar and restaurant surveys for two of my regular clients. I brought photocopies of my receipts." I pulled the pages out of my bag and passed them across the table to her. "So the coroner has determined time of death?"

Dietrich gave me a guarded look, set the receipts aside, and nodded somewhat curtly.

"That's all for now," she said, rising from the table. "I'll be in touch if I have any other questions. Please remain available."

"Is that another way of saying don't leave town?"

Dietrich was not amused. I made sure she had my office and home phone numbers, and she walked me back out to the lobby.

I lit a cigarette as soon as I'd locked myself in my car. I felt as though someone had run a thousand volts through my adrenal glands. My hands were shaking and my skin was clammy. Hearn had been murdered because he could point the finger at Laura's killer. I was certain of that. Maybe he'd even tried to blackmail the person who'd hired him.

When I got back to my office I pulled the flash drive out of my purse, popped it into the computer, and added the details and timing of Hearn's murder to the file.

When the mail carrier stomped into the office I almost had a heart attack. I gave her my outgoing mail and accepted the small stack she had for me. When she left, I locked the door behind her and looked through the mail. There was a payment from Kate Howard. I noted the amount and slipped it into my wallet.

I checked the magazine in the Glock and took a spare mag out of my gun drawer, making sure it was also fully loaded. I toyed with the idea of having an alarm installed and decided to price them. For the first time since I'd rented the office I felt exposed and vulnerable, being surrounded by floor to ceiling windows and glass doors.

Since I wasn't having dinner with Anderson, I could take care of my regular clients. I checked the schedule and grabbed some forms, then locked up the office.

I wanted to change clothes before going out, so I headed down the companionway to the docks. Elizabeth was out on her steps talking to K.C. She watched me for a minute and then said, "What's wrong, honey?"

"What makes you think anything's wrong?"

"Aren't you having dinner with Detective Hottie tonight?"

"We're having dinner tomorrow night instead. You know that PI from San Mateo I told you about? The one who tried to mug us at the *Fanny Pack*?"

"Of course."

"Well, he's dead."

"Oh," she said. "Your hair looks great."

"Did you hear what I just said?"

"I heard you. What's your point?"

"He was murdered, and the case file on me was taken from his office."

"Did he have a computer?"

"Yes."

"So?"

"I don't know yet. The police have to check the files."

"How was he killed?" she asked.

"He was strangled with fishing wire."

"Gross. You think he was killed because you talked to him?"

"Yeah, I do."

"What are you going to do?" she asked.

"I'm thinking about getting an alarm for the office. Maybe hiring a bodyguard. I'm carrying the Glock," I patted my purse, "and I'm hoping to get a good night's sleep."

"You must be getting close."

I nodded. "I just wish I knew what I was getting close to."

"Have you eaten today?" Elizabeth has a way of simplifying things. "I have low fat lasagna."

"That sounds great, but I have to get some bar and restaurant surveys done. You wanna come?"

"Absolutely. As long as you don't keep me out too late."

We had drinks in three different bars, nibbled at dinner in two restaurants, and talked more about the investigation. I told Elizabeth I was taking the pictures of Charles and Fred to Kurt the hairdresser and Betsy the librarian the next day, and that I was having dinner with Fred on Friday. She approved of Bill, even though they hadn't met, but asked what I hoped to gain by having dinner with Fred again.

"I don't know. More insight into his character, I guess. Maybe a chance to search his car."

We arrived back at the marina at half past ten and even before we got out of the car we heard D'Artagnon barking. If he sees, hears, or smells anyone he doesn't recognize, he sounds an alarm that can be heard throughout the marina. Thinking of Ralph Hearn's death, I wondered who was on the docks that didn't belong there. I was glad I'd locked my pilothouse before going out. I don't normally lock the boat, but I'd been feeling paranoid since the attempted mugging.

I walked with Elizabeth to her trawler and thanked her for coming out with me. On the way to my boat I stopped to scratch behind D'Artagnon's ears and asked him what he'd been barking at. He responded by leaning his forehead up against mine. D'Artagnon does this a lot. It's an expression of affection, like a canine hug, and it always touches my heart.

Chapter 26

D'Artagnon started barking again at 2:40 Thursday morning. His tone was so outraged that I briefly considered going outside to see what was bothering him, but I was too tired to get out of bed and after a few minutes he stopped. I drifted back to sleep and dreamed I was being stalked by a faceless man with a hatchet.

I slept until 7:00 and woke up feeling anxious, still caught in the nightmare. I rolled out of bed, showered on board, and lingered over coffee and low fat lactose free yogurt while I watched the morning news. The murder of Ralph Hearn was a featured story.

At 9:00 I walked up to the office to check my e-mail and phone messages before going to the Mane Line to show Kurt the pictures of Charles and Fred. As I inserted my key in the lock the door swung open. I sucked in a breath and drew the Glock from my purse holster, dropping my bag on the ground.

All my senses went on high alert. I felt goose bumps erupt on my arms and neck. I knew I'd locked the office last night. My heart beat like a jackhammer as I stepped over the threshold, and my vision seemed to expand, taking in everything at once. The notepad on my desk was slightly askew. My swivel chair had been moved away from the desk. I always push the chair up against the desk before leaving to conceal the Ruger holstered under the lap drawer. The color printer near my wall safe had been moved a few inches to the left and the framed photo that covers the safe was slightly crooked.

I checked under the desk for my Ruger. It was still there.

At first glance nothing appeared to be missing. I walked slowly through the office. The computer, the printers, the fax machine, the microwave, the TV, and the VCR/DVD player were all in place. I reached the hallway and saw that the bathroom door was closed. I never close the bathroom door. It's a tiny room and I get a little claustrophobic in there, so I lock my front door to insure privacy, rather than closing the door when I'm in the bathroom. Fortunately, the bathroom door faces the hallway and is not visible from the front of my office. My claustrophobia stems from childhood punishments; being locked in my bedroom.

I held the Glock in my right hand, took a deep breath, and flung the bathroom door open, crouching to make less of a target. The door slammed back against the wall and I could see in an instant that the room was empty, but there was no doubt someone had been in my space. The marina complex employs a janitorial service, but they only clean the public restrooms and the hallways. They don't even have keys to the offices.

I walked back to the front door, retrieved my purse, and locked the door.

There was a message on my machine from Bill, asking me to give him a call when I got in. He'd called at 2:20 a.m. That was odd. I knew I'd given him my home number.

I booted up the computer and checked the file on Laura. All my files are password protected, but I checked the properties anyway. It hadn't been opened since I'd saved it the day before. I unlocked the Pendaflex drawer and took out the folder on Laura's case. It was just a bunch of notes, some pictures, Laura's AMEX statements, the phone bill, the printed pages I'd photographed of the murder book, and the CIS reports.

Something felt funny to me. Handling the folder, I got goose bumps on my arms again. It's easy to pick the lock on a desk drawer. Maybe the intruder had left his scent on the paper. Pheromones are subtle, yet they influence our every response to each other.

I picked up the phone, put it down again, and took out my cell. I called Bill Anderson and told him the office had been broken into.

"Have you got your door locked now?" he asked.

"Yes."

"Keep it locked. I'll be right over."

"Can you bring a fingerprinting kit with you?"

"Sure, but stay put, and don't open the door for anyone until I get there."

While I was waiting for him to arrive I paced behind my desk, smoked a cigarette, and tried not to touch anything. I let my mind drift over the events of the past few days, trying to remember everything that had happened; lunch with Betsy from the library, my visit with Kurt at the Mane Line, the second trip to Derrick's office, the phone call with

Fred Wulf, the confrontation with Charles Spencer, Ralph Hearn's death, my interview with Detective Dietrich, and my growing attraction to Bill.

I decided it was probably safe to handle the coffee pot.

When Bill arrived I noticed dark circles under his eyes and offered him a cup.

"Please," he said, glancing dubiously at the Glock positioned on my desk blotter.

"Black?"

"Yeah, black is good."

I poured us both coffee and as he tasted it a vague smile crossed his face. I buy good coffee. It's one of my indulgences. I sat down behind my desk.

"Nikki, there's been another murder," Bill said.

My heart started pounding again. I tried to set down my cup, but my hand was shaking badly and I splashed some coffee on the desk blotter.

"Oh God," I croaked. "Please tell me it wasn't Kurt."

Bill stared at me. I felt my eyes heat up and tried not to cry.

"You knew him?" he asked.

I sat there fighting the tears, unable to speak. The guilt was overwhelming. Eventually I collected myself enough to respond. "I told you he cut my hair yesterday," I said, absentmindedly touching my head. "I was going back today to show him pictures of Fred Wulf and Charles Spencer. He said Andrew McConnell had been dating a man, and he could identify him. Someone must still be tailing me, but I swear I haven't noticed anyone since Sunday night." I took a breath. "How was he killed?"

"You don't want to know. Is there more coffee?"

"You're going to tell me. I have a right to know. And you'd better get someone over to the library to keep an eye on Betsy at the reference desk."

"What? Why?"

"Because I talked to her too. Weren't you listening yesterday? She worked with Barbara Herbert. I took her to lunch. I was going to see her later today with the same pictures. She probably won't be able to ID the guy Barbara was with. She only saw him once, across a dark parking lot. But if I'm being followed, anyone I've questioned is at risk."

He handed me his empty cup and took out his cell phone.

I refilled his cup while he called the precinct and arranged for someone to keep an eye on Betsy. When he hung up I looked at him expectantly.

"It's ugly," he said.

I sat back down, lit a cigarette, and inhaled deeply. "Okay. I'm ready."

"Apparently Kurt was drinking at the I-Ching bar last night. Toxicology says someone slipped him some triazolam. It's a tranquillizer, also known as Halcion."

"I know what Halcion is. They've already done the autopsy?"

"Yeah."

I remembered the Guinness I'd spilled on Fred at *The Wall* and got a queasy feeling in my stomach.

"He was drinking Jack Daniel's, according to the bartender," Bill continued. His voice was dispassionate, and he was watching my face, gauging my reaction. "His body was found in the alley behind the bar by a homeless couple. It's the same alley where Barbara Herbert was killed. Something had been driven through his left eye and into his brain. Probably an ice pick. He'd also been raped, uh, sodomized."

I was wrong. I wasn't ready to hear this at all. I got up and ran for the bathroom. When I finished vomiting coffee and yogurt into the toilet, I brushed my teeth and rinsed with Listerine. I returned to my desk and lit a fresh cigarette.

"You said he'd been raped. How do they know it was forced?"

"Trauma to the surrounding tissue. Trojan Supra condom, again."

"Kurt was a big guy."

"He apparently had enough of the drug in him to make him passive, plus his blood alcohol level was extremely high."

"I can't believe this is happening. It's all my fault."

"We don't know for sure that there's a connection."

"Oh, *please*. Kurt described the man Andrew was dating to me. He said he was very GQ and full of himself. That sounds like Fred Wulf. Have they found a file on me in Hearn's computer?"

"No, but he didn't use his computer much. All of his current case files were handwritten."

"Can you post a surveillance team outside Wulf's house, and one outside Charles Spencer's? And Derrick Howard should be watched too." Might as well cover all my suspects at the RCPD's expense while I was at it. Rod Howard lived in San Francisco. I wondered if Bill could have someone watch him too. My head was spinning. I took a deep breath.

"We've been watching Fred Wulf and both Derrick and Rod Howard," Bill said. "Apparently Fred and Derrick stayed home last night."

"There's a side entrance to Wulf's garage."

He frowned at me and checked his notebook. "His lights were on until midnight, then they went out one room at a time. His Jag was parked in the driveway all night."

"He could be using automatic timers on the lights and maybe he rented or borrowed another car, or slipped out the side door and took a cab. Hell, he could have walked to Redwood City. It's only a couple of miles. What about Derrick?"

"He and his wife were visible through the front window until ten-fifteen, then the living room lights were turned off and lights in an upstairs bedroom toward the back of the house went on. The upstairs lights went out at ten-thirty."

"And his car was in the garage all night?"

"The garage doors were closed all night. Rod Howard went out, but didn't leave San Francisco."

"You're probably going to be too busy for dinner tonight."

"I've gotta eat," he said. "I just won't have as much time as I would have liked." He stood and walked around the desk. When I got up he wrapped his arms around me. "Don't take it personally, Nikki. It's not about you. I'll see you at eight." And he kissed me on the forehead.

I was speechless. There was some profound chemistry here and it had been a long time since I'd experienced profound chemistry. Then I remembered Kurt and plopped back into my chair.

"Lock the door behind me," Bill said, as he exited. He stood outside the office until I got up and threw the deadbolt latch.

After he left I sat at my desk for several minutes feeling dazed. Then I added Kurt's death to the growing file on Laura Howard. It was obvious to me that all the murders, starting with Laura's, had been committed by the same monster. I read through the file again, wondering about the people I'd met since taking this case. In reality, any one of them could be the killer.

It struck me that Bill and I had both forgotten to do anything about the fingerprints in my office. Oh well. If it was the killer who broke in, there probably wouldn't be any prints.

After typing up the previous night's reports, I secured the Glock in my purse holster and drove to the library.

Chapter 27

As I pulled into the library parking lot I remembered that Betsy didn't start work until 12:00. It was barely 10:00. Since I was already there, I decided to go inside.

To my surprise, I discovered Betsy working alone at the reference desk. There was a plainclothes officer seated at a nearby table; a clean-cut man in his early thirties, dressed in jeans and a polo shirt. He was reading a paperback novel and he looked up whenever someone approached. He glanced at me briefly, then went back to his book. I guess I didn't appear threatening to him.

"Hi, Betsy," I said. "I thought you didn't come in until noon."

"Normally I don't, but Carlie is out sick today."

I decided not to waste words. I took the envelope out of my purse and placed the pictures of Fred Wulf and Charles Spencer on the desk in front of her. Betsy looked down and furrowed her brow.

"I assume you want me to tell you if either of these men is the one I saw with Barb that night."

"Yes," I said. "If you can."

She picked up each picture and studied it, then shook her head. "I'm sorry. I'm just not sure. It could be this one," she pointed at one of the photos of Fred, "but it was dark. I'm really sorry."

"That's okay," I said, tucking the pictures back into the envelope. "Thanks for trying."

The officer looked up again as I left, and checked out the next person in line. It appeared Betsy was in capable hands. If someone was following me, I hoped it was obvious that she hadn't been of any help.

I went back to the office, locked myself in, and reread and printed my entire file on Laura Howard. I decided to hide a hard copy of the file in case something happened to me, the flash drive, and my computer. It was fifty-one pages long. I stuffed it into a large manila envelope, which I set by the door so I wouldn't forget it when I was ready to leave.

I glanced outside as I put the envelope down and noticed a man standing near one of the pillars, smoking a cigarette. I hadn't seen him in the complex before. He was over six feet tall and had red hair and fair skin. He was heavy set, wearing a dress shirt with slacks, but no tie or jacket. He was turned so that my office was peripherally visible to him, but he wasn't looking directly at me. I wondered if he was the link between me and the killer, or if maybe this was the killer himself. I decided to find out.

I slung the pistol purse over my shoulder, and, turning my back to the door, compulsively press-checked the Glock to be sure it was loaded and had a round in the chamber. I snatched up the envelope, exited the office, and locked it behind me. After locking the door I tried the knob, just to be sure. When I turned around the red-haired man was gone.

I walked casually to the parking lot, unlocked the 2002, and got in. I drove to the marina management office and parked. I checked the box where I receive my personal mail. Nothing but junk mail. As I was getting back into my car I noticed a midnight blue, late model Volvo with tinted windows pulling into a space nearby. The windows were too dark for me to see who was driving. When I pulled out of the lot the Volvo did not follow.

I drove to the gym, just around the corner on Veterans Boulevard, and parked at the farthest corner of the lot near Whipple Avenue so I could watch the street where Bair Island Road exits onto Whipple. After about a minute the blue Volvo drove out, and sure enough, it made a left on Veterans, then a left on Convention Way. It didn't enter the fitness center lot, but it was nearby. This led me to the conclusion that whoever was driving the car was not actually tailing me. They didn't have to. They had attached a transmitter to my car.

I drove straight to the Redwood City Police Department, parked in front of the main entrance, locked the car, jogged up the steps, and blew into the lobby.

L Ketteridge was behind the front desk. I asked her if Detective Anderson was in. She grinned happily, said she would check, and winked at me.

Three minutes later Bill entered the lobby, looking worried. How could someone this sensitive handle the job he had to do every day?

"What's up, Nikki?" he asked.

"I think there's a transmitter somewhere on my car," I whispered. "Do you have one of those bug detector thingies?"

"Yes," he said, moving me toward the door. "But not here. I'll bring it to dinner tonight. Can it wait that long?"

"I guess. I'm sorry to bother you. I'll see you later."

"It's no bother," he said, squeezing my arm. "Be careful."

He held the door for me and watched until I was safely inside my car.

I scanned the small parking lot as I drove to the street. The Volvo was nowhere in sight. I felt like an idiot. I was supposed to be this big, tough detective, and I didn't even have the hardware necessary to check for transmitters. I thought about taking a drive to Radio Shack to pick something up, but decided to play cat-and-mouse with my tail instead.

I went to the Albertson's market in San Carlos, parked in a side lot under a tree, and walked back to the street. I hid behind a fenced-in dumpster at the corner of the building and waited. Two minutes later the Volvo drove into the main lot. It made the rounds of the various parking areas, slowly cruising up and down each aisle and, eventually, rolled around the side of the building where my car was located. The driver returned to the main lot, and parked. No one got out of the car.

I entered the store and purchased some lunch items to restock the office fridge, taking my time at it. I know from personal experience that the most maddening part of any surveillance is waiting for something to happen.

Driving home I kept checking my rearview mirror, but he wouldn't be close enough to spot. He didn't have to be.

I hadn't gotten the license plate number and I was kicking myself for that as I unlocked the office door.

I unpacked the groceries and decided to give the office a thorough cleaning. I needed to wash away the feeling of having my space violated. I dusted file cabinets, washed walls and baseboards, cleaned the toilet, wiped the bathroom shelves, and even cleaned the refrigerator. When I'd exhausted myself I locked up and walked down to my boat.

CHAPTER 28

AT 6:30 I HIKED up to the marina facilities to shower. As I passed Elizabeth's trawler I noticed that her door was closed. She was probably working late. When I came out twenty minutes later, her door was open. I dropped my shower bag on the dock, climbed aboard, and peered inside. "Anybody home?"

Elizabeth came up from the stateroom.

"Hi, honey." She grinned at me. "Ready for your hot date?"

"Yes and no. I printed a hard copy of the Howard file. Can I leave it with you?"

"Sure. Can I read it?"

"If you have a strong stomach. That hairdresser I told you about was killed last night, I'm being followed again, and my office was broken into."

"Jesus, Nikki. What have you stepped in?" Her smile was gone.

"I wish I knew. Will you be here for a while?"

"I'm not going anywhere."

Back aboard my boat I blew my hair dry and carefully applied smoky green eyeliner, mocha shadow, black mascara, and cherry red lip gloss. I dressed in jeans and my favorite green blouse. When I was satisfied with my appearance I stuffed the large manila envelope into a grocery bag and walked to Elizabeth's. I went inside so no one could see me give her the file, and I closed the door behind me. Elizabeth was sitting at the galley counter and she looked a question at me.

"I don't know who might be watching and I don't want anyone to know you have this," I said.

"Okay."

"After you read it, hide it."

"I have the perfect place." Her eyes twinkled.

"Lock your door," I said. "I know you never lock your door, but this is serious. Please lock the door, and keep the windows closed and locked too."

"Okay," she said again.

We embraced longer than usual. I didn't like involving Elizabeth in something this dangerous, but she was one of the few people I knew I could trust. I stepped outside and waited until I heard her deadbolt slide into place.

When Bill arrived for our date I was waiting in the office with the lights off and the door locked. Even though I was expecting him, I jumped when he knocked. Maybe I should cut back on the caffeine. I turned on the lights and unlocked the door. Bill came in with a fingerprinting kit under his arm.

"Let's get this out of the way first," he said, holding up the kit.

"Oh, well, actually I cleaned today. I figured if it was the killer who broke in, there wouldn't be any prints anyway. Sorry."

"You cleaned *everything*?"

"Yeah. Sorry."

"Let's go to dinner, then."

"What about my car? Can you check it for transmitters?"

"I knew I was forgetting something. We'll have to stop by my house."

That's when it first crossed my mind. It was a ridiculous notion and I was almost ashamed to have it, but what if Detective Bill Anderson wasn't what he appeared to be?

We took his Mustang and drove across town in silence, each absorbed in our own thoughts. Bill lived in a cream-colored stucco house on Madison. The garage was a separate wooden structure behind the house, with sliding doors that opened horizontally.

He parked in the driveway and we entered the house through the laundry room, which opened onto the kitchen. He had one of those antique gas stoves that collectors are always looking for, and the kitchen was spotless. Why did I keep meeting men who were more into housekeeping than I was?

"Make yourself at home," he said. "I'll be right back."

I watched as he went inside the garage, partially closing the door behind him. It was a warm evening. Why he would want to close the door, even part of the way?

I walked around the house, just to get my bearings. Moving through the living room at the front of the house I appreciated the absence of the usual knickknacks that most people collect.

There were two bedrooms, one at each end of a long hallway, with a bathroom between them. The bedroom at the front of the house had been converted into a studio. Mounted on stands were an electric guitar and an acoustic with mother-of-pearl inlays. An amplifier was set against one wall and on an adjacent table were three mixing boards and a high-end recorder. Judging by the investment he'd made in equipment, I guessed he was probably talented, or at least dedicated.

I went back into the kitchen and opened the refrigerator, scanned the contents, and found nothing out of the ordinary. I had no valid reason to suspect Bill of any wrongdoing. This is just something I do when I'm left alone in the home of someone I'm curious about. I checked the kitchen trash. It had recently been emptied and there was nothing much in it, just some used paper towels and an empty egg carton.

I looked out the window to see if he was coming. He wasn't, so I went into the rear bedroom and opened each of the dresser drawers, feeling under the clothes. The nightstand to the left of the bed contained a small box of Trojans, and yes, they were prelubricated Supra. I felt a chill. Maybe every male in California used these condoms. Bill seemed like such a dedicated cop. He couldn't possibly be the killer, could he?

I replaced the box in the nightstand resisting the temptation to count the number he had left in the box. The nightstand on the right revealed a Smith & Wesson .38 Special. I didn't touch the gun, but carefully closed the drawer and went back into the living room.

I sat down on the sofa, my pulse racing, certain that he'd walk in any instant and guess what I'd been up to. Not that there's anything wrong with snooping around someone else's house. I just don't like getting caught at it. After about thirty seconds I went and checked the window again. The garage door was still partially open.

I went into the bathroom and looked in the medicine cabinet. Bill used the same Artic Mint Listerine that I did. He had a bottle of aspirin, a jumbo-size bottle of Aleve, Crest toothpaste, some KMS hair gel, a full four ounce bottle of Grey Flannel cologne, a toothbrush, shaving cream, a razor, and a comb. The contents of the medicine cabinet were casually organized, and I was relieved to see it. I'd been afraid I would find all the labels facing forward, like I had at Fred's house. The bathroom trash basket contained an empty shampoo bottle, the box that the Grey Flannel had come in, and an empty toothpaste box. I wondered if I should be flattered, new toothpaste and cologne. Could be a compliment, right?

I decided to go outside and see what was taking him so long. As I approached the garage and reached for the sliding door, Bill stepped out into the daylight, looking startled to see me. He quickly closed the door behind him. Okay, this was definitely getting weird. I can understand being embarrassed about an untidy garage. I sometimes feel insecure about people seeing the mess on board my boat, but I make no effort to hide it. It's just something about me that my friends have to accept. Love me, love my clutter.

"Sorry that took so long." He held up a black wand. "I couldn't remember where I'd put this thing. Shall we get going, or would you like a drink first?"

"No thanks. I'd really like to get the debugging over with so we can go to dinner."

"I was thinking," he said, "since I have to drive you back to the marina after dinner anyway, why don't we eat first and take care of your car after? It would save driving time."

If I didn't know better I'd have sworn he was stalling, maybe giving someone enough time to remove the transmitter from my car. And I didn't know better. Would the police stoop to planting a bug on my bumper to keep track of where I was going in the course of an investigation they weren't having any success with? Was the Pope Catholic? Plus there were those incriminating condoms.

I felt a profound sense of disappointment. I was growing fond of Bill and, like most people, I assumed that my instincts and hormones would never lead me astray. If I was attracted to him, he had to be a good guy, right? Maybe I was letting my tendency to distrust everyone get the better of me. I decided to stop jumping to conclusions and wait to see what happened next.

"Okay," I said. "Where are we going?"

"Gypsy Cellar. Hungarian food and, if we're lucky, a violin player."

"That sounds great."

The Gypsy Cellar was a quaint little restaurant on the corner of Jefferson and Middlefield. Bill had made reservations, but we didn't need them. The place was practically deserted. We were seated at a window table with a lovely view of the traffic on Jefferson.

After a few minutes we were approached by a waitress in her sixties wearing a white peasant blouse, a red skirt, a colorful bandana in her hair, and sensible shoes. She served us ice water and handed each of us a menu, then asked if we'd like anything from the bar. Bill ordered a Corona and I asked for a glass of Chablis. I don't normally drink wine. I'd probably have a headache tomorrow. I was punishing myself. Try as I might to quiet my imagination, I now suspected that Bill was not what he seemed on the surface, therefore I felt there must be something wrong with me because I liked him. This is the way my mind works. Being aware of the process doesn't always put a stop to it.

We silently looked over our menus. Everything looked good and, although I hadn't felt like eating all day, I now realized that I was starving. When our drinks were served I ordered the stuffed chicken breast and a dinner salad. Bill ordered lamb chops and a Caesar salad. We handed the waitress our menus and she ambled off toward the kitchen.

I sipped my wine, looking at Bill over the rim of my glass. He was tough-guy handsome, rather than pretty like Fred. His eyes were warm but shrewd, and they met mine without hesitation.

"Sorry," I said. "I guess I'm not very good company tonight."

"You have a lot on your mind. Did you call any of the bodyguards I recommended?"

"Not yet. I'm not sure I can afford one. Besides if this maniac is serious about taking me out, I don't think a bodyguard will do much good."

"You may be right, but any protection is better than none. They don't charge that much. You should give it some thought."

"Maybe I'll call, just to get prices."

Of course if I had an off-duty police guard with me they wouldn't *need* to plant a transmitter on my car. They'd know every move I made. Being suspicious, even paranoid, keeps you on your toes and causes you to examine everything, question everything. It also gets you in trouble if your suspicions are unfounded, and it totally prevents you from enjoying the present moment. I drained my wine glass and looked around for the waitress. She was nowhere in sight.

"So what's your next move?" I asked.

"I assume you're referring to the case," he said, with a wolfish grin.

I grinned back at him in spite of myself, and nodded.

"We've questioned everyone on your list and gotten basically the same answers you did. I took a look at Fred Wulf and Rod Howard's prints. Both were in the database. Wulf's right index fingerprint might be a match to the partial we got from Laura's zipper pull. Also his right thumbprint looks like a match to a partial the Menlo Park PD got off Andrew McConnell's belt buckle, but that's not enough to justify a search warrant. There isn't much we can do except watch and wait. I assume you already know about the indecent exposure charge."

"Yes. I ran a background on Wulf. Why aren't the partial prints enough to justify a warrant?"

"Not enough points."

"So your plan is to wait until he kills again?"

Bill flinched. "Even if there were enough points to verify that the prints are Wulf's, that would only prove that he knew both victims. Of course, there was that phone call." He took a sip of his beer, looking distracted.

"What phone call?"

His eyes focused on me again. "The day after Barbara Herbert was killed we got an anonymous call on the tip line.

The caller described someone he'd seen leaving the alley where the victim was found. Wulf matches the description."

"And that, combined with the partial prints, still isn't enough evidence for a search warrant?"

"I'm afraid not."

Unbelievable. It might not be enough to convince a judge, but it was enough for me. Fred had just moved to the top of my list.

Bill spotted the waitress and waved. When she approached he requested another glass of wine for me and coffee for himself.

A few minutes passed before the waitress returned with our drinks and salads. I was dismayed to discover that I'd lost my appetite. I picked at my salad, drank more wine, and watched the traffic go by.

When Bill had finished his salad, our entrees were served. Even without an appetite, the chicken breast was hard to resist. It was plump and moist, stuffed with rice, goat cheese, butter, and basil. The asparagus was slightly al dente, just the way I like it. I ate more than half of my dinner and finished a third glass of wine. I asked for a doggy bag for my leftover chicken, thinking of D'Artagnon.

After dinner we stopped in the parking lot to check out the sunset and Bill casually draped his arm around my shoulder. I wanted to relax and enjoy the intimacy, but I couldn't.

We didn't talk much during the drive back to the marina. Bill pulled into the boat owners' lot and parked in a vacant space right beside my 2002. How had he known where I was parked? Had he seen my car before? Maybe on one of my visits to the police department. I couldn't remember. I'd had too much to drink.

Bill picked up the wand and asked me to pop the hood. I got out my keys, unlocked the BMW, yanked the hood latch, and went around to open it for him. A BMW's hood is hinged in the front so you have to lift from the end nearest the windshield. He automatically lifted the hood as though he'd done it a hundred times before.

"You ever own a BMW?" I asked.

"No. I like American cars."

I stood there and watched him run the wand over the engine. When he'd finished, he closed the hood and asked if I had a jack.

"Of course," I said, sounding more defensive than I'd intended.

I unlocked the trunk and got out the jack. Bill cranked up the front of the car and asked if I had a towel or a blanket that I didn't mind getting dirty. I keep a beach towel in the back seat for sunny days. The leather upholstery gets really hot. Bill took the towel and spread it on the ground under the elevated end of the car.

"What about a flashlight?" he said.

I took my Maglight out of the glove compartment and handed it to him. He crawled under the car and rolled onto his back, then ran the wand under the engine. After a few minutes he got up, handed me the wand, followed by the towel and the flashlight, then lowered the jack. I thought that was going to be it, that I was right, and he had stalled me long enough for someone to remove the gadget from my car.

He carried the jack to the rear of the 2002 and started cranking it up. He spread the towel out on the ground, lay down on his back again, and scooted under the car until only his legs were visible. They were nice legs...

I crouched down and watched him move the wand slowly under the middle of the chassis. When he shifted to his left and started running it under the trunk area I heard a sharp beeping sound, like one of those travel alarm clocks. Bill pressed something on the handle of the wand and it stopped beeping. He set it on the ground, fished a handkerchief out of his pants pocket, and pulled something off the bottom of my car.

He scooted carefully out from under the car and sat up, shining the flashlight beam on what was in his handkerchief.

"This is the little culprit right here," he said.

It was no bigger than a dime. In fact it looked like a dime; a smooth, matte black dime.

"It's tiny," I said. *Brilliant, Nicoli.*

"Yup. Mind if I check it for prints?" he asked.

"No. Please."

Bill stood up, gently wrapped the bug in his handkerchief, and slipped it into his pocket. He reached under the car and retrieved the wand, then handed me the flashlight and kissed me on the lips.

"Take care of yourself, Nikki," he said. "I'd like to get to know you better."

I was still trying to get my brain to generate a response as his car disappeared around the corner of the building. Definitely some chemistry there. I couldn't stop smiling, and I couldn't help comparing the experience to kissing Fred the other night. Bill's kiss didn't make me feel threatened, and it definitely left me wanting more.

I lowered the jack, folded up the towel, and tossed everything in the trunk. I collected my purse and my doggy bag, locked the car, patted the hood affectionately, and wandered through the gate and down the companionway. I was feeling a little dazed and I didn't hear Elizabeth's door slide open.

"Hey, how'd it go?" she asked, stepping outside.

"What?"

"Your dinner with Detective Anderson. Where did you eat?"

"Oh. Gypsy Cellar. Stuffed chicken." I held up the bag.

"Are you okay? You look kind of stupid."

"I'm fine. I think I'm falling in lust."

"*Outstanding.* Tell me everything."

We sat on Elizabeth's steps and I confessed to her that I'd begun to suspect Bill. I explained my thought process, gave her the whole story, so she'd understand and not think me a complete imbecile.

She said, "You're kidding."

I flushed with embarrassment. It was ridiculous after all. I told her about the bug under the car, the red-haired man I'd seen outside my office, and the Volvo that had been following me.

"Clearly, someone thinks you know something," she said.

"I just wish I knew what they think I know. Did you read the file?"

"Of course. I think you should focus on Fred and Charles."

"I think so too. But tell me why."

"Because Laura had sex with whoever killed her. I know you think she was into risk taking, and she may have been kinky, but I don't think she would willingly have sex with her own father no matter what happened when she was a kid."

"I'm not so sure about that. Maybe she was conditioned by her childhood experiences to behave like a victim. You know some people become addicted to chemicals produced in the brain by recurring emotional trauma. Laura may have become addicted to the experience of being abused, or victimized."

"We don't know Rod was telling the truth about Laura being molested."

"What about Rod?" I asked. "He really needs the money, and he'll inherit a bundle now."

"Yeah, and he *was* only her half-brother, but you've described Rod to me. He doesn't sound very attractive."

"What's your point?"

"If you were Laura and you were seeing someone who looked like Fred, would you meet your unattractive half-brother behind a dumpster to have sex with him?"

"Probably not, but lust is in the eye of the beholder. What about Frank?" I asked.

"You said Frank told you Laura wasn't into sex, so I think we can assume that Laura wasn't into sex with Frank," Elizabeth answered. "No accounting for taste. I think he's yummy."

"I noticed. Maybe he found a way to spice it up. What about Candy? Maybe Laura was bi."

"What are you thinking? That she used a strap-on or something?"

"It would explain the absence of foreign pubic hair," I said. "Some of those dancers shave everything.

But if you used a strap-on, why would you also use a condom?"

"I don't know. To keep it clean?"

You have to be really good friends with someone to have this kind of conversation.

"I can see Charles had a motive," I said. "He was jealous, and maybe afraid his wife would find out he'd been stalking Laura, but why would she have sex with a guy who was too tame for her in college?"

Elizabeth thought for a minute. "Maybe she got interested again when he got married. It would increase the risk factor."

"For him, not for her. What would Fred's motive be?" I asked.

"Why does there have to be a motive? Maybe he and Laura were having kinky sex and he got a little carried away and accidentally killed her."

"And then he stabbed her three times to cover up his mistake?"

"You are so sarcastic sometimes. You might be right, though. Fred is compulsively neat, and Laura's murder was messy, wasn't it?"

"Very." I grimaced, remembering the crime scene photos. "What about the other murders? There are similarities between Laura's murder and the murders of Andrew the hairdresser and Barbara the librarian. Then somebody hired that PI Hearn to follow and assault me, and now he's dead. And I'm convinced Kurt was killed because he could identify the man Andrew was dating."

"Maybe the question is, can we picture Charles or Fred dating Andrew."

I tried to imagine it. "I don't know. They both seem straight to me."

"Fred could have an alter ego who isn't compulsively neat," she muttered, almost to herself.

"Wait a minute. What if he *isn't* compulsively neat? What if he's just compulsive about having things in order, you know, because he likes to be in control. Even though the killings were messy, the crime scenes were controlled. There was almost no evidence. Just a few partial prints. Also, the rubber band holding the plastic bag over Laura's head had the word *organic* printed on it. When I was in Fred's house I searched his fridge. All his veggies are organic. *And* Bill told me they got an anonymous phone call after Barbara Herbert was murdered. Someone saw a man matching Fred's description leaving the alley where she was killed."

Elizabeth's eyes lit up. "Oh my *God.* What are they doing about that?"

"Nothing. Bill says there isn't enough evidence to justify a search warrant."

"I guess that makes sense, if the tip was anonymous. Tell me about Charles's office. What did his desk look like?"

I tried to remember if everything on his desk had been lined up, but all I could think of was how his face had changed color.

"I don't remember. I guess I could pay him another visit, but I'm not sure he'd invite me back to his office again. We didn't exactly hit it off."

"What about me? I could pretend I have some money to invest, ask him for advice, get a look at the office, and then tell him I'll get back to him."

"What if he's the killer?"

"People ask for advice before investing all the time. I think a stock broker would be more than happy to meet with a potential client."

"But you work in Sunnyvale. He's in Palo Alto. When would you have time?"

"I don't start work until nine. Didn't you say he goes in early?"

"He went in early the day I followed him. That doesn't mean he's there early every day."

"So I'll drop by his office tomorrow morning and if he's not there, he's not there. If he is, I'll tell him the Howards recommended him."

"I don't know about that. What if he checks with them?"

"He's not going to call them while I'm waiting in the lobby. You worry too much."

"Okay. Just be careful."

I hugged Elizabeth goodnight and shuffled off to my boat.

I undressed, leaving my clothes in a heap on the floor, and climbed into bed. As I was drifting off I heard a familiar scratching noise on the pilothouse door, followed by a high-pitched whine. D'Artagnon. I struggled out of bed, located the doggy bag with the leftover chicken, and climbed the steps. I opened the door and he wiggled inside, his nose elevated toward the bag. He must have smelled the chicken when I walked past his boat.

I fed it to him one bite at a time and he swallowed each mouthful without chewing. When all the scraps had been devoured he licked my hands and gave a full body wag as he leaned against my legs. I scratched above his tail and around his ears, and then I sent him home.

I sank back into bed with a smile on my face and was almost instantly asleep.

Chapter 29

The Dream Machine woke me at 6:00 on Friday morning, the acoustic guitar CD reminding me of Bill Anderson's guitars. My wine headache wasn't as bad as I'd expected it to be.

While the coffee was brewing I dialed my office number and checked my messages. Fred had called to confirm our dinner date, saying he would meet me at my office at 7:45. He'd made a reservation at Castaway out at Coyote Point instead of the Garden Grill. He said he thought it would be more romantic. I love Castaway. They always have fresh salmon, and the view of the coast is spectacular. I was a little creeped out by the romance part. The evidence was pointing to him and, even if he wasn't the killer, there was something disturbing about Frederick Marcus Wulf.

I was in my office when Bill called at 9:00, asking if I'd contacted any of the bodyguards he'd recommended yet. I said I hadn't, and he made me promise that I would do so by the end of the day.

I spent my morning scheduling bar and restaurant surveys with my regular clients.

At noon I got a call from Elizabeth.

"Nikki, the guy has almost nothing on his desk. Just a pen and pencil set, a picture of his wife, and two empty trays. There wasn't a wrinkle in his suit, tie, or shirt, and every hair was gelled into place. I can't believe you didn't notice! I would have called you sooner, but I've been on a conference call all morning. Anyway, he is totally obsessive-compulsive, and he nearly broke my fingers when I shook his hand. What an asshole."

"Did he seem suspicious about your reason for being there?"

"Not at all."

"Good. Thanks, Elizabeth. I owe you another pair of shoes."

I had a Cobb Salad at a client's restaurant in Palo Alto, jotted down survey notes in the car, and then drove to Nordstrom where I bought Elizabeth a hundred-dollar gift card. I didn't spot the blue Volvo until I was leaving the Nordstrom lot. It was parked in a remote corner, under a tree.

Driving back to Redwood City, watching my rearview mirror, I figured out why I hadn't spotted the Volvo earlier. It was nowhere in sight. There had to be another transmitter somewhere on my car. Why should that surprise me? He would have noticed the original bug was no longer tracking me, and simply attached a new one.

Back at the office I left a voice-mail message for Bill, telling him there was another transmitter on my car, then I typed up an invoice for Kate. I edited out the molestation and prostitution details from the file, as well as the notes from my conversation with Frank regarding Laura's apparent lack of sex drive, and then printed it. Since I couldn't verify what Rod had told me about Derrick molesting Laura, I didn't want to destroy Kate's faith in her husband unnecessarily, much as I disliked him. I couldn't see what difference it would make if Kate learned now of Laura's arrest for propositioning a Vice cop, and she certainly didn't need to know that Laura hadn't enjoyed sex with Frank.

I enclosed a note telling Kate I was getting close to something, and that I'd keep her posted. Hope springs eternal.

I gave the package to the mail carrier when she delivered my mail, then I re-locked the office door behind her and called one of the numbers Bill had given me for a bodyguard.

"Lieutenant Quinn," said a husky female voice.

"Lieutenant, my name is Nicoli Hunter. I'm thinking about hiring a bodyguard and Bill Anderson recommended you."

"Oh yeah, he said you might be calling."

"How much do you charge?"

"Sixty an hour plus mileage."

I thought about it. I could afford this.

"That sounds reasonable," I said. "What hours are you available?"

"From six p.m. until two a.m. I have to get *some* sleep to do this job, but not much."

I liked her instantly.

"How much notice do you need?"

"Twenty-four hours would be good, but if it's an emergency I can make do with an hour's notice."

"Okay, thanks. I'll let you know."

Before we hung up she gave me her cell phone and pager numbers. I felt better just having spoken with her. Maybe this wasn't such a bad idea. Even if it didn't keep me alive, I'd feel more secure and sleep better at night.

At 6:00 p.m., I walked down to Elizabeth's boat. She was on her dock steps sipping a cocktail and cuddling K.C.

"Hi, sweetie," she said.

I handed her the gift card.

"Oooh, Nordstrom! *Thank* you."

"You earned it."

"I've been thinking about Fred," she said. "How neat his house was. Even his garage was organized. Where would someone like that keep things he didn't want anyone to find?"

"I wish I knew."

"What about a safe deposit box or a storage locker? Is there any way to find out about things like that?"

"I could ask Michael to do a little hacking for me."

Michael Burke and I had been sweethearts from kindergarten through the second grade. I used to beat him up on the playground every day. He proposed to me, and I accepted, when we were five years old. We had the top two IQs in our first grade class. His was four points higher than mine. We don't see much of each other anymore, but we stay in touch. He lives in the Santa Cruz mountains and is something of a recluse. He's also a computer guru, earning his living as a white hat hacker, testing network security systems, and repairing computers that have been virus-damaged.

"What do we do if he has a storage locker?" I asked. "Cut off the lock and search for evidence?"

"Maybe. Where else would you hide a knife?"

"I'd like to get a look in the trunk of his car."

"And how do you plan to do that?"

"I don't know yet. Can I have a glass of water?"

"Help yourself," said Elizabeth.

I got up and went inside the trawler, took a glass from the rack, and located a jug of spring water in the fridge. I filled my glass and went back outside.

"Maybe I can slip out during dinner and pick the lock on his trunk."

"Where are you going for dinner?"

"Castaway."

"Valet parking," she said. "You'd have to find the car first, in the dark."

"Shit, you're right."

"I have an idea." Elizabeth's eyes danced. "Spend the night with him, and when he's asleep get his keys and search his trunk."

"Very funny."

"You could slip the valet a twenty and ask him to bring it around."

"That would take too long. I need a shower."

I gave her the empty water glass, kissed her on the cheek, and trudged down the dock to my boat.

After showering I put on a black western-style dress with a silver belt buckle. I decided to go the whole nine yards and pulled on a pair of black cowboy boots with silver tips on the toes. They hurt my feet, but they looked great. My image in the mirror looked amused.

At 7:30 I was ready to go. As I approached the companionway I noticed Elizabeth's door was open. I reached across the deck and knocked on a window. She came outside and whistled at me.

"Wow! Why are you wasting this on Fred?" she asked.

"You think it's too much?"

"No. You look beautiful."

"Thanks."

"Have you got your gun?" she whispered.

I patted my purse. "You need to close and lock your door and windows until this case is resolved, remember?"

"Yeah, yeah. Whatever you say. Have fun, Nikki, and be careful." She shook her index finger at me.

"I'm always careful. I'll stop by after dinner if you're still up."

"I'll be up," she said.

I walked to the office and let myself in, locking the door behind me. I turned on my desk lamp, leaving the rest of the office dark. I wasn't sure how I felt about Fred being in my office, so I planned to scoot him out as quickly as possible.

While I was waiting I booted up the computer and sent Michael Burke an e-mail asking him to research Frederick Marcus Wulf. I included Fred's social security number from the paycheck stub I'd lifted, and asked him to look for any information on banking, safe deposit boxes, and storage locker rentals. I also asked if he'd like to get together for dinner.

I was turning off the computer when there was a knock on my door. I looked up and saw a tall masculine silhouette. As I approached the door I could see it was Fred, nicely dressed, as usual, in charcoal slacks, a dove gray shirt, and a slate gray cashmere pullover. His eyes seemed to glow in the dim light.

I unlocked and opened the door, then went back to my desk to get my purse and switch off the lamp.

"What time is our reservation?" I asked.

"You look nice," he said. "Eight-fifteen."

I turned back toward the door and saw that Fred was now halfway inside my dark office, blocking my path to the exit.

"Thank you," I said. I looked him in the eye and smiled. "Shall we go?"

He hesitated for a moment and then stepped aside.

Fred's Jag was parked near my office and I wondered if he'd been here before. The car was unlocked and Fred opened the passenger side door for me, waited until my dress and I were safely inside, and closed it gently. During the drive to Castaway, he asked me how my week had been.

"Interesting," I said.

"Oh?"

"First this PI from San Mateo who was following me got killed. Then I got my hair cut by a guy named Kurt who knew Andrew McConnell, that hairdresser who was murdered? You probably heard about it on the news. Anyway, I asked Kurt some questions about Andrew, and that night *he* was killed."

I watched his face for a reaction. There was none.

"I was pressuring the PI to tell me who his client was, and I think he was going to, but someone killed him first. Kurt had seen the man Andrew was dating and might have been able to identify him. I was going to show him some pictures, but I never got the chance."

"Were you going to show him a picture of me?" Fred asked.

My heart skipped a beat. "Of course," I said.

He turned his head away from the road long enough to make eye contact. He was smiling, but it wasn't a happy, carefree kind of a smile. It was feral. I felt an involuntary shudder run the length of my body.

When we arrived at Castaway a college age cutie dressed in black trousers, a white shirt, and a red vest opened my door and helped me out of the car, then accepted Fred's keys and issued a receipt.

As we walked to the front of the restaurant, Fred took my arm. I wanted to jerk away from him, but I steeled myself and went on with the charade.

We were seated at a window table with a panoramic view of San Francisco Bay. A busboy served us ice water and warm French bread, and a few minutes later our waiter approached. He introduced himself as David and handed us menus. Fred ordered a double Glenlivet up, and I ordered coffee. David told us about the evening's specials, and then left us alone to look over our menus.

When our drinks were served we ordered dinner. I asked for the steamed clams, the salad bar, and the grilled swordfish. Fred smiled sardonically at my appetite, and ordered the Caesar salad with grilled shrimp. David collected the menus and departed.

I looked across the table at Fred. "Do you mind if I ask you a few more questions about Laura?"

"Ask away." He took a generous sip of his scotch.

"You were sleeping with her, right?"

"Yes." The look on his face was beyond condescending. It was arrogant.

"Did she ever ask you to put your hands around her throat while you were having sex?"

Fred abruptly stopped smiling and moved his intense gaze toward the Bay. He didn't say anything for a minute. Then he slowly turned back to me. His eyes had lost their glow and there was something else, maybe fear.

"I told you she was bored," he said. "She was looking for excitement."

"You didn't answer my question," I said quietly.

Fred silently took another sip of his drink. Just when the tension was getting palpable, David arrived with my clams. He told me I could help myself to the salad bar anytime I was ready, and pointed it out to me. Before he could get away, Fred ordered another double Scotch.

The clams were served in a butter and garlic broth, and they were tender and juicy. When I'd finished them Fred was still giving me the silent treatment, so I decided to step outside and grab a smoke.

"I'm going to the ladies' room," I said, rising from my seat.

Unless I missed my guess, our entrees wouldn't be served until I returned. I walked past the restrooms, slipped out the front door, and lit up. I stood beside a small waterfall in the courtyard and looked out at the deep blue sky above the parking lot. The sun was setting and it was an unusually still evening. A peripheral flash of color caught my attention. I turned to get a better look, and couldn't believe my eyes. There was a petite, strawberry blonde person bending over the open trunk of a silver-blue Jaguar XJS that was parked up the hill. I watched as she switched on a penlight.

"*Jesus Christ,*" I whispered.

I glanced quickly at the parking valet. He was leaning against the booth, contemplating the boats in the harbor. I tossed my cigarette in the fountain and, taking out another, sashayed over to the booth and asked him for a light. The kid responded with all the requisite hormones, his hand shaking as he held a plastic lighter to my cigarette. I stood with my back to the Bay, keeping him turned away from the uphill parking area and Fred's Jag.

"Been working here long?" I asked.

"Two weeks." His voice cracked.

"You're very good at your job." I smiled. "How are the tips?"

"They're great!" he said, with enthusiasm.

He was adorable, but it took tremendous self-control for me not to look past him at Elizabeth. As I made small talk I remembered the night she had broken into Fred's house. She'd given me back the Glock, the phone, and the camera, but not the lock picks. I mentally slapped myself on the forehead.

When I didn't think I could wait any longer without arousing Fred's suspicions and the valet's expectations, I thanked him for the light and went back inside. As I passed the waterfall I glanced up the hill. The Jag's trunk was closed, and Elizabeth was nowhere in sight. I blew out a sigh of relief as I hurried back into the restaurant.

Fred looked annoyed as I approached the table and sat down.

"Sorry that took so long," I said, with a self-deprecating smile. "Irritable bowel syndrome."

Fred grimaced and waved an impatient hand in the air. David must have been watching, because our entrees were served immediately.

The swordfish was moist and firm with a subtle garlic and lemon flavor. On the side were rice, carrots, and green beans. I ate half of the fish and watched Fred nibble at his shrimp salad and guzzle his scotch.

When Kate received the report I had mailed she would probably tell Derrick about Fred and Laura. I decided not to broach that subject tonight. I pushed my chair back and said I was going to check out the salad bar. Fred gave me a look I can only characterize as disdainful, undoubtedly remembering how I had heaped my plate at the Chart House.

I collected a few leaves of romaine, some spinach, Greek olives, and mushrooms, and topped the whole thing with oil and vinegar. I passed on the more filling food groups. When I arrived back at the table I noticed that Fred's salad had been cleared and he was starting on his fourth double scotch. And he was driving.

"I'm sorry if my questions make you uncomfortable," I said. "I have to ask. It's my job."

He remained mute, drinking his scotch and brooding.

When I'd finished most of my salad I waved David over and asked for the check. He took a black leather folder from his apron pocket and placed it on the table. I paid with cash to save time. I was anxious to get away from Fred, and even more anxious to question Elizabeth.

"Had enough of me for tonight?" I asked, as we walked toward the door.

Fred gave me a sideways glance, but said nothing. Could he have snuck out while I was chatting with the parking valet and seen Elizabeth at his car?

When the valet brought the Jag around, Fred opened the door for me. I got in and watched him tip the young man, who was now ignoring me in favor of cash.

The drive home was quiet until we reached the Whipple Road exit.

"Should I drop you back at your office?" Fred asked.

"Yes, thank you. I have some paperwork to finish up."

He pulled into the marina lot and just sat there as I climbed out of the Jag.

He said, "Goodbye, Nicoli," and drove away as soon as I'd closed the car door.

That sounded final. I wasn't interested in Fred, and he might be a psycho-killer, but I still found his behavior unsettling. I don't take rejection well, even if I don't care about the person who's rejecting me.

I entered my office, locking the door behind me, and turned on all the lights. I sat down at my desk and smoked a cigarette, waiting ten tortuous minutes before turning off the lights and locking up again. I walked back out to the parking lot and looked around for the Jag. I didn't see it anywhere, so I hurried down to my boat, noting Elizabeth's closed door as I passed her trawler. Three hours in cowboy boots was all I could stand. I hastily changed into jeans, a Hawaiian shirt, and a pair of comfy old boat shoes. I left my dress and purse on the bunk, and jogged back to Elizabeth's with only my cigarettes and lighter in hand.

I ran past D'Artagnon, who was out on the deck of his boat, without even stopping to pet him, and immediately felt guilty about it. I'd make it up to him later.

I knocked on Elizabeth's door and waited. After a moment she called out, "Who is it?"

"It's me."

She slid the door open a crack. When she saw me, she opened the door the rest of the way, glancing over my shoulder at the companionway. She looked panicky.

"Hi, Nikki," she said. "How was dinner?"

"Are you out of your fucking *mind?*"

"Come on aboard," she said, grabbing my wrist. She pulled me inside, then closed and locked the door behind me.

"I saw you in the parking lot!"

Her eyes got as big as saucers. "You *saw* me? Oh my *God.* Did Fred see me too?"

"I'm not sure. He might have. What were you *thinking?* You broke into his car in a public place for Christ's sake!"

"I'm sorry. I just couldn't help myself. I searched his trunk. I forgot to give you back those lock picks, and after you left tonight I kept thinking about what you said. Anyway, I drove out to Castaway and saw there was only one parking valet on duty, so I thought, what the hell? Nikki, I found the knife."

"You what? Slow down a minute. You mean you found *a* knife."

"Okay, okay. I found *a* knife. And it's just the way you described it, with spikes on the hilt. He keeps it in a black garbage bag behind his spare tire. I think there's dried blood on it. And there's a broom handle in there with the top sawed off, a coil of fishing wire, a bloody ice pick, and a pair of red Victoria's Secret panties." She slapped the galley counter for emphasis, causing me to levitate off the settee.

Elizabeth got up and emptied the last of a bottle of wine into a pewter goblet. "You want some wine?" she asked.

I shook my head. I needed to keep my wits about me. I considered what she had said and reached for my cigarettes. "Do you mind?" I asked, referring to the smoke.

"No, go ahead." She cracked open a window as I lit up. "He's got a twelve-pack of Trojan Supras in his trunk too, and a box of surgical gloves." She swallowed some wine. "So, what do we do now?"

"First tell me you didn't touch anything."

"I'm not a complete moron," she said. She walked to the sink and picked up a pair of pink Playtex gloves. "I wore these."

"Atta girl," I said.

I moved over to the window she had opened, and exhaled smoke through the gap.

"We need to *do* something," she said, handing me a coffee cup to use as an ashtray.

"I'm thinking."

"You're *thinking*? What do you mean you're thinking? What are you thinking about? I'm telling you I found a bag full of evidence in the trunk of Fred's car!" Her face flushed and she started pacing. "Oh, wait, I know you. You're thinking he somehow found out what each of the murder weapons was, and then he went out and bought a spiky knife, and a broom, and some fishing wire, and he's baiting you. Like this is some kind of a *game*. That's what you're thinking, isn't it?"

Even under pressure, Elizabeth has one of the quickest minds I've ever known.

"It's exactly the kind of thing he would do, just to prove how superior he is, and to mess with me. We can't assume anything until Bill has the evidence tested."

"I don't *believe* this! There was nothing on the news about the knife having spikes on it. And what about that anonymous phone call the police got? He's the *killer*, Nikki! Let's call Bill right now and tell him what I found. Let him decide what to do about it."

"I've got his cell number in my purse. I'll call him as soon as I get home."

D'Artagnon chose that moment to let loose with a long series of angry barks. Elizabeth and I looked at each other. We were both thinking the same thing. What if Fred *had* seen her looking in his trunk? What if he was here now?

"Jesus," she said, putting a hand over her heart. She picked up her wine glass, which had somehow become empty. "I'm going to have another glass of wine. Are you sure you don't want anything?"

"No, thanks."

Elizabeth checked the door to make sure it was locked, and then got out her corkscrew and opened a bottle of something Italian. She took a clean goblet from the hanging rack over the sink and filled it, then sat down next to me. We waited in silence for a few minutes. D'Artagnon had stopped barking. That was a good sign. He'd probably seen someone up on shore he didn't recognize.

Eventually Elizabeth said, "Since I found the evidence illegally, how will Bill justify the search warrant?"

"I don't know. That might be a problem. Maybe he can follow Fred around until he commits a traffic violation. He drives really fast. Can the police search your car if they stop you for speeding?"

"I don't think so."

I put out my cigarette, and set the cup in the sink.

"I left my boat open with all the lights on. If I don't go back soon the mosquitoes will move in."

"Okay," she said. "I'll be awake all night. Call me after you talk to Bill."

We hugged each other at the door, and when I was outside I heard Elizabeth lock it behind me.

CHAPTER 30

D'ARTAGNON WASN'T OUT ON deck when I walked past his boat on the way to mine, and I still felt guilty about ignoring him earlier. I continued down the dock and stopped in my tracks when I saw that my Cheoy Lee was completely dark. I always leave the lights on. I even sleep with the lights on. I don't like the dark.

I looked around and saw that all the dock lights and some of my neighbors' lights were on, so it wasn't the electricity. I checked my shore power to make sure someone hadn't turned it off as a prank. The switch was in the *on* position. Unless all the bulbs on board my boat had burned out simultaneously, someone had gone aboard and turned off my lights.

My heart started pounding. I should have hired Lieutenant Quinn to guard my body. I should run back to Elizabeth's boat and call the cops. That's what I should do, but what would I tell them? *I can't go home because the lights are off?* I could imagine the stories that would be circulating around the RCPD the next morning. Not that I cared what the local cops thought of me, much, but ever since I was a kid I've had trouble walking away from confrontations. I blame my father for this. When I was little he convinced me that no one would respect me if I turned away from a fight. Even if I got the shit beat out of me, it was better than being thought of as a coward. Now, as an adult, I know there's no shame in being afraid, especially if you have a good reason, but I still respond to the stimuli.

I walked down the concrete finger to my dock steps. Listening intently I cautiously climbed aboard causing as little motion as possible. Someone had closed my pilothouse door. I knew I'd left it open, and there wasn't enough of a breeze tonight for it to have swung shut. I silently opened the door, and stepped inside. The hatch was open, as I had left it.

The companionway steps on my Cheoy Lee are steep, and if you walk down them facing forward you have to arch your back in order to avoid clobbering your forehead on the top of the hatch. Normally I back down the steps, but tonight I didn't have the nerve. I was shaking and my knees felt rubbery.

Inside the boat I couldn't see a thing. I felt my way into the stateroom, flipped on the light and flinched at the sudden illumination. My pistol purse and dress were on the bunk where I'd left them. I picked up my purse and reached for the Glock. It wasn't there. I unzipped the main compartment, looking for the flash drive. Also missing.

"*Shit!*" I whispered as my heart moved up into my throat and cut off my supply of oxygen. D'Artagnon had been barking at an intruder, and now whoever it was had the flash drive with all my notes on it, and my new Glock. "Mother-fucking *shit*!"

I dumped the contents of my purse onto the bunk, just to be sure. Okay, now I was sure. Someone had gotten past the secure gate and had been on board my boat. Maybe they were *still* on board. I should slip back outside, run to Elizabeth's boat, and call the police.

I stepped into the galley and turned on the light. Derrick Howard was sitting at my galley counter, holding my Glock in his lap. He was the picture of serenity, dressed in black, his hair covered by a watch cap, and he was wearing latex gloves. The expression on his face was so tranquil it was chilling.

I bolted for the companionway and made it to the base of the steps, but he was too fast for me. He grabbed me by the hair and dragged me backwards.

"Sit down, Ms. Hunter," he said. "We're going to have a little chat, and then we're going for a walk."

He let go of me and I perched on the edge of the galley settee. I rubbed my scalp and squinted up at him. "You mind if I smoke?"

I felt terrified, helpless, and indignant. I needed to dull down the emotion so I could think. I needed nicotine.

"Go ahead," he said.

I took the cigarettes and lighter out of my shirt pocket, and lit up. Under the right circumstances a cigarette can be a decent weapon. These were not the right circumstances.

"This is your party," I said, exhaling smoke and nodding toward the Glock. "What do you want to talk about?"

He pulled the flash drive from his hip pocket and held it up. "I assume this contains the details of your investigation?"

I said nothing.

"How many copies did you make?"

"Why do you care? There's nothing on it about you," I lied.

"How many?"

"Three," I said.

He smiled, pleased that I had chosen to cooperate.

"Where are the other two?"

"One is up in my office, locked in the desk, and one is in my safe deposit box."

Of course I didn't have a safe deposit box, but I had a bunch of flash drives in my desk and I was hoping to buy some time.

"Which bank?" he said.

"First National."

"Did you sign the signature card Nikki or Nicoli?"

"Fuck you," I said.

"Later," he replied, and I froze, realization washing over me. He was going to rape me and kill me, and make it look like Fred had done it. He'd take some trophy from the scene and plant it in Fred's trunk with the others.

"Have you shared the information with anyone?" he was saying.

I thought about that for a moment. He'd kill me no matter what, but if I said yes, there was a chance he'd kill others.

"No," I sighed. "I haven't even printed it yet."

"Well, that's something anyway."

He sat down opposite me and my mind began displaying images of Laura after death, pre-lubricated condoms, a spiky knife, Kurt in the alley...

"Is there anything you'd like to know before you die?" he asked.

So, Derrick wanted foreplay. Fair enough. I did have questions. Lots of them. I nodded and filled my lungs with smoke.

"Shoot," he said, and grinned sardonically.

"Why are you killing all these people? You have a beautiful wife, a successful career, a great-American-dream life. What the fuck is your problem?"

Derrick seemed unperturbed by my verbal assault. He tilted his head slightly to one side, perhaps deciding whether or not to respond. Finally he said, "Laura had started going to a therapist, recovering memories from her childhood. She confronted me, and said she was going to tell Kate. She even threatened me with public exposure. It would have ruined my business, and the notoriety would have been extremely unpleasant. So..." He flipped his free hand as though it should be obvious why he'd chosen to kill his own daughter.

This guy was bat-shit-crazy and a complete sociopath. I shivered involuntarily before repeating my question. "Why the others?"

"To lead the police to Fred, of course. They should have been onto him weeks ago."

"The anonymous phone call," I blurted out.

"Very good, Ms. Hunter. Yes, I made that call. I told the police I saw Fred leaving the alley where the librarian was killed. And they did nothing. If you and your little friend hadn't come along, there's no telling how long this might have taken."

So I wasn't the only one who had seen Elizabeth in the parking lot.

"Were you jealous of Fred? Is that what all this is about?"

"Of course not," he said. "But I didn't care for the way he treated Laura."

Can anyone spell *irony*? The man who had abused Laura as a child, violated her innocence, and who had killed her rather than have his guilty secrets exposed, was offended by the way another man had treated her.

"He likes to have sex in public places," he continued. "Did you know that?" I shook my head dumbly. "I was following her the night they had sex behind that dumpster. It was dark, but they wouldn't have noticed me if it had been broad daylight. Afterwards, he just got in his car and left. It was like that with all of them."

All of them?

"I need him to be arrested for these murders, and you're my insurance. When your body turns up, your redheaded friend will run screaming to the police about what she found in Fred's trunk, and that cop you had dinner with last night will do whatever it takes to get a conviction. End of story."

I felt a lifetime of rage against injustice hit the surface. It felt better than fear, so I let it come. I couldn't allow Derrick to get away with this. I had to do something to make sure he got caught, even if I didn't live to see it happen. I took a deep breath and forced myself to continue talking.

"Why Kurt?" I asked. "And why Barbara and Andrew? How were they connected to Fred?"

"Kurt described Fred to you perfectly. I thought it would be more incriminating if he was killed before you showed him the pictures."

"Wait a minute. How do you know he described Fred to me?"

"My assistant was getting her hair cut in the next chair. She's a terrible gossip."

"Your *assistant* is involved in this?"

"Oh, *God*, no. That was just a coincidence."

I felt my jaw drop. "Unbelievable." I stubbed out my cigarette and lit another. "You know, the police were watching your house the night Kurt was killed. They saw your bedroom lights go off. How did you manage to slip out of the house without disturbing Kate?"

"She's a creature of habit. Takes a Halcion with warm milk every night before bed. She has insomnia. So I just slipped an extra dose into her milk. Once she was asleep, I went out the patio door and walked to Redwood City."

"Did you know you were being watched?"

"No, but it pays to be cautious."

"What about Andrew and Barbara? Where do they fit in?"

He looked puzzled for a moment, like he couldn't believe I didn't get it. "Fred was having sex with them too. One night I followed him when he left Laura, and he went and hooked up with the hairdresser. One right after the other.

"That night he screwed Laura behind the dumpster he put a bag over her head. I could tell she liked it." His eyes glazed over as he spoke, remembering. "I thought the timing was perfect. After he left I came out from where I was hiding, and she started to scream. I punched her in the face to shut her up, and that knocked her out. I fastened the plastic bag back over her head. When she was dead I stabbed her a few times so I'd have something with her blood on it to put in Fred's trunk."

He watched me for a reaction. I didn't give him one.

"Were you wearing gloves that night?" I asked.

"I got in the habit. Started keeping surgical gloves and condoms in my car."

He seemed to enjoy talking about his crimes, almost as though he was proud of himself, and he hadn't been able to share his obscene little discourse with anyone else. I'd read about this. Psychopathic killers have an overwhelming need to take credit for what they've done. They want to brag about it. Telling someone, anyone, makes them feel god-like. At least it was giving me time to think of a way to disarm him. Also, I have to admit to more than a little morbid curiosity.

"Why did you rape Kurt before you killed him?"

"To keep the pattern consistent. I'd never done that before. Fred seems to like it, so I thought *why not*? It was interesting. You know what else he does? He brings a plastic bag with him on his little adventures, and when he's done, he puts the used condom in the baggie and takes it with him. He has sex in public, but he doesn't want to litter."

I glanced at the gun he held in his lap and noticed that Derrick had an erection. I felt a wave of nausea, but determined to forge ahead rather than surrender to panic. I swallowed a couple of times before speaking.

"There was no foreign pubic hair found on any of the victims, even though they'd all recently had sex."

"He shaves everything." He stood up, adjusted himself, and began pacing. "So I started shaving too."

"There were no defensive wounds found on Andrew. No sign of a struggle."

"You'd be surprised how docile people become after sex. Or maybe you wouldn't." He winked at me.

The man who was planning to rape and kill me was *flirting* with me?

"As soon as Fred left I moved in and finished the hairdresser off. It was so fast he never even knew what was happening."

Jesus.

Derrick abruptly stopped pacing and turned to face me. "It's time to go," he said. He gestured with the gun, indicating that I should stand. "We'll stop at your office first."

I stayed where I was. "Derrick, your daughter is dead. You killed her, and four other people to cover it up. I'm assuming Hearn was trying to blackmail you, so you had to get rid of him?"

Derrick nodded curtly and motioned with the gun again.

"The police will find some evidence linking you to one or all of those victims," I continued. "You are going to get caught."

"Don't underestimate me, Ms. Hunter. I've been very careful. Now get up."

I put out my cigarette, stood, and moved slowly toward the companionway, wondering if an elbow to the solar plexus or a heel-stomp on the instep would cause his trigger finger to convulse.

He must have read my thoughts. "Don't be stupid," he said. "Just get your ass up those stairs."

"Wait," I said over my shoulder. I turned toward the stateroom. "I'll need my keys to get into the office."

Keys make an excellent weapon when gripped firmly and directed at the eyes. Plus I had a canister of pepper spray in my bag.

"I already have your keys," he said, grabbing me by the hair again. He jerked me back against him and gave me a shove toward the steps. When he released me I spun around, coming up under his gun arm and grabbing his wrist with both hands. I pushed upward, trying to loosen his grip on the Glock, but he was a lot stronger than I was, even with the adrenaline rushing through my system. He wrenched free and slammed the gun into my forehead. I staggered backwards, dizzy from the blow, and fell to my knees.

I wiped the blood from my forehead and glared up at my captor. If he wouldn't let me near my purse and the pepper spray, maybe I could get close enough to scratch his face. Get some DNA under my fingernails for the forensics people to discover after I was dead, and leave some marks he wouldn't easily be able to cover. Of course I was feeling reluctant to piss him off just now. One more push and he might kill me first and search my office for the fictitious flash drive later. I was in no hurry to die.

He pointed the gun at me and took a step back. "Let's go."

I leaned against the steps and pulled myself up. My forehead was throbbing and my legs felt like they wouldn't support me. I climbed up into the pilothouse with Derrick close behind me.

I keep a machete next to the door in case there's an earthquake and I need to cut the dock lines in a hurry. I looked down at it as I passed through the small room. I was afraid I wouldn't be fast enough.

The fear was paralyzing me, keeping me from taking any action that might save my life. Like a deer caught in the headlights, I could see my own doom coming and was too frightened to get out of the way. I'd never been in a life and death situation before, and I was disappointed by my reaction, but that did little to change the panic I was feeling.

I walked out the pilothouse door. The night air was bracing. I took a deep breath and thought about jumping in the water. I felt lightheaded, I'm a poor swimmer, and the Bay water is icy, even in the summer. Besides, I didn't have a clear shot at the water from where I was standing. Instead I pushed off hard from the deck, jumping over the steps onto the dock and hoping to throw Derrick off balance with the motion of the boat. He was behind me, his forearm around my neck, before I could take two steps.

"Behave yourself," he muttered in my ear.

He held the gun in his left hand, the muzzle pressed against my jaw, as we walked down the dock. His other hand gripped the waistband of my jeans. The gun I could handle, but the feel of his gloved fingers on my lower back was intolerable. Held at this angle, the gun was likely obscured by my hair. In the dark, the matte black Glock wouldn't be visible from more than a few feet away.

I remembered the loaded Ruger I keep in the office under my lap drawer. He'd have to give me my keys to get into the office, or risk the time it would take to try each one. The same thing would be true with the desk. Surely he'd trust me to unlock a drawer. After all, he had my gun.

I tried dragging my feet to slow things down.

"Keep moving," he whispered. "I'd hate to have to kill any of your neighbors."

I walked on, periodically wiping the blood from my head wound to keep it out of my eyes.

When we reached the end of the dock and turned left I felt rather than saw the black streak in front of my face. It was like a hot gust of wind and it landed, teeth first, on Derrick's left wrist. Everything dropped into slow motion while a dozen things seemed to happen at once.

D'Artagnon's body slammed into Derrick and the impact knocked me aside. The Glock went off with a deafening crack and a flash of light, and I felt the burn on my temple. I sat down hard on the concrete dock as the gun flew out of Derrick's hand and skidded away. Derrick hit the dock next to me full force. I scrambled on hands and knees after the gun. D'Artagnon released his grip on Derrick's wrist and was leaning toward his throat when Derrick backhanded the pup hard enough to knock him into the water just as I retrieved the Glock.

I pulled myself up into a shooting crouch and pointed the gun at Derrick. Assuming I wouldn't shoot an unarmed man, he lunged at me. This time I was ready for the attack, I was pissed, and I had a weapon. I sidestepped to my right and slammed the Glock into his left cheek as he turned. He covered his face with his hands and I kicked him in the balls as hard as I could. When he bent at the waist clutching his injured package I clobbered him on the back of the head with the Glock again. Good thing I didn't have my finger on the trigger.

With Derrick temporarily incapacitated I reached over the side of the dock, grabbed D'Artagnon's collar, and helped him climb out of the water. He shook himself nose to tail, spraying salt water all over me, licked my left hand once, and then promptly clamped his jaws around Derrick's exposed throat.

D'Artagnon's people, Kirk and Jonathan, had appeared on deck, wondering what the hell was going on. I told them briefly how he'd saved my life, shouting to compensate for my inability to hear due to the proximity of the gunshot, and asked if I could borrow a cell phone. Kirk fished his out of his pocket and leaned over the rail to hand it to me.

I felt the dock vibrate rhythmically behind me and turned, expecting to see another neighbor awakened by the commotion. Elizabeth came running down the dock in a short cotton nightgown and bunny slippers. She looked back and forth between me with the Glock in my hand and Derrick with D'Artagnon at his throat. She was speechless. Elizabeth is rarely speechless.

I quickly dialed 911 holding the phone tight against my ear with one hand, still holding the gun on Derrick with the other. I got a recording. A moment later a California Highway Patrol operator came on. I asked to be connected to the Redwood City emergency dispatchers.

I explained the situation to the dispatcher and asked her to page Detective Bill Anderson. She assured me that help was on the way.

Finally Elizabeth spoke. "D'Artagnon must be getting tired. Should we call him off?"

After a moment's consideration I decided she was right. He'd probably need a tetanus shot too.

"Good boy, D'Artagnon," I said. "You can let go now."

He wagged his tail, but did not release Derrick.

Kirk told him to drop it, but he maintained his grip. It finally took both Jonathan and Kirk to drag the snarling, slobbering beast from Derrick's throat. Remarkably, the skin on his neck was barely broken. What a good dog.

Bill arrived a few minutes later, followed by four uniformed officers. After they'd heard my story a still dazed Derrick was cuffed, Mirandized, and taken away in a patrol car with lights flashing. Bill stayed behind to take my full statement, and to make sure I was okay.

Once Derrick had been removed and I'd given a full report of events to Bill, I started shaking badly. In spite of the balmy weather my teeth were chattering and I began to feel the head wound. I sat down on the dock and wrapped my arms around D'Artagnon, who licked my face causing me to dissolve into tears.

I waited until the uniforms gave me a receipt for the Glock, which was being taken as evidence, so I could reclaim the gun when the case was resolved. Then I allowed Elizabeth to drive me to the emergency room. Bill had gone to the station to handle the paperwork.

My forehead didn't need stitches, but the doctor used a butterfly bandage to hold the split flesh together. He cleaned and bandaged the gunpowder burn on my temple, and suggested I have the stippling removed by a plastic surgeon as soon as possible. He examined my eyes, telling me how lucky I was, and said the ringing in my ears would probably dissipate in a few hours.

When we got home from the hospital, Elizabeth walked me to my boat. The emergency room doctor had given me a couple of Norco for the pain, and I was feeling a little bit wobbly. She helped me get out of my clothes and gently tucked me into the bunk.

"You want me to stay, honey?"

"I'm fine. But thanks for asking." I glanced at the bedside clock. "Is it really two a.m.?"

"Yes. I'm taking tomorrow off. I'll check on you in the morning. Get some sleep."

She kissed my bandaged forehead, and let herself out.

I dozed for a while, but when my cell phone sounded from my purse I nearly jumped out of my skin. Who would be calling at this ungodly hour?

I dug the phone out of my bag, and looked at the number on the screen.

"Elizabeth?"

"Hi, honey. I just wanted you to know I let Detective Hottie in the gate. He's on his way."

"Okay. Thanks."

"No problem. Sweet dreams," she said, and giggled before hanging up.

I grabbed a short terry cloth robe off the floor and covered myself before climbing up the companionway and sticking my head out the pilothouse door. Standing on the dock next to my slip was Detective Bill Anderson, illuminated only by the light shining through my port holes.

"You coming aboard?" I asked.

"If you're not too tired for company." He looked pretty ragged himself.

"Come on in," I said. "I'll make coffee."

Bill smiled at that. Probably remembering the Kona I'd served him when he came to my office. He followed me down the companionway, mirroring my actions by backing down the steps. I enjoyed the view as he descended. Bill Anderson has an exceptionally fine ass. My face flushed as I busied myself with the coffee maker.

Bill seated himself at the galley table, watching me in my little terry cloth robe as I fussed with the filter. When

I'd finished the set up and switched on the machine I turned to face him. He scooted over a little and patted the settee. I eased down beside him.

He stroked my forehead gently with his fingertips, sending little jolts of electricity all the way to my toes. "Are you okay?"

"No," I said. "But ask me again in the morning."

He gave me a slow smile. I licked my lips self-consciously and his eyes lowered to watch the motion. Then he leaned in and kissed me.

Epilogue

Derrick Howard was charged with five counts of first-degree murder with special circumstances, and was convicted in less than six weeks. I think the process was accelerated because the judge refused to allow the media into her courtroom.

It turned out Derrick *had* left a trace of his DNA behind. One of his eyelashes had been found inside a knife wound on Andrew McConnell's back.

My testimony made a difference too. Derrick had confessed everything to me, and PIs are excellent witnesses because we're trained to commit details to memory. The second PI Derrick had hired was also a witness. This was the tall red-haired man I'd seen outside my office who had followed me in the Volvo. His name was Jim Sutherland, and he testified that Derrick had requested that he follow me and give him daily reports. The night I'd found Derrick aboard my boat he'd called Jim on his cell phone and told him the job was over and he could go home. Jim had stuck around long enough to see one of my neighbors let Derrick in the gate, and he'd been on shore watching as Derrick led me down the dock, not to mention the chaos that followed.

Derrick is appealing his sentence now, and will probably continue to do so for the next decade. His attorney tried for a diminished capacity plea based on Derrick's personal history of childhood sexual abuse at the hands of his father, but the D.A. was able to prove premeditation. When the press published Derrick's photograph, the owner of a knife shop in Oakland came forward and testified that Derrick had purchased the knife with the spikes on the hilt the day Laura was killed.

The morning after Derrick was arrested I had received an e-mail from my friend Michael Burke, saying that Fred did his banking at Wells Fargo and did not rent a safe deposit box or a storage locker. He asked if I was interested in hearing about Fred's indecent exposure arrest. I e-mailed him back, thanking him for his help, and took a rain check on any additional information about Fred. This was out of character for me, but I'd had enough of other people's insanity to last me a while. Michael and I made plans to have dinner.

Fred called my office during the height of the media circus that surrounded me, saying he'd been fired after details of his sex life hit the tabloids. He asked if I'd like to make it up to him. I declined.

I never did get a return call from Gerald Kuhlman, and he remains something of a curiosity to me, although it didn't surprise me that he chose not to represent Derrick at trial. An attorney who represents politicians has to be careful about his image.

Kate came to court every day, and when it was over, outside the Hall of Justice, she slipped me an envelope with three thousand dollars in it.

"A little bonus," she said. "I can never thank you enough for what you've done for Laura. I should have known what was going on in my own family. I should have seen what a monster Derrick was. Maybe the signs were always there and I just ignored them. I'll never forgive myself for not protecting her, but I hope she can somehow forgive me."

"I don't think you can blame yourself for not seeing through his mask, Kate. Sylvia didn't even know, and she's his sister, and a psychologist." But we both knew she would blame herself for the rest of her life.

I considered refusing the reward, but I had earned it.

We shook hands and parted on the courthouse steps. I silently wished her luck with what was left of her future.

D'Artagnon and I have been taking long walks in the Bair Island Nature Preserve. I also took him with me the day after Derrick was sentenced, when I brought flowers to Laura's grave. He sat on the ground next to me while I told her about what had happened since her death, that her father hadn't gotten away with it, and that it looked like he'd spend the rest of his life in prison. I cried over the injustice of what had happened to her. After that visit, in spite of my tears or maybe because of them, I felt a sense of peace.

When the trial was concluded Bill took some vacation time and I taught him how to sail. He learned quickly, once his stomach was empty. With practice he'll probably become a decent first mate.

~THE END~

Other Nikki Hunter Mysteries, by Nancy Skopin

Murder Over Cocktails

Dinner And A Murder

Murder A la Carte

Murder Served Hot

A Side Order Of Murder

Murder Alfresco

Murder Served Cold

Murder Al Dente

About the Author

Award winning author, Nancy Skopin, is a native of California who currently lives on the Oregon coast with her husband, Max Ferry, and their dog, Turq. An avid student of human nature, Nancy is happiest spending her days imagining the best, and the worst, that we are capable of, and translating those ideas into her Nikki Hunter mystery novels.

As does her central character, Nancy lived aboard a yacht in the San Francisco Bay Area for thirteen years, though she has recently settled on solid ground.

While researching her mystery series she worked for two years with a private investigator, learning the intricacies of the business and, specifically, the art of bar and restaurant "mystery shopping."

Visit Nancy Skopin's Amazon Author's page:
http://www.amazon.com/Nancy-Skopin/e/B00Y17LVBA/ref=sr_ntt_srch_lnk_1?qid=1466111557&sr=8-1

Or her website at: *http://nicolihunter.com/*

If you'd like to be notified when new Nikki Hunter mysteries are published, e-mail the author at:
NikkiMaxineHunter@gmail.com

Printed in Great Britain
by Amazon

18678538R00174